The Girl in the Photograph

The Girl in the Photograph

Kirsty Ferry

Book 3 – Rossetti Mysteries

Where heroes are like chocolate – irresistible!

Published 2018 by Choc Lit Limited
Penrose House, Crawley Drive, Camberley, Surrey GU15 2AB, UK
www.choc-lit.com

A CIP catalogue record for this book is available
from the British Library

ISBN 978-1-78189-406-4

Penguin Random House is committed to a sustainable future for
our business, our readers and our planet. This book is made from
Forest Stewardship Council® certified paper.

Printed and bound by Clays Ltd

For my family, as always.
I love you all

Acknowledgements

The Laing, in Newcastle upon Tyne, is my local art gallery and as well as having a rather nice coffee shop and some gorgeous Pre-Raphaelite artworks, it also holds two of my favourite paintings: *On the Beach* (1909) by Dame Laura Knight and *In the Spring* (1908) by Laura's husband, Harold. These paintings, Dante Gabriel Rossetti's poem *Sea Spell*, a book about Julia Margaret Cameron and Pre-Raphaelite photography, and a ruined house nestled in the cliffs on the East Coast Train line, somewhere near Berwick, were the starting points for this novel. I'd like to thank everyone who made it possible to weave all those elements into a story – especially Dr Barbara Morden, my tutor on an Open University arts course and something of an expert on Laura Knight and the Newlyn Group of Artists. I may have bent the truth a little as regards dates in Cornwall when the Knights were there (sorry Barbara!) but in my defence, this is fiction after all! I'd also like to thank Tom and Rosamund Jordan, who answered my questions and helped me join the dots and connect everything – including the Knights – to the Staithes Group of Artists.

And 'thank you' to everyone at Choc Lit for their time, energy and expertise in helping me bring this book to life, and another huge 'thank you' to all the wonderful readers who told me how much they'd loved this series and how they desperately wanted to know more about Jon, Becky, Cori, Simon and Lissy. After two whole books sorting everyone else's relationships out, Lissy really deserves a story of her own and I think she'll be very happy to find she has that in *The Girl in the*

Photograph. Thanks also to the Tasting Panel members who passed *The Girl in the Photograph* and made this possible: Karen M, Isabelle T, Hrund, Vanessa G, Sarah C, Sharon M, Helen D and Sharon H.

And, of course, as always, I want to thank my family and friends for all their love and support – for coffee, chocolate and wine duties, as and when applicable! You don't know how much all that means to me.

A Sea-Spell

Her lute hangs shadowed in the apple-tree,
While flashing fingers weave the sweet-strung spell
Between its chords; and as the wild notes swell,
The sea-bird for those branches leaves the sea.
But to what sound her listening ear stoops she?
What netherworld gulf-whispers doth she hear,
In answering echoes from what planisphere,
Along the wind, along the estuary?
She sinks into her spell: and when full soon
Her lips move and she soars into her song,
What creatures of the midmost main shall throng
In furrowed self-clouds to the summoning rune,
Till he, the fated mariner, hears her cry,
And up her rock, bare breasted, comes to die?

Dante Gabriel Rossetti

Prologue

She dragged the silver-backed brush through her hair, feeling the wild, salty, tangled curls stretch out and pull into the soft waves she was more accustomed to. She longed to be outside, rather than trapped in this gilded cage; she yearned to feel the sea breeze on her face and the sand crushing beneath her bare feet. She didn't belong here, with him, but she knew she had to stay, at least a little while longer …

Chapter One

'Seriously, it'll be fun!'

'Fun?' Lissy de Luca stared at her half-brother Jon Nelson and pulled a face. 'I suspect it's more fun for the photographer than the model.'

Jon was sitting on the sofa, right next to a picture window which was big enough for the afternoon sun to pour through the glass and make the little lounge in the flat above his Whitby photographic studio glow. 'Look, it's a project I've been thinking of for a while,' he said. 'You know Simon's having an exhibition in Mayfair and he's already said I can have some wall space. I think it'll be great to try and recreate some of the Pre-Raphaelite paintings in photography, and they'll go alongside Simon's work quite nicely. It's just a different form of art, that's all.'

Simon, an artist, and his partner Cori were friends of theirs who lived in London and Jon had just been telling Lissy about their joint plans. He was visibly fizzing with excitement.

'Well, his paintings are marvellous!' Lissy leaned forward and took a biscuit from a plate. 'He's got Cori to model for him and he can recreate all those pictures easily. They'll look so good. I can just see them now, up on that gallery wall. Wonderful.' She nibbled a corner of the biscuit, breaking into the chocolate shell with a view to stripping the chocolate off it in a neat, efficient manner before she hit the actual biscuit inside.

'So, basically, you're implying Simon's paintings are better than my photographs? Well, thanks sis, I love you

2

too.' Although Jon and Lissy had the same mother, they had grown up together in the household of Lissy's wealthy Italian father; but it had never made any difference to their relationship, which was based on the usual deep love and fiery spats between siblings.

In this instance, Lissy didn't rise to the bait. She licked the last vestiges of chocolate from the biscuit and popped the remaining shortbread circle into her mouth.

She stared at Jon as she chewed. 'I often wish I had a sister instead of a brother. Girls are less touchy.'

'Rubbish! Absolute rubbish. I grew up with *you*, remember, and I now live with two girls and no way are they less touchy!'

'You just proved it; you are far too touchy.' Lissy stood up and stretched. 'Well, as I was hoping to see Becky and Grace and they aren't here, I'm going to go.'

'Oh, sit down. They won't be long. Grace wanted to see the pirate ship so Becky took her out for a wander.' Jon suddenly perked up. 'Maybe she'll bring back some coffee?'

'What? Becky would juggle coffee *and* a three-year-old in a coffee shop, just to feed your addiction?'

Jon grinned. 'Hopefully.'

Lissy shuddered. She couldn't even contemplate such a horror. She loved her sister-in-law and her niece dearly, but surely there were limits? The thought of taking Grace into an exclusive café in London, where Lissy lived – well, in fact, an exclusive café anywhere – was inconceivable. There was a hot chocolate place along one of the side streets in Whitby with the blessing of outside tables. Lissy could just about cope with the child there. And that was only because she would usually feed her with a succession of marshmallows and strawberries dipped in chocolate, which did tend to keep her quiet, even if it made her rather sticky and unpleasant afterwards.

There was a jingle from way beneath their feet and it was Jon's turn to stand up. 'Customers. No rest for the wicked.'

He strode out of the lounge and headed towards the rickety old staircase that connected the flat to the shop. The studio dealt mainly with the tourist trade; people would come in to have photographs taken of themselves in period clothing and the twice-yearly Goth weekend celebrations were his busiest times. Luckily the queues of pale people dressed in black and discovering their inner vampire, courtesy of Bram Stoker setting part of his *Dracula* novel in Whitby, didn't bother his small daughter.

Grace often sat on the old wooden counter entranced by the vamps. Sometimes, it had to be said, her piercing, solemn stare would unsettle the customers more than they could unsettle her. It often took a double take for them to realise the thing that was 'off' about her – the fact that, like her father and aunt, she had one blue and one green eye, inherited from her paternal grandmother's line. Her unusual eyes were surrounded by the darkest, longest lashes, and when you matched that with her dark hair and her mother's English Rose complexion, Grace Eleanor Nelson was clearly destined for great, although not conventional, beauty.

'Hey!' Jon's voice, rising an octave and somehow simultaneously softening in tone, floated in from the tiny landing. 'Who is *this* coming up the stairs to my little house?'

'Cap'n Hook,' came another voice – a child's voice. 'But I want a crocodile. Tick tock!' The door to the lounge flew open and a mini-whirlwind came in, sporting a lop-sided eye-patch and brandishing a rubber dagger. 'Bang bang!' The whirlwind came to a sudden halt in front of Lissy and grinned through a mask of something unidentifiably, yes, *sticky*. 'Bang bang!' Cap'n Hook held the dagger aloft and pointed it at Lissy.

'Darling, *guns* go bang bang. That's a dagger,' said Lissy.

'It's a gun today,' replied Hook. 'Hallo.'

'Hello sweetie.' Lissy bent down, intending to kiss each side of her niece's face as she usually did in polite society, but the little girl had other ideas.

Grace threw her arms around Lissy's neck and lifted her feet from the ground. 'Mwaaah.' She smacked a wet kiss somewhere to the side of Lissy's mouth.

Automatically, Lissy put her arms around the child to steady them both and Grace snuggled in to her. 'Come see who Mummy found.' She pointed to the door and bounced in Lissy's arms. 'That way.' Lissy had no choice but to walk towards the staircase, breathing in the faint scent of chocolate and bananas the child was breathing out.

'I don't suppose your Mummy found anyone interesting?' she asked. 'Was it a princess? If it was a princess, maybe it was just a customer.' Grace adored the more elaborate Goths – she loved the long flouncy dresses and the lace gloves, stared covetously at the red lips and had, at times, to be physically restrained from touching the velvet chokers or veils the ladies displayed.

'No princess,' said Grace. She sighed and shook her head. Then she brightened. 'It's a prince!'

Lissy fully expected to see a pallid young man dressed in a top hat and a frock coat as she manoeuvred the unwieldy bundle expertly down the staircase and pushed the door open into the studio.

What she didn't expect to see, was Stefano Ricci.

'Oh, good God!' Lissy's face drained of colour.

Stefano looked at her, his heart thudding – maybe it was panic, maybe it wasn't. But, regardless, he hadn't been sure of what his reception would be. He did notice, however, that Lissy was as immaculate as she had always been. Her dark hair now fell to her shoulders from a severe side parting and a long, dark, choppy fringe hid part of her face. There were streaks of purple and pink in the fringe – on anyone else, Stefano knew, the highlights would be lost in the mass of dark hair. On Lissy, they lay exactly where they should.

He took a deep breath and smiled, bowing elegantly to her. '*Mia cara.*' Then he saw the look of thunder on her elfin face. 'Ah, why would you look so upset, Elisabetta? I have come from so far to see you again. And this – this little girl. She is a doll.' He turned to Grace. 'In my country, which is somewhere called Italy, we would call you *Grazia.*'

'*Grazia?*' The child tried the name out and appeared to like it. Grace was obviously not a shy child. She looked directly at him, a stranger to her, and jiggled, apparently letting her aunt know she wanted to be put back on her own two feet. 'Hallo, again.' She walked over to Stefano when Lissy had done her bidding and stood in front of him, waiting for him to answer.

'Hello,' said Stefano. He held his hand out solemnly.

Grace seized it and pumped it up and down, giggling. 'Mummy,' she said, turning to Jon's pretty chestnut-haired wife, Becky, 'he's nice. I like him.'

'I'm glad,' replied Becky, smiling back. 'He's Daddy's friend Stefano. Can you say that?'

Grace nodded. 'Yes.' She didn't elaborate however, and Stefano smiled.

'Good girl,' he said.

'Yes, I am,' replied Grace confidently. She tugged at the hand she still held and Stefano was curious as she pulled him slightly at an angle and pointed at her mother. 'But you must talk straight to Mummy. Her ears don't work right.'

'Grace!' That was Lissy scolding the child.

'She tries to help,' Stefano defended her. God, the woman looked good. 'How long has it been?' he asked, gently releasing Grace and taking a step towards Lissy with his hands outstretched. His camera was slung around his neck, and he felt the equipment bump against his body. He itched to take a photograph of Elisabetta. Nobody had ever compared to her.

'Not long enough,' said Lissy.

'Yet I think it has been far too long.'

'You *are* joking?' exclaimed Lissy. The child had run back to her now and was patting her legs, trying to get attention and probably hoping for another carry in her arms. She was half bending over to the child, ready to either pick her up or send her off with a flea in her ear, when she looked up at Stefano.

Flash.

'I thank you,' he said. 'You have made my first Pre-Raphaelite imagining come to life. You are the very image of Waterhouse's *Lady of Shalott looking at Lancelot*.'

'I don't believe you,' she hissed. 'You are sneaky and underhanded and ...'

'And you have never forgotten me,' interrupted Stefano, 'and you still feel a passion for me – otherwise, why would you still be so bothered to see me?'

Lissy, apparently, couldn't find an answer.

Chapter Two

Cornwall, Seven Years Ago

It had been the idea of Harold and Laura Knight that had drawn her to Cornwall. The Knights and their group of amazing, fabulous, talented Cornish artists, who had lived and worked there at the beginning of the twentieth century. But to Lissy, fresh out of an art history degree, Lamorna Cove had been highly disappointing. It was still disappointing a few months later, after she had lived and breathed Cornwall for a whole season and seen places with proper beaches.

She stood amongst what basically resembled a quarry and sighed. Where on earth was the beautiful Lamorna Cove beach she had seen in the pictures? Originally, she had wondered if she was just at the wrong part of the cove. Was there even another part? But the place still had some sort of strange draw for her, despite all that.

Taking a last look around, she clambered over the rocks and made her way back into the village. It was getting late and she was hungry and God she could murder a glass of wine. Something cold and white, she thought. But first ...

'Well?' He was standing there, hands in pockets, beside the car. That ever-present camera was hanging around his neck and the last rays of sunlight glinted off the lens.

Lissy's sharp eyes noticed the glint. 'Why isn't the lens cap on?' she asked. 'Did you take a picture?'

'You ask such silly questions, *mia cara*.' There was a smile in his voice as he moved towards her; two steps, that was all it took, and her heart began to somersault. His hair was still slightly damp from their swim earlier, and it was twisting itself up into dark curls that settled somewhere just below his collar. His eyes were almost black and his mouth – oh hell, his mouth …

Lissy's own lips curved into a smile and she stood, silently daring him to come closer. Because if she walked towards him there was no way on earth she would be responsible for her actions.

'You remind me of a *sirena*,' he said. 'A beautiful *sirena*, standing on the rocks. I do not know the word. A lady of the sea. A maid of the water.' He snapped his fingers, annoyed with himself, trying to get the word. 'What is it? The one that leads a man to the death?'

'A mermaid?' she tried. 'Half woman, half fish. All temptress.'

'Temptress. I like it.' He reached out and put his arms on her shoulders; cool hands on warm skin, sand and salt like fine grit pressing between them. Lissy shivered, despite the heat. She leaned forward, ready to properly tempt him by kissing him, and then she heard the shout.

'Hey! Lissy! Stef!'

'Perfect bloody timing.' She drew back from Stefano, his arms dropping away from her body. She felt something slip down her arms and looked in surprise to see the thin, red straps of her sundress hanging off her shoulders. 'What the …?' She looked at Stefano who looked back, a little smile playing around that perfectly sculpted mouth as he pushed his hands in his pockets. Seriously, did a man in cut-off denims ever look so bloody sexy?

'I tried.' He shrugged. 'It would have been fun. On the beach. Behind the rocks. Again.'

Lissy felt herself blush almost the colour of her dress and tugged the straps back up. 'You're terrible!' she scolded. 'I'm telling on you. Jon! Jon! Guess what?' She skipped out of Stefano's way and began to run over to the man who had called their names. Stefano caught her around the waist and pulled her back, laughing. Shrieking, she didn't resist.

Lissy and Stefano half stumbled, half tottered towards Lissy's brother, who was scrambling over some more rocks to get to them. He was another one who had a camera bumping around his chest area.

Jon smiled as he spotted them. 'I thought that was you two. I just got some brilliant shots around the corner. The light's incredible down here. I'm glad I came. Yeah. Could have been under better circumstances but – hey.' Lissy disengaged herself from Stefano and linked her brother's arm. This close, she could see his smile didn't really reach his eyes; a brave face, then.

'So she's really gone?' she asked quietly.

'Yeah. Um. We're going to stay friends, but …' Jon shrugged. 'She's packing. She's heading back to Sussex tomorrow. I'll give her time to leave, then it's not so awkward.' He pushed a wayward bit of hair out of his eyes and the smile slid off his face. He stared out to the sea, seemingly lost in the motion of the waves curling and breaking onto the cliffs.

Lissy watched his eyes follow the relentless movements of the tide and felt something like a lump of Cornish tin settle inside her stomach. 'Oh,' she said. 'I'm sorry.'

'That's okay. Mustn't have been meant to be,' he replied. 'Fran's great. I don't want to start putting blame on anyone …'

'But it's her fault, darling,' said Lissy passionately, squeezing Jon's arm. 'You're my brother. She's pretty damn stupid if she's willing to give you up.'

'We just want different things. I like Whitby. She likes Sussex. I mean – I *like* Sussex, of course I do. I love Sussex. But my heart – well. My heart's in Whitby. I can't describe it. I need to be in Whitby. I have to be up there.' He turned to her, his face a bit white and sickly-looking beneath his tan. 'I'm not sorry I came with her. I thought a holiday somewhere neutral might help. I'm pleased I did it. I'm pleased you decided to spend the summer here. At least I knew I had somewhere to stay if she kicked me out of the hotel.'

'I am sorry, my friend,' Stefano said. 'There is nothing so bad as when a woman stops loving you.' He held out his hand to Jon. 'Please let it be known that whatever happens, I am your friend.'

'Thanks.' Jon smiled, a proper smile that did indeed, this time, crinkle up the corner of his eyes. He shook hands with Stefano. 'And the same for you.'

'You are like a brother to me,' Stefano said expansively. 'I know I have known you only a few weeks, and I have known Lissy a little longer, but we are kindred spirits, you and I.'

'I'm glad you both took a break from your holidays to come on holiday,' said Jon, 'if you know what I mean? I'm not saying it very well, am I?' He took a deep breath. 'Let me try again. You guys – in Cornwall. Me – in Whitby. You guys – come to visit me. You guys – come back. Me – I try to make things work with Fran. And come and see you guys.' He laughed. 'God, it's not even funny, is it? It's too complicated to be funny.'

'Let her go.' Lissy squeezed his arm again then removed her hands, frightened in case he was going to take some sort of random hysterical turn in Lamorna Cove. 'Stay with us as long as you like.'

'Yeah.' Jon stared out to sea again. 'Have you ever read that Rossetti poem?' he asked, directing his comment to nobody in particular. '*Sea-Spell*. Talks about a man being battered on the rocks for love.' He threw his arms out to the side dramatically. 'I *am* that man.'

'Oh, for goodness' sake,' scoffed Lissy. 'That's like something out of a film.' She scrambled back to Stefano. 'Wine. I prescribe wine. And lots of it.'

Stefano lay stretched out on the lawn beneath the big apple tree in the garden of the cottage Lissy had rented for the summer. It felt like home now, and he spent more time there than he did in his own rented place; a small, white-painted terraced house tucked away between larger terraced houses within a fishing village on the south coast – just where it looked as if a giant had bitten a chunk out of the land mass.

Stefano's holiday home was beyond small. It was tiny. No, it was microscopic. Lissy had claimed she felt claustrophobic in the narrow lounge, and had demonstrated that she couldn't even lie flat across the width of the room. Stefano had bent down and scooped her up and shown her how easy it was for her to lie on the double bed in the miniature bedroom instead; they'd subsequently spent a pleasant couple of hours in that cool, echoing little room with the tang of salt in their noses and golden light playing across the whitewashed walls and the seagulls screaming in the bay across the road.

Oh, happy accident that he had met her on his first day in Cornwall; seen her sitting on the beach dressed all in white. He remembered walking up to her and standing beside her, beginning a conversation about the Newlyn artists and then listening entranced as she talked right back at him about art.

She had talked not only about the Newlyn artists, but about the Impressionists and the Pre-Raphaelites and how much she adored them. She was going to work in the art world, she told him; she had enough time and enough independence, thanks to a generous trust fund set up by her Italian father, to discover what she really wanted to do with her life, and in the meantime, she was going to enjoy every minute of her journey.

Her brother, Jon, was also a photographer. He lived in Whitby and was trying to set himself up in a studio. But she'd been doing some research and realised she could help him out, if he let her. He just needed to decide what he was going to do about his relationship first.

Before Stefano knew it; in fact, before they both knew it

really – they had fallen for each other. Properly. Indisputably. And frighteningly. And then she had dragged him up to Whitby one day, announcing, with a flash of that spontaneity and passion they both possessed, that she had seen the perfect premises for Jon. She needed to visit the place and was going to take Jon with her to make sure it was suitable, and Stefano had to come with her and that way he could properly meet her brother. So he did.

With Jon, it had been one of those instant, easy relationships; and when the man needed to have a heart to heart with Fran, there was no question of where he should take her. And it all had to be settled before Lissy signed the papers for the studio. Because, after all, what was the use of a studio and a flat in Whitby if Jon was going to make his life with Fran in Sussex?

Stefano looked at Jon now; saw him sitting on a bench in the shade, staring into a glass of wine with a cigarette dangling from his hand. A few small, probably biting, insects were flitting in and out of the glow the lit end of the cigarette gave off, but Jon was oblivious to their fiendish little presences.

'I did love her,' Jon announced. The wine was clearly taking effect, judging by the slight slur in his words.

'I know.' That was Lissy, stretched out on a picnic rug with her hat over her eyes.

'But I don't think Whitby was for her,' continued Jon. 'I don't think she loved me enough to give it a go.' He sighed and flicked some ash onto the path. The ash flared with orange sparks a little then died. 'I'm drunk. Good God.'

'There'll be someone else for you, darling brother of mine.' Lissy sounded drowsy now; soothing, yet drowsy. It was that sort of evening and still very, very warm. Stefano edged over to her and lay down beside her. He leaned across and flicked her hat off, then laughed at her indignant expression as those amazing eyes sprang open.

'I am sorry to disturb you.' He leaned in closer and moved her hair away from the side of her face. He brought his lips close to her ear and whispered: 'I wish I could take you right here, right now. But it would be too impolite and too heartless, no?'

Lissy gave a throaty giggle and rolled towards him. She lifted his hair away from his face and smoothed it back. Stefano could feel the pressure of her fingertips pressing down on the springy curls. He caught her fingers and, bringing them to his mouth, very carefully kissed them.

'Very impolite,' Lissy whispered back. Stefano felt a little shudder run all through her body and smiled.

'I think I'm really drunk, actually,' said Jon. 'Look, guys.' A clink as he put his glass down unsteadily on the grass and caught a pebble with it. 'I think I'd better go in.' He stood up and dropped his cigarette on the path, ground it into the cement with the ball of his foot. He stared at the dog-end for a moment. 'Crushed,' he muttered. 'Beyond crushed.'

'Oh, for God's sake.' Lissy sat up. 'Jon, go to bed. Right now. You'll have a stinking hangover tomorrow, but on the positive side, you know where you stand. You have to move on.'

Stefano laughed and sat up as well. 'Oh, Lissy, your sympathies do not last for long, do they? The poor man is broken and, as he says, crushed. Let him be.'

'Battered on the rocks,' muttered Jon. 'Totally battered. I'll be fine. I will be. 'Night, sis.' He leaned down and kissed her on the top of her head. 'Yeah. I'm not kissing you,' he said, pointing to Stefano.

'That's cool.' Stefano nodded. 'I don't want your kisses anyway.'

'Cool. 'Night, then,' repeated Jon. He turned and walked into the house, holding onto the door frame for support as he teetered indoors.

'God love him.' Lissy watched him go. 'He can't take alcohol that well. Never could. He'll be ill tomorrow. He'll be asleep in five, though, just watch.' Stefano dutifully watched the light of Jon's bedroom flick on for a moment, then flick off. 'That's it. He's in bed.' Lissy turned to Stefano and a sexy little smile played around her lips. Her odd, beautiful eyes twinkled in the dusk. 'Now what? What shall we do? It's not really very late, is it?'

'Not late at all.' Stefano pulled her close and nuzzled her neck, inhaling the scent of sun-tan lotion and the ocean. He thought he would never forget that smell as long as he lived. He felt the muscles in her cheek contract against the side of his face as she smiled.

'Excellent.' Her voice was suddenly husky. 'Let's make the most of it, then.'

And so they did.

Chapter Three

How could Jon have invited Stefano Ricci to Whitby? Lissy just couldn't believe it.

He knew how she felt about Stefano; how over the last seven years she had carefully constructed a barrier to keep him out of her life. He was well aware of what had gone on, both during her relationship with Stefano and even what had happened before that.

It was quite clear to her now that Jon had planned this, from the very first moment he decided to do that stupid project. He'd said he knew the right man to contact, the right man to help him out. But not for one moment had Lissy thought her brother would contact Stefano, of all people.

And to make matters worse, while they were all still in that studio, Jon had suddenly had one of his so-called brilliant ideas. 'Who's up for a wander down to the beach?' he asked. The evening was warm and sunny, and even with the sea breeze blowing gently in from the coast, the town was golden and inviting. 'We'll dig holes and build sandcastles.' This, obviously, to the child.

'Me me me!' Grace shrieked.

Lissy closed her eyes. 'Good God,' she muttered.

'That sounds lovely.' There was a note of amusement in Becky's voice. Lissy opened her eyes and glared at her best friend; her childhood friend, no less, who had eventually married her brother.

Becky smiled innocently at her. 'Doesn't it sound lovely, Lissy?'

'No,' replied Lissy. 'Why would I want to go down there

amongst all those horrible seagulls and nasty sand? It'll get in my sandals.'

'Sand and sandals, the perfect match,' said Stefano. He had taken up residence by the open door, dragging a chair across the studio and sitting there all lean and long-legged; clearly intending to block her way and, as a bonus, letting the summer air circulate around his bare feet. Those bloody bare feet. The last time she'd seen them, it had been a different summer evening and a different coastal town: Newlyn, in Cornwall.

The pebbly beach hadn't bothered Stefano. He'd stood there and watched her walk away – well, hobble and slip away as she teetered across the little stones, cursing at him loudly over her shoulder. He hadn't come after her; she didn't know if that was what rankled the most.

But he had this horrible habit of kicking his shoes off whenever he was near water or beaches or even fresh air, it seemed. At first it had been endearing. She loved the idea of walking barefoot with him along a sandy beach under the moonlight. But it had never become a reality – and to this day, she despised bare feet on the beach. And the thought of going to Whitby beach. With him. And his sodding feet.

No.

Just no.

But it seemed like one minute they had been in the studio and she was swearing that she wouldn't go. And the next —

'You dig in the sand, Antissy.'

Grace had never been able to get Lissy's name right. She was usually a remarkably clear little speaker for being three, but "Aunt Lissy" had always, somehow, escaped her. The child thrust the candyfloss pink spade at Lissy and sat down on the beach with a soft *flump*.

Lissy took the spade and made a few jabs into the sand while Grace's fingers crept over to the polystyrene carton of chips that by now had a faint layer of grit over them. She selected one and munched on it, watching her aunt all the time.

'It's so good when you're here,' said Jon. 'She loves playing with you.'

'Hmph.' Lissy knew her face was tight and her mouth all buttoned up; it was either that or she'd give in and break down and cry, and she'd sworn that she'd never let Stefano see her cry again.

Out of the corner of her eye, she saw a pair of bare feet come into view and she frowned even more. She jabbed the spade into the sand severely.

'No pebbles here, *bella*.' Stefano paused by her for a moment, and the camera made a soft whirr as he apparently took a picture of the sea. Then the feet turned towards her and he sat down, elegantly folding himself up like a deckchair right beside her. She kept her focus on the hole, digging and digging with more energy than strictly necessary.

'Dig t'Oztraylya,' muttered Grace, nodding approvingly and apparently satisfied with her aunt's labours.

'I won't find Australia, darling. Don't be silly,' said Lissy.

'Try. You never know,' murmured Stefano. God, his warm, Italian voice still had the power to make her toes curl, but she battered the feeling down as ardently as she battered the sand.

She worked at the sides of the hole, smoothing them down and patting them to firm them up. Grace knelt up and leaned in towards the hole, poking the end of a seagull feather into the sides and making the sand tumble down the walls in little trickles. Lissy put the spade down and sat back on her heels, sighing. 'Well done, darling,' she said. 'Well done for destroying Antissy's work.' Grace giggled and threw a shell into the hole. She began to chatter about buried treasure and Lissy watched her without really seeing her. Stefano was sitting there next to her. His presence felt like a big black storm cloud, ready to burst open and shower her with lightning.

'Please. You are still angry with me, after all this time?' He reached a finger out and lifted her multi-coloured fringe out of the way. He brought his finger down the side of her cheek and she flinched away. Stefano's gesture was almost tender. In fact, to anybody observing, it *would* have looked tender; but it did nothing but annoy Lissy.

'That won't work on me anymore, Stef. Forget it.'

'Aha – yet you still call me "Stef". You always used to call me "Stef".'

'I meant Stefano. Mr Ricci. Anyway. Forget it.' Lissy stood up sharply and brushed the sand off her pedal pushers. 'It's time I went. Becky! Jon!' She raised her voice and strode over to her brother and his wife. They had been ridiculously non-discreet and volunteered to go for ice-creams, leaving the other two adults and the child on the beach. Now they were heading back damnably slowly. Jon was saying something and laughing and Becky was looking up at him nodding in agreement. At Lissy's shout and her hurried movements, they turned her way, a twin expression of surprise on their faces. It wasn't often Lissy was riled; or at least it wasn't often she was riled and let people see it.

'I'm leaving,' said Lissy. 'I think I've exhausted this place. I hate beaches. You know that.'

'Oh, don't go,' said Becky. She hurried up her steps and drew closer. 'Look, we brought you an ice cream with a flake in it.' She held out a dripping mess to Lissy.

Grace suddenly appeared as if by magic between them all. 'I heard ice cream.' She smiled. 'With a flake. Please.' She held her hand out and Becky shrugged. She went to put it in the child's sticky little fist.

'Enjoy it, darling,' said Lissy. 'Aunt Lissy is going home now anyway.'

Stef appeared, clutching the pink spade in one hand and a floppy pink sunhat designed to look like a pig in the other.

'Please. Don't go just yet. Come. Walk with me to the pier and we can chat.' He plopped the hat on Grace's head and she shrieked with laughter, her hands coming up to the brim as Stefano pushed the hat gently down so it slipped and covered her eyes, the ice-cream wobbling dangerously before Lissy steadied Grace's wrist.

'I'm coming nowhere with you,' Lissy growled. 'I'm leaving and don't even think about following me.'

Of course he followed her.

'Elisabetta, I think we need to spend some time talking. We have a lot to say to one another.' He fell into step with her as she walked away from Grace and her ice-cream.

'I have nothing to say to you,' began Lissy, then she clamped her lips together as if she suddenly realised he had almost engaged her in conversation. Stefano chuckled. 'Damn you,' she muttered.

'You have already done that,' replied Stefano. Lissy faltered but kept on walking. He wondered what she would do when she reached the end of the pier – whether she would just keep on walking right off the thing and end up in the sea, or whether she would do a grand circle and end up retracing her steps back to the beach and safety and noise and people.

'No. Actually, no.' Lissy suddenly stopped and swung around to face him. Her eyes blazed in her sun-burnt face and he was drawn again to the unusual colouration of them – one sapphire, one emerald. 'Let's get this right,' she continued, seemingly oblivious to his desire. 'You damned yourself. You're the one who was with that woman. What was I supposed to do? Sit and watch while it happened? As if!'

'It was the biggest mistake of my life,' said Stefano. 'In fact, all the years after that – after her, without you, were the result of that mistake. I want to put it right.' He reached out and tried to take her hand. She shook him away and strode off again. He watched her stomp up to the end of the pier. It was the circuit she was going for then, not the throwing yourself into the ocean thing. That was fine. That was perfectly acceptable.

Stefano looked around and saw a wooden bench facing out to sea. As she couldn't stay at the top of the pier forever, she would have to come back to him at some point. He sat down on the bench, stretching his long legs out and crossing them at the ankles. He draped his arms along the backrest and leaned back, closing his eyes to catch the last of the warmth in the sun's rays on his face.

Even with his eyes shut he would know when she was passing him. He hadn't lived and breathed her perfume so intensely that summer without recognising it. Plus – he smiled to himself, feeling the heat relax his muscles – the gypsy in him would know when she scurried past. His grandmother had always claimed he had inherited his dark, passionate looks and his intuition from her Romany ancestors. Stef was inclined to believe her. Take Lissy, for example; you didn't walk into that sort of relationship by luck alone. The pull now towards her was as strong as it had ever been. And maybe that was what had drawn him to Newlyn that year; maybe he knew his destiny was there.

Of course, there was only one thing to query about that. He opened his eyes and stared into the cloudless blue sky. Lissy didn't actually *know* she was his destiny. He still had to convince her of that one and hoped her heart would believe it even if her head told her otherwise.

Cornwall, Seven Years Ago

Jon had stayed another day or so with Lissy. Then he'd gone back to the hotel and packed his own bags. Fran had left nothing of herself behind; not even a stray toothbrush or item of clothing that would be a perfectly acceptable reason for them to meet up again. It was definitely over. They watched Jon stuff the cases in the car and Lissy felt a little sorry for him.

'It's a long way back,' she said. 'Are you sure you don't mind driving? Fran isn't there to share it, remember.'

Jon smiled ruefully. 'Yeah. But at least I don't have to travel back via Sussex, do I? It's fine. I'll stop halfway, maybe rent a room somewhere if I need to. Have a mini holiday. Take some photos.' He shrugged. 'Or I might just head straight to Whitby. Get started in the studio as soon as I can.'

'Well remember – whatever you need, just let me know. I'll get it organised.'

'Thank you, Lissy.' Jon gave her a quick hug. 'Thanks for everything. You seriously didn't have to buy the place, you know.'

'I wanted to.' Then she grinned. 'I'm your landlady now; that gives me power. Isn't it marvellous? I told Daddy that I was going to do it. It's not fair that I got the rich father and the trust fund and you didn't. It's the least I could do. This way, you can set yourself up in business and I get to see that I've done something good. It's a start.'

'It is. And *you're* marvellous,' he said.

Then he was off.

Lissy slipped her hand into Stefano's as she watched Jon go and sighed as she waved. 'He can be an utter pain, but he's my pain. Do you know what I mean?'

'He's a good guy. There's a woman for him out there. His soulmate. He will find her.'

'Well I hope it's bloody soon.' Lissy sighed again. 'Come on. I want to go shopping. Shopping always makes me feel better.'

'Love always makes me feel better,' Stefano murmured. Lissy was aware of his warm body next to hers and her stomach did that squishy thing again.

But no – tempted as she was, she had to be sensible. 'Shopping,' she said. 'And I know exactly where I want to go.' She pointed towards the high street. 'I have it on good authority that there is a wonderful antiques dealer just down here and along one of the side streets. I'm going there.'

'You love your junk!' moaned Stefano. 'What is it about that stuff? What is it that draws you to it? You're like a moth to a flame.'

Lissy laughed. 'I just love it. I love the history of it and the stories it could tell.' She reached up and kissed him. 'Now are you coming shopping or not?'

'I shall grace you with my presence, *Signorina*.' Stefano bowed jokingly. 'Fear not.'

They meandered down the High Street hand in hand, until they reached the little antiques shop Lissy had talked about. It wasn't long before she had engaged the owner in conversation and spotted something she liked the look of.

'So what do you know about the history of this piece?' she asked. She was looking at a ring, which lay on a faded, red velvet cushion. The centre was a solitaire diamond; a round, brilliant circle which, when you tilted it, would probably look like a glorious diamond spinning-top from the side. 'I'm guessing it's Old European cut?' she continued. 'And maybe Edwardian, judging by the decoration on the shoulders?' The platinum ring was set with filigree leaves and flowers and what looked like tiny waves cresting over the decorations either side of the central gemstone. It was a very elegant, sophisticated piece of jewellery.

'That would be right, Madam.' The antiques dealer nodded in agreement. 'You have an eye for these items.'

'One of my abiding interests,' she replied. 'You'd be surprised what I can dig up in shops like this.'

'I'm sure, Madam. As far as this little beauty is concerned, we don't know a great deal about it. What you say is correct about it being Edwardian. It's probably a privately commissioned piece, maybe an engagement ring; but more than that, we can't tell. I bought it at an auction. I think it echoes the sea, don't you?'

Lissy looked at the ring for a moment longer, processing the information. She was aware of the dealer watching her closely.

'Do you want to handle it, Miss?' he asked. He was a sun-tanned, wiry-haired fellow with a face as round as a clotted cream scone. He smiled engagingly at Lissy and on some level she marvelled, as his white teeth completed the effect of a golden scone split and filled with the lovely local cream.

Then Stefano appeared at Lissy's elbow. 'What is the problem? Have you not agreed to instantly relieve the gentleman of his burden?' he asked, peering at the ring.

'No. Not yet,' said Lissy. For some reason, she was entranced by the ring, but it didn't feel quite right to take it. It seemed wrong that this particular ring, this token of someone's love, should have ended up in an auction and been sold onto an antiques dealer. Lissy didn't usually fuss about things like that. She was practical and, as she had said, had an eye for a bargain and a flair for spotting something unusual and interesting. But this piece, sitting on its little cushion, defied all her logic.

Stefano smiled at the dealer. 'I am sure Elisabetta would like to handle the item as she contemplates it. Please – allow me to pass it to her.' He held out his hand and the dealer dropped the ring into his open palm.

Stef turned towards Lissy and a glint of sunlight caught the diamond through the window. Lissy blinked as the rainbow flared and pierced her vision, flames seeming to lick around the diamond, turning its heart crimson and gold. She ducked her head and rubbed her eyes, trying to get the shards of light out of her pupils, and an image flitted into her mind of the ring being placed on the slim, right hand of a woman, her fingers curling around those of the person who had presented it. Then the fingers disconnected and the image faded and Lissy was blinking in the little shop again.

She sucked in a deep breath, feeling almost winded.

'I don't know if it was supposed to be an engagement ring or not,' Lissy finally managed to say, her voice sounding odd, even to herself. 'And if they *were* married, and it ended up for sale, it must have been a pretty bad relationship for them to get rid of it like that.'

'Does it matter?' asked Stef, looking bemused. 'If you like it, you should try it on.'

'No.' Lissy shook her head. The images had thrown her. She glanced at the ring in the palm of Stef's hand and knew it wasn't for her – not right now.

'I think I'd like to think about it,' she said, still staring at it. 'It won't run away. It's quite expensive anyway so I'll have to consider the cost.' That was a lie – it *was* expensive, but she could afford it.

'But someone else might buy it!' Stef moved his hand closer to Lissy. 'Are you sure?'

'It's beautiful and I probably *would* want it in the future, but I need some time to think. I'm getting a migraine, anyway. That flash caught me in the eyes and it's all twinkly now.' That, as well, was a lie. But it was the best she could come up with. The fact was, she wanted the ring, but she didn't want it at this moment. It just didn't feel *right*. 'I'll head home, I think, and lie down. It's the heat. And Jon splitting up with Fran. And the fact he's driving back all alone. I don't like to think of it.'

'Oh – my poor Elisabetta. Wait. I'll take you!' Stef's voice carried through the doorway into the street as she stumbled outside, rubbing her eyes again.

'No, it's fine!' she called back. 'I'll see you later.' And then she picked up speed and ran back the way she had come.

Chapter Four

Sea Scarr Hall, 1905

The man who was staying in the Dower House, a Mr Cooper, was supposed to be an artist. At least that was what Lorelei Scarsdale had been told. Her husband, Walter, was quite vague when she asked him.

'I have no real idea who he is.' Walter lined up his telescope to get a better view of the horizon. 'He simply pays the rent. I leave that sort of thing to the estate manager.' He leaned into the eye-piece, effectively dismissing her and thus ending their conversation.

Lorelei, for once, did not want to be dismissed so rudely. 'Is he part of the Staithes Group?' she persisted. 'They appear to be drifting away, somewhat. It would be so nice if he could help breathe some new life into the movement. After all—'

'Lorelei!' Her husband's voice was sharp, every inch of him a man who was accustomed to being in command. 'I told you, I do not know. Now, if you will excuse me, I have work to do.'

'But—'

'Please!' He swung around and glared at her. 'Leave me alone.'

Lorelei stared at him without speaking. She made her eyes go as wide as possible, knowing full well that their bright green – the colour of the frondy seaweed which floated in the rock pools down in the cove – unnerved him. Today, however, his eyes were flinty and harsh, glaring back at her.

Walter had once likened her to a witch, marvelling over her long, wavy black hair and her pale complexion; but that was before they were married and he had realised that they were quite incompatible. They were like fire and ice in the beginning. Only her fire had been dampened down by beatings and insults over the years, and she naturally shied away from his coolness. She sometimes thought that if she'd had sails or a steaming funnel, she would have interested him more.

The man who stood before her was so absolutely buttoned up on the face of it all, that she often wanted to rip his starched collar off and string him up by his silken tie. But of course, she could never do that. She cast a glance over his carefully waxed blonde hair and his tight little moustache and she wondered, not for the first time, what she had ever seen in him.

'Well?' he asked. Even his voice was clipped and horrid. 'Why are you still here?'

Why indeed?

'I'm sorry, Walter,' she replied. 'I'll go now.' Her voice, in contrast to his, still had a Yorkshire burr to it, despite his best efforts to educate her in the King's English. She turned on her heel and swept out of the room, daring, for once, to slam the study door shut behind her.

She headed down the corridor towards the main doors of the Hall before striding off down the steps and across the lawns. It was the beginning of the summer and the afternoon was warm, but even if it had been midwinter she was not going to stay in that house a moment longer than she had to.

Lorelei kept walking towards the walled garden – once through there, she could head straight across to the sturdy wooden door in the boundary wall and, upon opening that, feast her eyes on the sea and the cliffs and the cove that was theirs and theirs alone.

A small part of her acknowledged that she had been drawn into marriage with Lord Scarsdale in a bid to own this house and this view. Otherwise, there was absolutely no rational judgement to be made about why she had married him. She had been an artists' model, a nameless figure in the background of some of the best works of art the era had ever produced. She had worked in Cornwall and Paris and London, she had sat for Laura Johnson – who was now Laura Knight – and her new husband Harold. She had even posed for Monet, Renoir, Augustus John ... The list went on. And throughout her time in the background, she had developed her own talents and her own passion for painting.

And this passion was what her husband disliked so much about her. Lorelei was meant to be an ornament on Lord Scarsdale's arm and nothing else. She was not meant to think, speak, act or do anything to tarnish that image – that waxen, painted image of perfection that he demanded of her. She was not supposed to answer back, have an opinion or let herself fall into disarray. She must project perfection and propriety and obedience at all times; and God forbid she forgot to do any of that, or she would suffer the consequences.

She certainly looked the part of the objectified Lady Scarsdale he wanted – without being vain, she knew herself to be quite beautiful, which was why the artists had liked her. But she had never 'made it'; never become famous, like Lizzie Siddal, or Camille Doncieux, or Rose Beuret. And ultimately, it would have been wonderful to have been a model for Julia Margaret Cameron, but sadly, Mrs Cameron was dead and buried and there was no chance of that now.

So the idea that an artist had moved into the Dower House for the summer was absolutely, wonderfully appealing. The very idea of a kindred spirit, of someone she could talk to or learn from, or even perhaps work alongside, was exciting. Perhaps he would be a bearded, serious old man who had seen more and done more than she could ever hope to do. Perhaps the summer visitor had worked in Paris or London and knew the artists she aspired to be like; knew the artists she had sat for, even? How utterly divine, how utterly perfect, if for one summer, she could be herself again.

Lorelei had reached the door to the outside world now, and she pulled it open, pausing on the other side as she always did, catching her breath at the seascape that lay before her. The sparkling diamonds on the waves and that hushy-shushy noise as they broke over the rocks; the squawk of the gulls and the tang of salt drifting over in the crisp wind that blew in from the continent. How wonderful.

And how restricting.

There always seemed to be something just over the horizon, just out of reach for her, and it frustrated her like nothing else. She had thought that by marrying Walter, it would free her from her work and give her time to paint and enjoy the ideal of the artist's life which she had built up in her head. After all, the Scarsdales had an interesting poor relation who had apparently been an art tutor to one of the Pre-Raphaelites – or so the story went.

Lorelei wasn't sure. She had seen the wonderful portrait in the ballroom of a red-haired girl languishing in a field of daisies, so there was definitely a connection somewhere along the line. But the signature on the picture – Henry Dawson – was nobody she had ever heard of and she had no idea who the girl was. It was an interesting concept though, and to be honest, she had thought that having a connection like that to some of the most glorious artists in history, Walter would have been a little – no a lot – more accepting of her passions. But he wasn't.

Lorelei made her way towards the path that wound down to the cove and wished she had brought at least a pencil and her sketchbook. She never tired of this place; people – well, Walter – didn't understand her when she said it was always different. There was, of course, that Greek philosopher who advised you could never step into the same river twice, and that, really, was what she was trying to suggest to him. The water was constantly changing, the rockpools varied with the tides and one never knew what one would find washed up on the shore.

She ached to find, perhaps, a smuggler's barrel or a message in a bottle. Or a body. A body would be quite interesting, if rather disgusting. A body, she thought with a smile twitching at her lips, would jolly well chivvy *some* sort of reaction out of Lord Stuffy.

She kicked off her buckled leather shoes, the little heels of which would sink most dreadfully into the sand, and picked up her long skirt. Her intention was to reach the bathing machine, don the navy-blue bathing dress she kept there and swim out to sea as far as possible. Left to her own devices, she would abandon the bathing dress altogether – she had been a model, for God's sake, and there was not one bit of her that had not been sketched or sculpted at one time or another, so modesty was not the issue. Of course, the elderly artist in the Dower House might get a bit of a shock if he saw her swimming naked, come to think of it.

But the biggest issue was that her husband was quite possibly peeping through the windows at the cove using that ridiculous telescope of his. She did not see why he should be treated to a view of something he really didn't care for much at all in the privacy of their bedroom, through a lens which would magnify everything for his own pleasure.

No. The bathing dress it was.

Lorelei reached the bathing machine and danced up the six steps to the tightly shut door, which she wrenched open against the swelling of the wood. Inside, the place was like a dank, dim little barn, with one shuttered window looking out to sea. The first task was to fling the shutters open and she leaned out, closing her eyes against the wind that gusted across the beach. Walter would tell her it was too cold to bathe, but what did she care for his opinion?

Lorelei's next task was to rip her annoying, formal gown off and to drop it onto a chair in the corner. The frock was a ghastly shade of oyster trimmed with cream lace and she was not at all fond of it, but they had been to a luncheon with several of Walter's associates and therefore she'd had to dress demurely and appropriately. Then she untied her layers of petticoats until she was finally down to the awful corset, which subsequently came off and was dropped onto the floor with a grimace of distaste.

The bathing dress was stiff and cold, still salty from her visit two days ago, but she couldn't see the point of taking it to the Hall, having it laundered and ironed, then bringing it back down here. She had clean ones up there anyway, but it was just as easy to leave one here to use.

And the last thing she simply had to do was to unpin her formal chignon and let her thick, black hair tumble down her back. Then she plaited the heavy waves loosely, stopping half way down and tying the plait with a red ribbon that she kept in the bathing machine. Yes, it was more sensible to keep her hair pinned up for swimming, but she liked the feeling of it flowing behind her as she swam. It was not so pleasant afterwards, when it dripped down her back, but that's what the pins were there for. The plait could be wound up on top of her head and pinned in place and that helped a little anyway.

Lorelei left the machine, ensuring her towel was laid carefully on the steps so she could pick it up on the way back in, and headed down. Of course, the machine should really be *in* the water, so all she had to do to preserve her modesty was slip into the sea unseen – but that made no sense to her and she ran across the expanse of sand towards the waiting ocean. She waded out as far as possible, then began to swim with sure, confident strokes.

Walter hated coming into the sea, so she knew that as long as she was down in the cove and in the water, she was relatively safe from the violent man she had so casually married.

It was bliss.

Walter trained the telescope on the ocean, framing the little figure in the blue dress striking out to sea. Her dark plait was tied with a red ribbon that streamed out behind her, her strokes taking her over to a rock which he knew she favoured.

He shivered. He had never seen the appeal of the ocean. It was cold, it was salty and it was unpleasant, but she looked as if she belonged there. She was a veritable mermaid, and looked like her namesake. He could see her slim, toned arms ploughing up the water, her long legs keeping pace. He saw her breasts pressing against the wet fabric of her swimsuit as she rolled over and swam backstroke, her eyes blissfully closed while she moved through the water knowing, it seemed, exactly where she should aim for. A few yards away from the rock, she flipped over again, and he imagined those soft breasts suspended in the water, moving with the current ...

He altered the lens setting to keep her in focus and groaned as he felt a strong stirring of desire for her; then he flung the telescope away, disgusted. He turned from the window so he couldn't see her, and he couldn't be tempted by the filthy little whore he had married.

He didn't want to touch her ever again.

Chapter Five

'Hey, a penny for them, *mia cara*.'

Lissy stared straight ahead and hurried past Stefano. He had parked himself on a bench half way down the pier and there was no way – no way on earth – she could get past him effectively. And now, now he wanted to speak to her. Well, he knew what he could do with himself.

'May I walk with you?' He was off the bench and falling into step with her.

'No.' She hoped her curt response was enough to tell him he wasn't welcome anywhere near her.

'I am here for the duration, as they say, so you may as well get used to having me around.'

'Duration? What the hell do you mean? Have we declared war or something and I didn't know about it?' Lissy retorted sharply. Okay – she had answered him; been drawn into a conversation with him. Again. For God's sake …

'I am not at war with anyone. However,' Stefano said, shrugging, 'maybe you are at war with me, but it is nothing a peace treaty cannot resolve.'

'I beg to differ. Maybe you should have considered that before you allied yourself to someone else. It's going to take more than a simple peace treaty to make me forgive you.'

'But you did not know the full story!' Stefano lost his temper at last. 'You never listened. You never gave me a chance.' He grabbed her arm and pulled her roughly towards him.

'You just admitted she was a mistake! You just said …' Her words were cut off as he sealed her mouth with his. And suddenly it was like the last seven years had never happened and they were on the seashore at Newlyn and everything was lovely again ... She closed her eyes and couldn't help but let herself fall into the kiss and remember all those other kisses and all the times they had ...

And then, at length, he drew away from her, and his dark eyes burned into hers like embers.

My curse be on the day when first I saw
The brightness in those treacherous eyes of thine—

Oh, hell. Now she was quoting bloody Rossetti in her head. That poem about Lady Pietra degli Scrovegni. The image of the painting it belonged to flitted across her mind's eye, followed swiftly by an image of the very same model – Marie Spartali Stillman – in a photograph by Julia Margaret Cameron. It was her brother's fault; he wanted to do this damn project and he'd spent all afternoon talking about it and now it was all blending together and then she'd had too much sun and this had happened, this thing with Stef and so ...

'No!' She surprised even herself with force of the word. 'No. I won't let it happen again.'

He was still staring at her, but now he was looking as surprised as she felt. 'Why not, Lissy?' he asked quietly. She remembered how much she had liked the sound of her nickname when he said it. 'We both still feel the same. That just proved it. You cannot pretend.'

'I can never trust you again,' she snapped, 'and I don't need your explanations.' Lissy pulled away from him. 'I saw you with her. I saw you with a naked woman, hidden away in a secluded cove. What the hell was I supposed to think?'

'I ...'

'No! I don't want to hear it from you. You've had seven years, Stef.' Lissy was pointing her forefinger at him, astonished, on some level, to see it was shaking. But that wasn't surprising, really. Her whole body was shaking. With temper. Yes. With temper. Not with anything else. Like lust. Or passion. Hell, no. With temper. Purely temper. 'You've had seven years to come up with an explanation, Stef,' she repeated. 'Forget it. I'm leaving.'

Stefano stepped back as if she'd punched him. Lissy took the opportunity to push past him and hurry back towards the town; back towards the fish and chip shops and the amusements and the candy floss vendors. Back towards all the seaside tat that proved some people were enjoying themselves this afternoon.

Lissy cursed under her breath and began to run. The only place she could go was Jon's studio. And she had to get there before Stef did in order to jump into her car and drive away. She couldn't deal with any more of Stef today.

Stefano, sitting on the pavement outside the studio, looked up as Jon and Becky strolled towards him. Grace, tired out, was in Becky's arms, her thumb in her mouth and her eyes closed.

'Where's Lissy?' Becky asked.

Stef got to his feet as they came closer and smiled ruefully. 'I do not know. She ran away.'

'Ran away?' Becky repeated. She looked at her husband. 'Well, maybe that wasn't the brightest idea you've ever had, Jon.'

Jon pulled a face. He unlocked the studio door and gestured for everyone to enter. Stef stood back and Becky went first. She sat down on one of the chairs in the waiting area and rearranged Grace into a more comfortable position. The little girl's sunhat fell off and Stef stooped down to pick it up. He laid it on the chair next to Becky and wandered over to the window.

'Well her car has gone.' Jon moved behind the desk where

the till was. He produced a set of keys and began to take some of the money out, bagging the coins up and counting piles of notes. 'Either that or the bloody thing was towed away. I told her those yellow lines weren't the best place to park.'

'I think she might have been clamped if they caught her,' said Becky, 'and she would still have been here causing a fuss if that was the case.'

'She was probably annoyed that I used our space.' Jon smiled suddenly. 'I never thought of that. Well. She knows what it's like around here to park. I'm surprised she even brought the car.'

'We don't have an airport in the town. That's why,' said Becky. 'She might have taken the train, I suppose ...'

'Really!' Stef had had enough. He spun around and faced them. 'Does it matter how she got here? I want to know where she has *gone*. I need to talk to her. I need to speak to her and she needs to listen to me.' He turned back to the window and shoved his hands in his pockets, staring out into the street. He sighed and swivelled to face Jon and Becky again. 'Does anybody have any bright ideas?'

Jon moved over to him and clapped him on the back. 'Seriously, I have no idea, bright or otherwise, where she is. She could have driven back down to London for all I know. I didn't think to ask where she was staying.'

'She could have stayed here.' Becky nodded in the direction of the rickety old staircase up to the flat. 'The bed's always made. We always have coffee in, if nothing else, but she must have planned something. She didn't just call in on spec. We knew she was coming. She told us she was coming – as Jon clearly knew, because he invited you.' She pulled a face, perhaps wondering if that had been a good thing or not. 'But I guess she already had something sorted.'

'With Lissy, who knows.' Jon walked over and gently

stroked Grace's hair. The girl stirred in her sleep and snuggled into Becky. Stef thought she was a very endearing child and saw again, in his mind's eye, Lissy digging holes with her in the sand. He frowned, the images leading him to places he didn't want to go to, just yet.

'She might have rented a caravan for all we know,' Jon continued. 'The point is, she's run off and I think you're to blame, mate.' He suddenly grinned at Stef. 'How does it feel to still have that sort of power over her after so long?'

'Power?' cried Stef. 'She always had the power in the relationship. She's temperamental, that's for sure.' He frowned again and sat down, resting on the edge of a table and crossing his legs.

'That's not entirely her fault,' said Becky. 'You know about the guy she was with after Uni, don't you? It's understandable. She's only ever tried to protect herself since then.'

'Protect herself and organise everybody else's relationships,' said Jon wryly. 'Me and Becky, Cori and Simon – I suspect she thought of us all as projects in some way. She likes to take credit for us. It's the only way she feels in control, I think, because she can never control her own love life.'

'But I've never seen her so rattled before.' Becky shook her head. 'I seriously think she isn't going to forgive you any time soon, Stef.' Stef opened his mouth to defend his actions, but Becky shook her head. 'I don't want to hear about it. It's between you two. Now. Have you got somewhere to stay tonight, or is that a really stupid question?'

'No.' Stef sighed and re-crossed his legs. 'It is not a stupid question. I'm in a B & B. Well, it's more an apartment in the town, but it's like a B & B. I had hoped I would need a little space. I hoped Lissy might decide she would like to stay with me. You never can tell.' He smiled, mirthlessly. 'Oh, well. It was not to be. I just hope that she turns up somewhere.' He stood up and held his hand out to Jon. 'Goodnight, my friend. I will see you tomorrow. We must discuss the project. Your friends are also visiting, yes? Your artist friend and his partner?'

'Yes, Cori and Simon will be here at some point. We need Cori for some of the pictures.'

'It's just as well she's so good natured,' Becky commented, 'being treated like a sex object.'

'She's not a sex object!' Jon protested. 'She's like a model or a muse or something. And anyway, she's used to it by now. She's sat for so many of Simon's paintings. Come on, Stef, I'll see you out.'

'Thank you. And thank you for inviting me, Jon. It might have worked,' said Stef.

'It still might,' responded Jon. 'Don't give up just yet.'

'I have no intention of giving up. Lissy is what I want, and Lissy is what I will fight for. No more time wasting. I'd walk through the fires of hell to hold her hand properly again.'

And as he stepped out into the little cobbled street, Stef swore to himself that he wouldn't leave Britain this time without getting it all resolved.

He walked back to his apartment in the gathering dusk. The town was still alive, however, and every now and then black, shadowy figures would flit past him. The Goth tourists, of course; maybe seeing if they could raise the dead at the Abbey. Well, he wasn't interested in the dead. There was only Lissy who interested him, wherever she had disappeared to.

Not for the first time, he wished he could turn back time – roll back the years and be in Newlyn again with his Elisabetta. Yes, he realised now that he had made a huge mistake and knew what he should have done. It was just disastrous that Lissy had seen them, and it had all stemmed from there.

He walked up the steps and unlocked the door of the big, white Victorian house and headed up the stairs. He had rented the first floor. It seemed a bit of a waste of time and money now. It served him right; he shouldn't have been so conceited as to think he could come here and win her back without really trying.

He walked in the front door of the apartment and placed his camera down on the soft sofa, then headed into the kitchen. Pulling open the refrigerator, he took out a bottle of champagne. Yes, he had been very presumptuous. But as his love was not with him to share the champagne, he felt obliged to drink it himself.

Chapter Six

The Cove, 1905

Julian MacDonald Cooper watched the woman with the long, dark plait race lightly across the sand and strike out to sea. She was indeed a pleasure to behold and his intuition told him that she would make an excellent model and would be just as much of a pleasure to work with.

He wasn't sure who she was. He had just left the Dower House for a walk in the cove after a late lunch and he had come across this vision as he rounded the path down onto the beach. He understood it to be a private beach, so he wondered if she was a member of the Scarsdale household or a friend of theirs they had graced with access to the cove.

But he was determined to find out. He strode onto the beach feeling the sand between his toes. He never bothered with shoes or formality when he came down here. Formality was for working and impressing clients. Bare feet and an open-necked shirt would do him very well for the beach. He ran a hand through his longer-than-generally-acceptable dark hair and smiled to himself as he remembered the idea he'd had earlier today about finding a barber in Staithes.

That had never happened, had it?

Well, there was always tomorrow.

Julian had heard a lot about Staithes and the artists' colony that had sprung up about ten years ago. He feared their days were numbered though; their 1905 exhibition had been subsumed into the Yorkshire Union of Artists' work, and he had heard other plans were afoot to hold an exhibition in August – which would clash terribly with the Summer Exhibition at the Royal Academy in London. And the art aficionados would be down in the capital along with the wealthy patrons, not up here in a little fishing village on the north-east coast of England.

So that was why he had come down to Yorkshire from Edinburgh. Firstly, to observe how things were now, and secondly, to record Staithes and its colony for posterity in his favourite medium – photography. He already had a dealer lined up in North Yorkshire to buy and sell his photographs.

And that woman, who he now realised was swimming over to some rocks with the clear intention of climbing onto them, was just begging to be used as a model in some shape or form. But first, he conceded, he would actually have to speak to her.

'Ahoy there!'

Lorelei saw the figure on the shore waving to her as she settled on the rocks and felt a little burst of anger that her fun had been thus intruded upon. Then, as she watched him come closer to the shoreline, she realised that he was quite a stranger, and therefore very possibly the artist from the Dower House. From his confident stride and the way he held himself, this was no old man – no elderly gentleman who she could chat to. This was someone altogether much younger and much more vibrant.

She sat up straight on the rock and began to wring her hair out, twisting it and squeezing it between her long, artistic fingers. 'Do you have permission to be on this beach?' she shouted. 'It is private, and I'm afraid that you are trespassing. If that is the case, you may have to be shot.'

The man laughed and she could see he was wading out towards her, heedless of his trousers soaking up the sea water.

'I do have permission,' he shouted back. 'I'm renting the Dower House from the Scarsdales. I might ask you the same question. Do *you* have permission to be here?'

'Then I assume you are Mr Cooper,' stated Lorelei, ignoring his query.

'I am indeed Mr Cooper,' replied the man. He bowed elegantly, if a little mockingly, and she noticed with appreciation the fact that his hair fell over his face in a very Bohemian fashion.

'Then you are an artist, Sir.'

'I *am* an artist. But my medium is photography.' He took a few more strides towards her so the water was up to the middle of his thighs and he smiled. The deep brown of his eyes was very pleasing and Lorelei smiled back. 'Yet I do not know who *you* are,' he continued. 'Are you perhaps a mermaid or a siren, waiting for a sailor to clamber onto your rock and lapse unto certain death?'

'You are Scottish, Mr Cooper,' commented Lorelei, deliberately evading his questions. It would be rather fun to keep him guessing, she had decided. God knew she had little enough fun with Walter and she could never talk to him like this.

'I am indeed Scottish. And that is now three things you know about me, Madam Siren.' He held up his hand and began counting them off his fingers. 'I am Mr Cooper. I take photographs. And I hail from Scotland. Oh! No, my apologies. You know four things. You also know that I have permission to be on this beach, which is more than I know about you. I may have to report you to the Scarsdales after all.'

'Report away.' Lorelei slipped off the rock and began to swim diagonally across the expanse of water, cutting quite closely by him on an arrow-straight route towards the bathing machine.

'Incredible woman!' Julian called after her. 'I will discover your identity, have no fear.'

'Oh, I don't fear that!' she shouted back over her shoulder.

'And I am sure we shall meet again, sometime soon, Mr Cooper. *Adieu*!'

Lorelei emerged from the water and ran to the bathing machine, ducking down and picking up her towel from the steps. Once inside, she shut the door and dragged the chair across it. She wouldn't put it past the man to try and follow her in.

She stifled a giggle. If she was truthful, she wasn't actually sure if the chair was to stop him coming in, or her going out.

Julian wasn't going to move from that beach until she emerged – no power on earth would budge him. He sat down behind the bathing machine and crossed his legs. She had to come out at some point, and then he would pursue her to her destination. It wasn't very often one came across a beautiful, dark-haired mermaid in Yorkshire.

His waiting was rewarded about twenty minutes later when there was a scraping sound from behind the door and a creak as it was pushed open. The vision of loveliness descended the steps, looked left and right and began to walk back across the beach, towards the winding path which led to the Hall. Julian waited a little longer, watching her move elegantly and sensually across the sand. She had discarded the blue bathing dress and was clad in an oyster-coloured gown, which had lacy flounces instead of sleeves. It had clearly been crumpled up in that little hut. Slung over one arm was a messy froth of white material – her petticoats, he realised – and she was patting her roughly pinned up hair with her free hand.

The woman paused near the dunes and stared around her, looking for something. Then she bent down and picked something up from the ground – a pair of shoes – and she sat down on a tussock of scrubby grass to fasten them onto her feet, laying the petticoats untidily down beside her.

Now was his moment. He ran across the sand and caught up with her.

She looked up, surprise registering on her face. 'You waited? I didn't see you—' She blushed a little, betraying the fact that he was what she had looked for as she emerged from the bathing machine.

'Another question! And you have yet to answer mine.' He shook his head and folded his arms. 'Because I am going to follow you up to that Hall and demand your identity is revealed to me. I can tell by your clothes that you aren't a casual visitor to the cove. And you probably shouldn't be here, swimming around with nobody to hear your screams if you get caught in a riptide. So. Your name, please? And then I can let you leave.'

She sighed and stood up, gathering her petticoats together and folding them over her arms again, smoothing them down nervously. 'Yes. You are right. I have yet to answer your questions. I suppose I must tell you that you can't follow me up to the Hall and demand my identity because I am a completely different person up there. I am sure we will meet again, Mr Cooper. I look forward to it.' She nodded and turned away.

Julian couldn't help it. He reached out his hand and grabbed her forearm, pulling her back towards him. She flinched at the touch, stiffened, then stared at him, her eyes wide and surprised and the most magnificent shade of green he had ever seen. He noticed a smattering of yellowing bruises around the top of her arm and slackened his hold.

She followed his gaze and laughed in a slightly strained manner. 'Don't worry. A wave took me too close to the rocks. You haven't hurt me. It's just a bit sore today.'

'Damn waves. How dare they? Are you staying at the house, then?' he tried. 'Because I may be visiting later. I know there is some sort of event on tonight.' He pulled a face. 'I

44

wasn't going to go, but if you're there—' He let the words drift in the breeze.

The woman smiled and gently removed herself from his grip. 'I shall be there, Mr Cooper. Goodbye for now.' She inclined her head and began to walk up the path again.

Julian stood for a long time watching her graceful movements. She didn't so much walk as glide. He watched until she had disappeared out of sight. He itched to capture her in a photograph. And if he did nothing else that summer, he swore to himself that he would do that.

'Well I am glad to see you have decided to return.'

Lorelei closed her eyes and bit back a sarcastic retort. She knew she'd come off all the worse for it. Instead, she cursed under her breath and walked along the corridor, ignoring her husband who was standing in the study doorway looking as arrogant and pinched up as always.

An image of their tenant in the Dower House flitted unbidden into her mind as she put one hand on the banister to climb the stairs. She was embarrassed to feel her skin flush and a tingle spread across her body as she visualised Julian Cooper standing in the water, the sea lapping at his thighs and his hair blowing in the wind.

'Don't you dare ignore me!' The study door slammed shut, and she heard Walter marching along the hallway.

Lorelei's stomach clenched as he approached. He was obviously ready to continue the disagreement; and she knew what he was capable of when he was in a temper like this. She quickly took stock of her surroundings, judging which would be the fastest exit route from a well-aimed fist. With a sense of horror, she realised she was trapped in the long, narrow corridor and he was far too close, but the waft of whisky on his breath gave her hope that his reactions wouldn't be as sharp as usual. Alcohol, thank God, had that effect on him. But spending time with Julian had reminded her of the old Lorelei, and she found enough courage buried deep within that old self to straighten her shoulders and turn slowly towards her husband.

She might regret it later, but she was determined to face him down this time.

'Can I help?' she asked. 'Why the urgency to greet me? Has the ocean cleared of ships and I am the only interesting thing left to look at?'

'You look a mess,' he retorted. His eyes flicked up and down her body with distaste. 'And you appear to be in a state of undress.' She saw his fist clench and unclench and her heart skipped a beat. The bruises were never anywhere that really showed, and nobody would ever believe her anyway. Nor care – she had no family, no true friends left. She was alone.

'No, I'm not.' She held her voice steady with a great effort. 'I'm still wearing my gown and my corset – otherwise my dress wouldn't have fastened up.' She looked down at her hem which was filthy and yes, very much torn where it had caught on a gorse bush and she had tugged it away. The lack of petticoats had made the skirts too long and the vile gown hung at a quirky angle. But she liked the feeling of freedom.

She didn't, however, like the fact that Walter's whisky-soaked breath was coming faster and faster, and his hand continued to clench and unclench relentlessly. Just as his eyes went blank and he raised a fist towards her, she thought quickly and thrust the bundle of petticoats at him: 'Hold these, would you please, Walter.' Automatically, he grabbed the undergarments and held them for less than a second, until he realised what they were and threw them on the floor with a bellow. His fist lifted again, but Lorelei was too quick. She ducked out of the way and his punch landed in the plaster of the wall, making him hiss with pain.

'You common slut!' growled Walter. His face was mottled and angry and she knew she'd gone too far. 'Get upstairs now and clean yourself up!' A maid suddenly appeared around the corner and cowered into the woodwork, probably, Lorelei thought, saving her from another punch. 'You have sand and seaweed in your hair and it isn't even pinned properly. Someone must make you respectable. We are hosting a ball tonight and you will *not* be a vagabond.'

Lorelei laughed, a brittle, unnatural sound that had nothing to do with amusement. 'I'm so sorry, Walter. I'd never want people to think you'd married a vagabond. I had better go and get ready before the company arrives.'

She turned away and fled up the stairs, leaving the petticoats on the floor. She ran into her bedroom, her heart pounding, and locked the door, then hurried over to the mirror, shedding her clothing as she went.

The same face stared back at her as always, but she didn't feel the same. Not at all.

Chapter Seven

The Cove, Present Day

Stefano's 'love' was, at that precise moment, doing almost exactly the same thing as him. Only she had a bottle of mellow, red wine open in front of her. She was halfway down the bottle and didn't really intend to stop until she had emptied it.

Beside the bottle were the pathetic remains of a family size bar of chocolate. It was usually against Lissy's principles to consume so much chocolate in so little time, but needs must. She picked up the last two squares and popped them in her mouth. She had ceased tasting the sweet flavour about quarter of a bar ago; now it was basically an automated response as her jaws chewed and her mind wandered.

Unfortunately, her mind wandered to Lamorna, with the ever-present spectre of Stefano hovering around her thoughts. No matter how many times she thought about it, no matter how many times she pictured the scene in her head, it never changed. Her memories were horribly truthful.

She had come around the corner of the Cove to surprise him, knowing that he had said he would be working there that day. She'd been quite thoughtful – she had prepared a lovely treat, packed it all into a beautiful little wicker basket and she was going to surprise him. She had a bottle of wine with her, two plastic glasses and a selection of fruit and canapés, purchased from a deli. She had also brought, fresh from the local bakery, two piping hot scones wrapped in a chequered tea-towel, a tub of homemade (well, of course Lissy hadn't made it, but the lady in the bakery had) strawberry jam and a big pot of Cornish clotted cream. The image of the man in the antiques shop had stayed with her, and had made them both laugh when she'd admitted her thoughts to Stef. So she thought the scones were a nice touch.

Lissy clambered over the rocks towards the rock pools she knew were hidden there, and it was from that point where it all went completely downhill.

Lamorna Cove, Seven Years Ago

'Just tell me what to do. Tell me exactly what to do.' Her voice was throaty, sexy; it still made Stef smile, even from this side of the camera.

'*Bella* Kerensa.' Stef was sitting cross-legged on the rocks, the ideal angle for him to capture this alluring creature on film. 'You know exactly what to do.'

'You have to remind me,' said the girl. She was tall, blonde and had the curves and the pout to rival a young Brigitte Bardot. She was also a girl Stef had known for several years, on and off. On – very much on – when he came to Cornwall to work, and off when he was back in Italy, away from temptation. She was the reason he'd come back this time. The perfect woman to model for his latest series of photographs.

Currently, "Bella" Kerensa was stretched out languidly on a rock, lying on her back, stark naked, her fingers trailing in a crystal clear rockpool. 'I forget the simplest of instructions when you watch me like that.'

'I watch you as a professional,' replied Stef, framing the shot. 'I must watch you pose and stretch and roll over – yes! Yes, that is it. Exactly it.' He pressed the shutter as Kerensa rolled onto her stomach and raised herself up on her arms.

She lay on her front, bent her legs up and crossed them at the ankle, resting her perfect chin in her perfect cupped hands. Her eyelids were heavy with smoky colours and her lashes black and thick, layered with mascara. Her lips were palest pink, her blonde hair caught up in a 1960's style – a beehive, perhaps, that had half-tumbled from its pins as if after a session of lovemaking. Stef suppressed a smile as he took another picture. He knew what she looked like after such a session.

'*Bella*,' he murmured again. '*Perfetto.*'

Kerensa giggled and shifted so that she was on all fours.

She began to crawl over to him, her plump, shell pink lips slightly open, curving into a sensual smile. 'Your voice is my drug,' she breathed. 'Your accent – when you speak to me like that, I can't think straight.'

'Think only of the poses, the pictures,' replied Stef, clicking as she crawled closer to him. He felt a stirring somewhere he thought he should really reserve for only Elisabetta. But Kerensa slithering towards him made him catch his breath and click the shutter faster and faster as she approached, until she was right in front of him.

She laughed, softly, and took hold of the camera, moving it away from his face. 'Kiss me,' she whispered.

'Ah, Kerensa,' Stef said, groaning. 'I cannot, I cannot. She will kill me, I swear!'

'Who will? Who will kill you? There's nobody here except us. Just us.'

'Kerensa, no. I am here to work! Just to work!' he protested.

'We've always worked well together, Stef. Always. Nobody can see us.'

Stef stared at Kerensa, scanning her eyes, her nose, her lips, her perfect chin. 'I am here to work.' He tried to sound firm. Automatically, he lifted a hand and pushed a strand of hair away from her face.

On some level, he was cursing his Italian passion. On another – well – if they did it, it would be farewell, would it not? He had loved this girl, no strings attached, for a long time. He owed her something, surely?

No. No, he didn't. He tried to strengthen his resolve.

What he felt for Elisabetta – *that* was real love. That was the feeling you had when you knew you would throw yourself into the flames for her. You wouldn't hesitate to take a bullet for her; you wouldn't hesitate to sacrifice your life for her. It was Elisabetta he wanted, Elisabetta he needed.

'I have found someone else,' he told Kerensa. 'Her name is Elisabetta.'

'Elisabetta,' replied Kerensa. 'Hmm.' She leaned forward and before he could move away she had placed her slick, pink lips on his, biting the bottom one gently. She pulled away from him, fixing her eyes on his. 'Where did you meet this Elisabetta? And when?'

His lip throbbed and so did somewhere else but he ignored it. 'I met her here. I met her some weeks ago—'

'Some weeks ago? Not long then.' Kerensa kneeled up and shuffled closer to him. She wrapped her arms around his neck and pounced, swiftly wrapping her legs around his waist and smiling into his eyes. He put his arms around her body to steady them, terrified they would tumble off the rocks and hurtle into the sea below.

'Kerensa, stop it!'

'Some weeks ago,' Kerensa repeated. 'But you've known me so much longer.'

'Yes, but I cannot know you like *that* anymore, *bella*.'

'Really?' she asked, a smile curving her lips. 'Well, let's see about that, shall we?'

She pressed herself against him and he closed his eyes. Oh God! Maybe he could stave her off with a kiss? Maybe he should just push her gently away? Maybe he could—

But the thought never had time to crystallise. There was

an unholy shriek from the top of the rocks. Stef looked up, mortified. Kerensa followed his gaze.

Then she laughed. 'The fiery Elisabetta, I presume,' she said, and went back to the task in hand.

Whitby, Present Day

Lissy hadn't waited to see any more. 'What the *hell* are you *doing?*' she had screeched from her perch at the top of the rocks. Now, when she thought about it, she realised she must have looked less like an avenging angel and more like a velociraptor swooping in for the kill.

She had sworn particularly nastily at the pair of them, and reached into the basket full of treats. 'This is you *working?* This is what you *do?* A bloody naked woman and my boyfriend wrapped around each other?'

'Lissy! It's not what it seems. Kerensa is an old flame. We knew each other—'

'An old flame? I bet she's the reason you came here, isn't she? What was I? Just a distraction until you *reconnected?* How could you, Stef? I refuse, I absolutely *refuse* to be used by anyone. I'm not going to be just a *distraction.*'

She hurled the first thing that came out of the basket at him. It happened to be the jar of jam. It just missed him and shattered on the rocks. Stef let out a yell and tried to shift away from the shards of glass. The woman rocked on his lap and ducked her head, laughing, clinging tighter. Lissy followed through with the tub of cream. Next were the scones. The fruit was easy to launch, and she didn't care two hoots about that hitting either of them on the sodding head.

'I trusted you. I really trusted you!' Lissy shouted. 'How could I be so stupid? You're all the same!'

The Sixties sex-kitten was still laughing, shaking her head

as if Lissy was to be mocked or pitied or something, hanging onto him like a bloody limpet, curling up closer around his body, despite his futile attempts to unpeel her.

'No, Lissy! Please. We were just saying goodbye—'

It was completely the wrong thing to say.

'Doesn't look much like it's goodbye from here!' yelled Lissy. 'It looks like you're making up for lost bloody time, happy that I'm not around. Forget it, Stef. Just forget it. I hate you! In fact, no. I don't hate you. I have no feelings for you at all. None. It's finished. It's over. Go off with her. I really don't care.'

She closed her fingers around the bottle of wine and pulled it out of the basket, but common sense kicked in at that point; she hung onto the bottle and threw the basket at them instead. It skittered across the rocks and fell into the deep pool with a *splosh*.

'And you can collect your things from my cottage,' she shouted as her parting shot. 'Actually, no. I'll dump them on the sand for you. Then your girlfriend here can help you pick them up – and if you're lucky, the tide won't have come in and swept the whole bloody lot away!'

True to her word, she had dumped his belongings on Newlyn beach, the closest beach to her cottage. And he'd turned up for them, without the mystery woman in tow. He'd come with his right foot all bandaged up too; hobbling along saying he'd stood on some of that strawberry jam glass and cut himself. But so what?

If he hadn't been so fickle, things might have turned out quite differently. And as she watched the sun drop into the ocean from the terrace of yet another rented holiday home, a few miles up the coast from Whitby, Lissy let go of all the anger and all of the hurt and cried over Stefano Ricci for the first time in seven years.

* * *

Just a bit further down the coast, in his own holiday apartment, Stefano had reached the bottom of his champagne bottle – he had dispensed with a glass and drank straight out of the thing – and was now staring out of the window. He couldn't see much, just the big old houses opposite him, a few of which had themselves been converted into B & B's and boutique hotels. He wished he had taken rooms closer to the beach.

He always felt happier and freer by the ocean, probably due to the fact he had grown up near Portofino, a picturesque harbour village in Northern Italy. He had numerous happy memories of lazy days and hectic nights on the Italian coast, part of a large, noisy family, the third child of five. He was now thirty-seven years old and had seen his sisters love, marry and have children – not necessarily in that order. His family owned a large villa by the coast, his father's fortune coming from vineyards, and he had been a confident, spoilt, only son. It seemed a world away now, diving into those crystal depths and seeing the statue of Christ the Abyss beneath the ocean, simply as a rite of passage.

Stef had always been artistic and discovered a deep love of photography in his early twenties – and an even deeper appreciation of the models he met in that industry. Some, he had slept with. Some, he had kissed. One he had thought he loved – briefly. And he'd tied himself to her in a fit of rage after Lissy refused all contact with him – no emails, no phone calls, nothing.

Kerensa was the one he had lived with, sometimes laughed with and often fought with for six of the seven years he and Lissy had been apart. But those high-octane years and the meaningless affairs on both sides had finally made him take stock and realise he needed more. He wanted more. He wanted what he'd had with Lissy. Kerensa was a beautiful mistake, that was all. They parted as violently and as passionately as they had begun, and he apologised to her for wasting six years of her life. She had told him, eventually, that she wanted children. And he'd suddenly realised he wanted them too, but with Elisabetta, not Kerensa. He'd never been able to forget Lissy. He'd never wanted to destroy himself for Kerensa – but he'd happily throw himself off a cliff to save Lissy.

Lissy and he were going to head east, that long-ago summer, and tour the Cornish Riviera in a battered old VW campervan. The names of the beaches didn't exactly roll off his tongue; Lissy had laughed at his attempts to say words like *Mevagissey* and *Polkerris*. She had begged him to take her on a basking shark safari and they had spent hours looking at maps and plotting their route. But in the end, they'd never gone. Was it too late now?

Stefano dragged himself away from the window and the painful memories and headed into the little second bedroom. He had created a portable, makeshift, digital photography studio in there, by warrant of his laptop. Unlike Jon, Stefano embraced digital photography and was renowned in his field for creating the most astonishing pieces of digital artwork. He had some things to finish that he had been working on before he came to England, and also, within his portfolio, he had one or two precious pieces he just couldn't leave behind. It was these he turned to now, pulling them out of the folder and examining them. He intended to find a use for them here – how, he wasn't sure, but he was going to do it.

But first, he thought, he needed to sleep. Time and tide waited for no-one. And if he managed to sleep, at least the awful, lonely, Lissy-less night would pass more quickly.

Chapter Eight

Sea Scarr Hall, 1905

The company that night consisted of a selection of Walter's friends and acquaintances attending a ball to celebrate the coming-out of seventeen-year-old Miss Florence Percy, the daughter of a Scarsdale cousin from Northumberland.

Lorelei had tentatively suggested to Walter that, as a display of wealth and grandeur, the Scarsdales should host a ball so little Florrie could cut her debutante teeth before visiting London to represent the family. Walter had, surprisingly, agreed. He was, he had said, hoping it would encourage Lorelei, the current Lady Scarsdale, to act as she should be expected to. Then he had invited everyone he knew, telling her there was no room left for any of her friends, if indeed she even had any friends, which he doubted.

Sadly, he was right, but it galled her nonetheless.

Lorelei's greatest hope was now that Julian MacDonald Cooper should attend. Then she would have at least one person there that she knew. She was ten years older than Florrie, but almost ten years younger than her husband and his acquaintances – Florrie's mother, Mary, for example, was only two years or so older than Walter, and thus it was that she, Lorelei, did not fit into any category easily; she was neither fish nor fowl. Julian, it had seemed, was around her age, though. Which was encouraging.

Lorelei sighed and stared at herself in the mirror; yet another formal gown – white, this time, and eminently virginal to show off her sweetness and purity as lady of the manor.

It had probably been a bad choice. But she did quite like the dress. She smoothed down the frills on the skirt and stood up a little straighter. Her eyes drifted to the window where the evening sun was just beginning to stain the sea rose-gold and orange, and wondered what Julian's reaction would be when and if he came.

For a brief moment, Julian wondered whether he should have gone back into Staithes and found that barber after all. Then he decided the answer was no. These people were nothing like him, and therefore he should not be judged by their standards.

Julian hadn't met Lord Scarsdale, although the estate manager had been a decent enough fellow. He hadn't said anything directly derogatory about his employer, but Julian had a sharp mind and soon gathered that the man didn't hold his lordship in any great respect. Lord Scarsdale paid his wages, of course, but the man didn't get involved with the estate as much as he should. The estate manager had come with the territory, if you like – and Walter was apparently a poor substitute for his father, the previous Lord Scarsdale.

So as Julian walked up the path to the Hall and was almost knocked over by a carriage speeding down the driveway, he determined he would only stay long enough to see the Siren, satisfy himself of her identity and leave. He smiled to himself. He wondered whether the Siren would come away with him. Maybe she wouldn't be missed if she was a minor guest – the thought of her leaving with him was enticing, anyway, and that was what put the spring back into his step and gave him the energy to climb the steps and walk through the great doorway into the foyer.

'May I introduce you to the company, Sir?' A butler or a footman or whatever the hell you called them had appeared silently out of nowhere and blocked Julian's path.

'No, thank you. I'm only renting the Dower House. My name is Julian MacDonald Cooper and I *have* been invited, I assure you.' He produced an invitation card, which seemed to satisfy the Gatekeeper. Heimdall. That's who he reminded Julian of – the watchman of the old Norse gods, ready to blow his horn and summon the rest of them when their enemies appeared, on their way to raid Asgard. He ducked his head to hide a smile as Heimdall moved away to let him pass.

Julian walked across the black and white tiled hallway and followed the sounds of invited guests towards a large room at the back of the house. A couple drifted past him and nodded, the female eyeing him curiously and the male taking her arm and pulling her closer to him in a proprietary fashion.

Yes, Julian thought he probably looked a little out of place here – he hadn't brought any clothes suitable for a ball, that was for sure; so he had worn his three piece, chequered business suit and reluctantly donned a tie and a starched white collar for the occasion. The man who had just passed him had worn a very dapper dinner suit and the lady dripped with lace and diamonds, her silhouette so "S"-shaped that Julian wondered vaguely how she could even stand upright. She must be incredibly well balanced somewhere in her underskirts, in fact, she might be …

His train of thought came to a sudden halt. There she was; his Siren of the Rocks, dressed in a white, frilled gown – but instead of looking as trussed up as the guest in the corridor had, there was a distinct lack of "S"-shaping in her carriage; just a woman wearing a beautiful dress, the skirt falling gently from her waist and pooling onto the floor. Her hair, black as the midnight sky, swirled high onto her head and a cluster of white lilies-of-the-valley were tucked into the side.

God, she was enchanting.

Julian found that he couldn't move. His feet literally seemed to be stuck to the floor and he just stood there, staring at her. As if she could feel his eyes on her, she turned her head and met his gaze.

As she caught his eye, her skin turned a delicate shade of

pink and her sea-green eyes widened slightly. A smile touched her lips for just a second, then she dipped her head and turned away, melting into the crowds.

She couldn't believe he had really turned up. Next to the boring friends of Lord Stuffy he was a breath of fresh air. He drew the attention of quite a few women in that room, but she had been pleased to realise he looked at her and her alone.

Terrified that her blushes would draw attention to her, she ducked her head and retreated to the coolness of the shadows. She hadn't gone very far when Florrie appeared, seemingly out of nowhere, and stood in front of her. Florrie and her mother had arrived only a couple of hours beforehand, the girl a veritable whirlwind of excitement and raring to go. She had barely been introduced to her bedroom, before she was demanding her ballgown be organised and rejecting all suggestions of a nice rest before the party.

'Who's that man who just came in?' Florrie's blue eyes were wide and curious, her fair hair slipping sideways out of its elaborate chignon.

Lorelei smiled and reached out, tucking a bunch of feathers more securely into Florrie's hair. 'Well now, that's our summer tenant. He's a photographer, by all accounts.'

'But what's his name?' the girl persisted. 'Is he famous? He's rather a buck.'

'A *buck*?' exclaimed Lorelei, wondering how the child knew such slang – yet he *was* very handsome. It seemed, then, as if it wasn't just the older ladies who found Julian attractive. 'Please don't let your mother hear you using that sort of word, darling. And whether he is famous or not, I don't know. He's called Mr Cooper and I'm sure he doesn't want any attention drawn to him tonight.' *So just stay away from him*, she wanted to add.

'I *dream* of having a man like that fall for me,' said Florrie with a beatific smile. She clasped her hands together and fixed her eyes on Lorelei. 'Do you think there will be men like that in London?'

'Hundreds of them,' replied Lorelei. 'All waiting for you.'

Florrie laughed rather too loudly and a man nearby glared at her. She covered her mouth with her hands. 'I must learn to control myself,' she said, her voice muffled, her eyes blinking owl-like above her chubby fingers.

'Treat this as a practice event,' advised Lorelei. 'If you do anything socially unacceptable here, you will remember not to do it when it matters.' *When, for instance, there are men around you, who you can set your sights on properly.*

Florrie nodded and let her hands drop from her face. Her fingers clutched at her satin skirts and she sighed, staring over Lorelei's shoulder. Lorelei just knew she was staring at Julian.

'He's looking over here,' said Florrie. 'Oh, my!'

'Darling, we are right next to the champagne. Of course he's looking over here. The poor man must be thirsty. I'm the hostess. I will take him a drink. You go off and enjoy yourself.'

'Oh, but don't you have servants for that sort of thing?' Florrie asked. 'Because if you don't, I could take it and—'

'*No!*' Lorelei knew her voice was too sharp and the girl's face fell. She softened her tone and tried again. 'No, Florrie. This is your evening. You are here to socialise and enjoy yourself. Whatever would your mother think if she saw you serving drinks?'

'But you're going to serve them,' Florrie tried again.

'And as I said, I am the hostess. I make the rules,' said Lorelei. 'Now shoo. Go off and find someone to dance with you. Actually ...' She caught sight of her husband's solicitor and his family. 'Archie there is a lovely young man. Archie!' She raised her voice and the solicitor's twenty-year old son looked across. He was a shy young man, prone to a slight stoop due to his height and rangy with it. But his brown eyes were kind, his reddish hair too long and verging on the Bohemian, just like Julian's and his face was sweet. Lorelei knew he would look after Florrie. 'Archie. Come and meet our guest of honour.' The boy blushed and shambled over and Lorelei quickly introduced them properly.

Once she was satisfied that Florrie's attention had fully shifted to Archie, Lorelei reached out, took two champagne flutes and hurried across to Julian, keeping to the shadows at the edge of the room.

She was coming towards him. She had two champagne flutes in her hands and much as he knew very little about this sort of social occasion, he did wonder whether it was *de rigueur* for the female guests to serve the male ones. And whether they usually hugged the shadows in such a fashion. Maybe that was why she was doing it.

'You came,' she said, when she was standing right in front of him. There was an awkward pause when Julian felt a little frisson of electricity pass between them, then he smiled and held out his hand for the glass she proffered.

'I did indeed,' he replied. 'I'm delighted to see that you came as well.'

The Siren laughed and shook her head. 'I had no choice, really.'

'Ah. When you're a guest of the Scarsdales, I assume it is expected of you,' said Julian. 'That is the way I feel anyway and I'm well enough away at the Dower House to be practically invisible.'

'I'm not a guest,' said the Siren.

Julian waited for her to expand, but she just fixed him with those eyes and stared at him, quite curiously, he thought.

'One of the family, then?' Julian persisted.

'Yes,' replied the Siren. 'You could say that.'

Julian caught sight of the man he assumed was his host:

an insipid-looking man with neatly waxed blonde hair and exuding an air of buttoned-up authority.

Julian grinned. 'Well you look nothing like *him*, thankfully. I take it you must be related to a different side of the family, perhaps to someone on his wife's side?'

'I *am* the different side of the family. Unfortunately, that man happens to be my husband.' She bit her lip and dropped her head as if embarrassed. 'I'm sorry. I shouldn't have said that about him. About it being unfortunate, I mean.'

Julian stared at her, aghast. 'Unfortunate? My God, it *is* truly unfortunate. I think I had better leave.' He felt his face colour and looked around for somewhere to put his untouched champagne. Bloody hell. Of all the women to bump into around here and to take a liking to, he had to find the lady of the manor. Well, at least that was his question answered regarding her identity.

He wished he was still ignorant about that one.

'No. Please. Please, don't leave.' Lady Scarsdale or whoever she was reached out an elegant, white-gloved hand and touched his. There was a definite shock of something which frazzled up towards his shoulder at that point. 'I'd like you to stay.' She cast a look around the room desperately. 'I really would like you to stay. Look. The doors are open onto the terrace. Come outside with me. I can't bear being cooped up in here a moment longer anyway.'

Julian opened his mouth to protest, but his feet were unwilling to turn away from the woman and his eyes certainly didn't want to lose sight of her any time soon either. Like an automaton, he found himself following her towards the huge glass doors and before he knew it, he was outside on the stone terrace at the back of the Hall, overlooking the gardens.

Julian was simply staring at her as if he had been struck dumb. His mouth kept opening and then he would shake his head and close it again, all ready for the cycle to repeat. Lorelei felt utterly miserable.

'I'm sorry,' she said, quite pathetically. 'I was enjoying the anonymity of it all.' An ironic thing to say, she thought, for a woman who wanted more than anonymity in the paintings she had appeared in.

'Yet I still don't know your name,' said Julian eventually. In what might have been a fit of pique, he ripped his necktie off and began twisting it between his fingers. 'All this time. You just didn't tell me and you let me find out like this. At a bloody stupid ball in your bloody big house.' He let go of the tie and pushed his hair away from his face.

'All this time?' repeated Lorelei, watching the movement covetously. 'There, now, I beg to differ. It's simply been a few hours since we met. Not long at all.'

'What are you called?' he asked, quite sharply, bringing her attention back to his face. His deep brown eyes, even darker in the evening light, seemed to hold a glint of steel as he stared down at her.

'Lorelei. My name is Lorelei.' She held his gaze in just as steely a fashion.

'No, it's not,' snapped Julian. 'Tell me the truth.'

'It *is* Lorelei!'

'Oh, yes. Like the famous Siren. Like a mermaid. Of *course* your name is Lorelei.' Julian bowed dramatically. 'No coincidence, then, that I found you sitting on a rock in the middle of the sea, eh?'

The Scottish accent was magnified deliciously as Julian Cooper became more agitated and sarcastic.

'No coincidence at all,' replied Lorelei. 'I like sitting on that rock.'

'Waiting for unsuspecting sailors to crawl up onto it and be lashed to their death, eh? Or unsuspecting photographers. *God*!' He shook his head. 'Unsuspecting photographers.'

'I'd like you to tell me more about your photography,' tried Lorelei. 'I'm very interested.'

'No, you're not.' Julian shook his head sadly. 'I'm just someone who is different and interesting to you. A summer visitor who you can play games with. I don't like games. And now I really do think I should be going. Goodnight, Lady Scarsdale.' Lorelei thought there was a slightly venomous tone to that comment. 'I shall try to keep out of your way over the next few weeks. Running an estate like this cannot be an easy task and I am sure you are extremely busy.' She saw him look into the seething mass of gowns and suits which clogged up the ballroom and he looked distinctly unimpressed with it all.

'No. You're not just a summer visitor. You're an artist – a photographer. Disbelieve me if you will, but I have a great affinity for such people.'

'I would like to believe you, Lady Scarsdale – indeed, I may wish to linger here and discuss the arts with you a little longer. But I see your presence is required within your ballroom. Your husband looks rather agitated and seems to be searching for you.' The formal tone of voice didn't suit Julian and Lorelei narrowed her eyes. Then she turned to look inside the room and felt them widen in horror.

'Oh, no. Oh, the stupid girl,' she cried. Florrie was hanging onto a very worried looking Archie and her hair had tumbled completely out of its chignon. Archie tried to stand her gently upright and she stumbled again, laughing and bumping into one of the dinner-jacketed guests, who then spilled his drink over his gargantuan and over-flounced wife. 'I told Cook that punch was too strong. Goodness only knows what she added to the stuff,' moaned Lorelei. She turned to speak to Julian, to beg him to bear with her a little longer, until she sorted the carnage out – but he had vanished into the night.

All that was left was his necktie, dangling over the balustrade. Lorelei quickly picked it up and tucked it into her bodice, then hurried into the ballroom to attend to Florrie's disgrace.

The whore had disappeared. God, it was impossible to keep her in one place. She had begged him to host this ridiculous ball, for the stupid, fat daughter of his delicious cousin Mary, and she had vanished into the night, like the vermin she was.

Mary. *Ah, Mary.* She was the woman his harlot of a wife should aspire to be like. Mary – a true lady: elegant, decorous, obedient. *Yes, Walter. No, Walter. Please, Walter, whatever you want, Walter.* Not like the bitch in heat he had married, yelping her pleasure out into the night after they'd coupled. Disgusting. He'd known then, that first time, what she was like. He should have thrown her out there and then.

He had watched the strumpet in the ballroom, flirting with the men, nodding to them as she passed, swaying her hips as she walked. Provocative. Filthy. He scanned the room, repulsed by the disgraceful behaviour of that little piglet Florence. Where the hell was his wife when he needed her? Where the hell was she?

His eyes drifted across to the doors leading out onto the terrace. There she was, a sliver of white, talking to yet another man. He was about to stride across and drag her back in, when she turned and saw him.

That was better. She had started to hurry towards him and the man had melted away. She looked contrite, as she should do. He narrowed his eyes. Did she look contrite enough? If she didn't, he would damn well make sure she felt extremely sorry later tonight. His breath caught as he momentarily thought of the pleasure that would give him, then he stamped the feeling down.

Look what she did to him. Look what she made him think about.

The disgusting little tramp.

Chapter Nine

Lissy watched through narrowed eyes as Jon pulled up behind the studio in his car. She heard him swear through the open window.

'Unbelievable,' he said. 'The woman is shameless.'

'And she doesn't even look guilty,' added Becky. 'That's a skill in itself.'

Lissy had deliberately parked squarely in Jon's parking space and had no intention of moving.

'What time do we have to leave our house to get our parking space?' asked Jon, getting out of the car and slamming the door behind him. 'Eh, Lissy? What bloody time?'

Lissy's eyes slid away from Jon and Becky; she tilted her head, looking behind them, trying to see into the car. 'Where's my god-daughter?'

'Nursery,' said Becky. 'And don't try to change the subject. How long have you been here?'

'Too long. Because you're *late*!' Lissy turned to face them. 'I hardly slept, okay? I kept thinking of Stef and what he did and how you had the audacity to invite him here. So yes; I took your car space out of protest.' She tried hard to keep the wobble out of her voice. This pathetic person she was turning into was not the image she usually projected; but bits of the shiny, varnished Lissy seemed to be crumbling hourly, just like the old cliffs in Whitby. Whoosh. One day, she'd end up in the sea and simply float away, broken into pieces.

'Well you can just *un*protest and get the hell out of my space,' said Jon. 'I have appointments booked today and I can't miss them. Oh, and Stef is coming over later. We need to

66

discuss the plans for the photo shoot, so Cori and Simon can just fall in with it all. Stef has some great ideas about it; he's done similar things before. Do you realise how successful he's been with his photography?'

'I've not made it my business to follow anything he's done.' Lissy was thrown for a second as she thought about Stef coming here and the possibility of seeing him again. Despite herself, a few butterflies rose up in her stomach, then subsided. 'I don't care what he's been up to and as far as I'm concerned, he can go back to Italy and back to that woman.'

'So what are you doing here today, then?' asked Becky. 'I'm sure you guessed he'd have to come back to see Jon, and perhaps you were maybe planning to casually bump into him? Casually have another slanging match that doesn't achieve anything? Just for the simple reason that you want to see him, but you don't know what to do about how you feel? He's Stef. He's not a married man, you know, like that arse who screwed you over after Uni. We're a long way past that one now.'

The comments took Lissy by surprise; they were so close to the mark that they were enough to break down her last, fragile defences. 'Oh, Becky!' She gave up. She sat down on the edge of a flower trough at the corner of the building and put her head in her hands. 'What am I going to do?' She looked up at her best friend, who was possibly one of the only people that knew the real Lissy hidden beneath the London veneer. Even Cori, for all they'd been to university together, didn't know the half of what had happened afterwards. 'I'm lost. I'm absolutely lost. I always have been as far as he's concerned. But how can I ever trust him again?'

'It's okay.' Becky sat down next to her. 'Whatever went on, went on – but I think you know what you have to do. Between you, you have got to sort it out.'

Lissy took a deep, shuddering breath. 'Part of me doesn't want to. Part of me says I don't care anymore.'

Becky smiled and looked at her friend. 'Lissy. You do care. You care loads. If you didn't, you wouldn't be in this state.'

'But a big part of me wishes he would go back to Italy and stay there,' said Lissy. 'Whatever he says won't make up for what he did. I can't believe *you*,' she said, looking at Jon, 'even brought him here. But I'm sorry, Becky. You're right.' Lissy sighed and gave Becky a quick hug. 'He *has* got a hold on me. I wouldn't give a toss if I didn't care so damn much. I still can't believe that he would throw away what we had for *her*.'

'Well, if you feel that strongly, you have to try to salvage something,' said Becky.

'Maybe. But I can't think about it now.' Lissy ran her hand across her eyes to wipe the tears away. *Oh, but she could think of him, she could think about those lips and those eyes and how his hair felt, soft and springy, between her fingers ...* 'I have tried to do something nice for you. Even though you all think I'm awful. And I did it before he came here, so it's got nothing to do with that, just so you know. Let me show you.'

Lissy dug her hand into her pocket and brought out a crumpled piece of paper.

'Paper, Lissy?' teased Jon. 'I haven't seen you use paper for ages. The information's always in your phone.'

Lissy rolled her eyes heavenwards and ignored her brother; she opened the paper up and smoothed it out. 'Sometimes, you have to use it. Look.' She directed her comment pointedly to Becky, thrusting the paper at her sister-in-law. 'Directions.'

'Directions?' Becky looked confused. She took the paper from Lissy and scanned it. Then she looked up at her and frowned. 'I don't understand. This place is just up the coast, isn't it? I know how to drive north. And if I keep the sea to my right I can't go wrong, can I? But why would I want to go to Staithes?'

'It's not quite Staithes. Look again. There.' Lissy jabbed her forefinger at the map.

Jon came over and peered at it as well. 'What's that? A little bay?'

'Not just *any* little bay.' Lissy looked at Jon. 'It's *my* little bay.'

'What?' Jon stared at her. '*Your* little bay?'

'Yes. Well. It's mine for the summer anyway. I've rented this house here.' She pointed to a small square marked on the map. 'The bay – or cove, rather – belongs to the land. It's private. All sheltered, but with a lovely sandy beach and some rock pools and things. Staithes had a fabulous artists' colony, you know, back in the late 1800s. They were all inspired by the Impressionists. Harold and Laura Knight had a studio there ...' Lissy suddenly stopped speaking and ducked her head.

'The Knights,' remarked Jon, 'from the Newlyn Colony – down in Cornwall?'

'That's right,' muttered Lissy, without looking up. Cornwall. Of course Jon would remember that. Of course he would.

'Interesting,' said Jon.

'Not really.' Lissy lifted her head up and glared at him. 'I did all of this before Stef came, remember? I can't just abandon Cornwall to him and my memories and the Knights are just a link, that's all. What I was trying to say, was I knew you wanted somewhere for that stupid photography project, so I did some investigation and this was too good a chance to miss. It's mine all summer, including the beach. Oh, and it's got a beach hut thing on the bay as well. With a little garden out the back.' She mimed the shape of a square and looked at Becky. 'For the child. You can pen her in.'

Becky burst out laughing. 'Pen her in? Grace? Seriously?'

'Why not?' asked Lissy. 'It'll keep her perfectly safe, won't it?'

Becky just shook her head. 'Grace won't be penned anywhere. But good luck if you want to try it.'

'Oh,' said Lissy. 'Well. That's a disappointment.'

'It's a nice idea though.' Jon was clearly trying not to laugh. 'Thank you for thinking of her. And of us. We'll pop up after work and have a look, if that's okay? Now – please, Lissy, will you move your car? I'm blocking the access and people need to be along here to get to their own buildings. And my first appointment is in half an hour, so I really need to get set up.'

Lissy sighed and nodded. 'All right. Oh – are you going to tell Stef about me coming here?' Her stomach churned at the thought. Did she want Stef to know she'd been there? Did she want him to think she was bothered? *Was* she bothered? She didn't want to answer that one.

'Well,' Jon said gently, laying his hand on her shoulder and squeezing it, 'he'll have to know you sorted the location out, won't he? And he'll have to come with us as well, if he's working with us. Is that okay?'

'I suppose so.' Her voice shook, just a little. 'I'll just have to keep it professional. Either that, or I'll just ignore him.'

'You could, but, to be honest,' said Jon, looking up, 'if you don't move your car right now, Stef is going to catch you anyway.'

Lissy shrugged his hand off her shoulder and followed his gaze. A tall figure was ambling along the street in the distance. He was unmistakeable. Her heart hammered in her chest and she felt her cheeks burn.

'I'm off. Don't tell him I came. And *don't*,' she said, directing her multi-coloured gaze at Becky, 'tell him I'm parking up at the Abbey instead. And please don't tell him I've decided to spend the morning at the Abbey. I'll never forgive you if you do, okay?'

And with that, Lissy hurried away and disappeared into the alley behind the studio. She started the car up and pulled away, heading towards the Abbey car park at the top of the hill. She had known Becky a long time – a very long time –

and Becky was, to all intents and purposes, deaf as a post; which was sometimes very useful for them both.

In this situation, for instance, Lissy hoped that Becky hadn't heard her request. And if Becky had, by some miracle, heard her, Lissy trusted that she would pretend she hadn't.

Whitby Abbey

There she was, just as he had anticipated – wandering amongst the Abbey ruins, stopping and reading the interpretation boards, looking up at the columns of stone and broken arches.

He lifted his camera and framed her perfectly in the right-hand side of the shot, capturing the moment as she inspected a little bunch of trailing flowers growing out of the brickwork, an archway just behind her.

The image of *The Gardener's Daughter*, he thought. Or at least, his own interpretation of the famous Julia Margaret Cameron photograph. He walked right up to her, and she didn't even move from the spot; didn't turn to face him.

Still inspecting the tiny purple flowers, holding onto the one she had delicately captured between her fingers, she spoke as if to the flower: 'How did you find me?'

'Becky told me where you were.'

'I asked her *not* to tell you,' replied Lissy.

'She said she didn't hear your request.'

'Then surely, if she said that, she knew there *was* a request, so she should have respected it.' Lissy let the flower drop and it bounced against the warm brickwork, quivering as it settled, and she turned to Stefano.

He waved his hand around his ear and shook his head. 'She said not. She said it is a terrible affliction she has. I did not pursue it further.'

'She's a dreadful liar,' said Lissy. 'By that, I mean she's a good liar. She's just simply terrible. I know what I'm trying to say. What are you really doing here?'

'Looking for you. And hey! I found you!' He spread his hands out and smiled.

'Whitby's not that big a place. You could have wandered around all day and you probably would have found me anyway.' Lissy started walking away from him, passing a stone-lined hole in the ground. 'Don't fall in there. I'm not pulling you out.'

'What is it?' he asked. He raised his camera, ready to take a photograph.

'It's a grave, for dead people.'

'Oh.' He lowered his camera without taking the shot. 'I see.' He fell into step beside her. 'Pretty nasty.'

'Oh, it's nasty when you lose a two-year old and find them lying in it.' Lissy stopped and turned to him, raising a finger and pointing it at him. 'But don't ever tell Becky that happened. She doesn't need to know her daughter thought it was a bath and demanded to know when it would be filled.'

Stef laughed and took hold of Lissy's finger, then encased her cool, soft hand in his. Her nails were painted a glossy, deep violet today; they looked amazing. They'd always been amazing. He remembered them digging into his back as they … but no. Not here. Not in this sacred place. Lissy didn't pull her hand away immediately, anyway. She waited a good three seconds, so that was a start. She could easily have slapped him there and then. Instead, she walked off in front of him again.

Stef took a couple of longer strides to catch up with her and tried some more general conversation. 'Jon mentioned you found a location?'

Lissy nodded without looking at him. 'I did. It's perfect for what Jon wants.'

'Would it be perfect for what *I* want?' he asked.

'It depends on *what* you want,' she replied. 'It's very

secluded. You could do your photo shoots there and not be disturbed. There's a beach hut so people can get changed in it. It's rather fabulous.'

'Ah, yes, they mentioned the penning in of the child at the beach hut. *Grazia* does not strike me as a child who would be penned. She is a free spirit, I think. Rather like her *Zia* Elisabetta.'

'I'm a very good Aunt Elisabetta. I tried to cover all eventualities and make it inclusive for her. Of course, I might have just stayed away from the whole thing, had I known you were coming to England.'

'Why?' He stopped suddenly and reached out, pulling her towards him. 'Do you still hate me so much? You said all feelings for me were dead. You told me in Cornwall you would never feel anything for me again. Is that still the case? Because to me, right now, that does not seem to *be* the case.'

'I don't hate you. Not anymore. The only thing I feel for you right now is contempt. *Disprezzo*. I still can't get over what you did.'

Stef had always been delighted that Italian was Lissy's second language, thanks to her father. He missed their vibrant, fast conversations in his native tongue. It was good to hear her use it again.

'Please. Let us talk about it,' said Stef. 'This is a good time to do it, and a good place. You know that here, in the Abbey grounds, I will be nothing but truthful. You never gave me a chance ...'

'And like I said, you've had seven years to think of an excuse,' she interrupted him. '*Lasci perdere*, Stef. Forget it. I don't want anything from you. I just want this project to be over and done with, so my brother gets the recognition he deserves. He's a good photographer and with that wall space in Simon's exhibition – well. It could open up all sorts of doors for him.

'That's the only reason I waited for you up here,' she

continued, 'to tell you that. I won't be awkward or silly or spoilt about you being here and I'll try my best to be all grown-up and professional. It's all for Jon and I'm going to have to put aside what happened with us, or I'll have to leave everybody and go back to London, and I don't really want to do that just yet.' She glanced at the grave and her mouth turned downwards and he wondered if she was a little more attached to Grace than she cared to admit.

'But you *did* wait for me up here. I have to hold onto that, Lissy. It's the only thing I have right now and it means a lot. You could have left a note. Or banned me from coming; told me to do *my* shots on the Whitby beach.' He laughed. 'Oh, yes. That would have been fun, with the children and their ice-creams and the terrified people from the *Experience of Dracula* crying as they run to the beach past the *zucchera filato* stalls ...'

'The candy floss stalls.' Lissy half-smiled. 'We had some good times in Cornwall. The best candy floss ever. I don't want to forget any of that. I just wish ... I just wish things could have turned out differently.'

'I too wish it hadn't happened,' said Stef quietly. 'We ...'

'No!' Lissy shook her head. 'Stop it. I can't do this. I have to go.' She twisted away from him and began to run across the grass.

'Lissy!'

'No, Stef!'

'But—'

It was impossible. She'd gone. He had to let her go. He'd do more harm than good if he went after her today. But she'd waited for him and they'd had a reasonable conversation, so that was good. That was very good.

'I won't give up, Lissy,' Stef promised quietly as he watched her disappear. He was going to do his utmost to win her back.

Oh, yes, Stefano Ricci had a kernel of a plan, and he was damn well going to carry it out.

74

Chapter Ten

The Dower House, 1905

Julian had spent a largely sleepless, frustrated night staring out at the cove. He had thrown off and discarded his suit, then thought better of it as he had a meeting with a gallery owner that week and a crumpled suit would not be a very good advertisement for him.

From the terrace, he could see the rock which Lorelei – if that was indeed her name – had been sitting on, and despite everything, he thought it could not have made more of a perfect setting for a photograph of her; the woman sitting on the rock, her long black hair cascading down her back, naked to the waist ... oh well. Maybe that was going a little too far, but the overall idea of her as a true Siren of the sea was an encouraging one.

'Knock, knock.' The voice was soft and came from below him, to the left. Julian looked down, surprised at the interruption, and felt his face harden as Lady Scarsdale was revealed in all her glory.

Today, she was wearing a coffee-coloured gown with geometric peach-coloured trimmings around the skirt and a huge, peach satin rose, pinned just under her right breast. A band of tiny cream flowers on a green ribbon the colour of her eyes wound their way along the neckline and a peach satin ribbon was tied around her waist. Her black hair had been pinned up neatly away from her face and her pretty green eyes were troubled.

'I brought a gift,' she said. Dragging his gaze away from her overall personage, Julian saw that she was raising a small wicker basket up to him. The contents were covered in a blue and white chequered cloth and looked strangely knobbly beneath it. 'Apples,' she continued, 'and some strawberries from the kitchen garden. My favourites. Oh, and a pot of cream from our Jersey cows. You can't have strawberries without cream. Or champagne, really. So I brought some of that as well, since you missed out on it last night.' She lifted the basket a little higher and tweaked the cover back. Julian saw the bottle sticking out of the corner, the fruit packed around it and a couple of books in there as well. His necktie from last night was tied in a bow around the handle. A nice touch, he thought sarcastically.

'So now you are Lady Bountiful, not only Lady Scarsdale. And you have come to pay your respects to the starving artist who is renting the Dower House. I thank you for your concern, Lady Scarsdale, but I'm not starving and I don't need your charity.'

'It's not charity. And don't call me Lady Scarsdale. I hate it. It's too formal. Call me Lorelei or call me nothing at all. I don't really care.'

'Why are you here?' asked Julian, turning and facing her properly.

She looked up at him for a moment, then walked around the side of the terrace and up the steps onto it so she was next to him. 'I don't like being talked down to.'

'Me neither,' said Julian.

They stared at each other in silence, then she spoke again. 'Let me show you this. Just give me five minutes of your time and I shall leave. But I insist on talking to you in those five minutes.'

Julian nodded and leaned back against the balustrade, folding his arms. Truth be told, paradoxically, he wanted to spend those five minutes in her company even though he had decided that he wanted nothing more to do with her.

She placed the basket down on a small table and peeled

back the cover fully. She lifted the bottle out and stood it carefully next to the basket, along with the pot of cream. Then she took the handful of books out and opened the first one. It fell open easily at a page with a lot of writing on it and a title in beautiful cursive script.

Beneath the title, Julian saw the word "Monet". Unable to help himself, he leaned forward and read the cursive script. It was the name of one of Monet's famous paintings – a crowd scene depicting something like a party at an outdoor garden in Paris and the information pertaining to it at a Paris exhibition.

Lorelei left the book open at that page and placed it on the table, then she did the same with the next book; and the next. And the next. Soon, she had a line of books open and Julian saw that they were all programmes for art exhibitions by famous artists – the French Impressionists, the Slade School and some of the later Pre-Raphaelites.

The woman eventually opened the last one and stood straight.

She turned her attention away from the books and looked directly at him. 'These are all programmes for various art exhibitions. The most recent one is this one, which was down in Cornwall.' She tapped one of the books with her slender fingertip. 'The common denominator is that I was painted into all of these pictures. I met my husband at this last exhibition. I think he was excited to find a woman that others admired, but sadly that novelty soon wore off when he realised I was a human being with feelings and needs, rather than the sweet, silent girl depicted in these paintings.

'I was very young in most of the pictures, to be honest. Young and naïve. But I love art. I love the atmosphere of a working studio or being around artists in the open air. I love the process of being painted. To be so close to Staithes was a dream come true anyway – even though I haven't really managed to find out much about it – and when I discovered that an artist was moving into the Dower House over the summer, I was beyond excited.

'I had two major ambitions in my life. One was to be recognised as an artist in my own right and one ridiculous one was that I could claim to have been a sitter for Julia Margaret Cameron, who of course is long dead now, God rest her soul. But I can still try to achieve the first ambition. And I'm sorry if I misled you. I was naughty and I do apologise.' Lorelei frowned and looked back at the programmes. 'I'll leave these here for you to look at and you can leave them behind when you go home. You may find something of interest in them to pass the time. I shan't bother you again, Mr Cooper.'

The woman turned away, lifting her skirts deftly and nodding her head in a farewell.

She had barely made it to the top of the steps when Julian called her name. 'Lorelei!'

She turned and stared at him in surprise. 'Not Lady Scarsdale, Mr Cooper?' There was a bite to her words and he felt himself colour.

'No. Lorelei – if you will allow it. I think perhaps it is I who should apologise. I misjudged you and you clearly had your reasons to be "naughty" as you say. I didn't realise you were so *au fait* with the art world. I actually *saw* this picture ...' He tapped the same one Lorelei had done. '... during the exhibition in Cornwall. I'm sorry we didn't meet then.'

Lorelei paused and blushed slightly. 'Things may have been quite different if we had indeed met then,' she answered. 'I was at the opening night. I had to be, really. Walter was there as well. The rest ...' She shrugged, seemingly in resignation. '... is, as they say, history. I can't change it now.'

'That's a shame.' Julian moved towards her. 'I went on the fourth night. How close we must have been. Tell me, do you still want to know more about the Staithes movement?'

'I would love to know more about the Staithes movement, but I've yet to find anyone who will humour me.' She laughed bitterly. 'My husband isn't at all interested and it's not seemly for Lady Scarsdale to wander around the town questioning people.'

'Would it be seemly for the Scarsdales' guest to escort his hostess into the town, then?' asked Julian. 'Perhaps do a little preparation work first? Perhaps get to know his hostess a little better, now they have found a common ground in Monet?' He was as surprised as she apparently was that such an invitation had come out of his mouth.

'I don't know,' she replied, those sea-green eyes widening. 'I'd like to think so. But I couldn't get away today. Florrie is here for the rest of it and we are having a tea party for her at four, before they leave for the evening sleeper train. The poor girl is still in bed. The punch really didn't agree with her last night.' She suddenly smiled, her beautiful, perfect face taking on a mischievous look that had Julian staring at her in awe. 'You should come to the tea party. I do believe Archie's family are coming, but Walter informs me that he, Walter, will not be attending anyway, so I will have nobody to talk to. Be at the Hall for four, sharp.'

Julian found himself nodding assent, speechless as Lorelei blew him a little kiss and practically danced down the steps onto the beach. He watched as she picked up her skirts and ran up the winding pathway back to the Hall.

Four o'clock then. Oh, yes. He would definitely be there at four.

The Cove, Present Day

Lissy thought she had done very well with the house near Staithes. She sat on the terrace, mistress of all she surveyed

– at least for a few weeks. It did seem absolutely perfect for their purposes – or so Jon had said.

'I like it,' he told her, walking along the shoreline. 'It's a really good place to work. I think we can do a lot here.' They hadn't spent very long with her that night; Grace needed to get home, apparently, and get ready for bed. Lissy couldn't quite understand what the urgency was for taking her home, but it was clearly important to Grace.

'Routine,' Becky told her, cuddling the fretful, tearful little girl. 'She needs to be home. She needs her bed.'

'But she's three!' Lissy protested. 'How does she know what she wants at the age of three?'

'She knows,' said Becky, quite darkly. 'She knows *exactly* what she wants.' Lissy looked at Grace, saw the red face and the tear stains and the runny nose and decided not to argue. She patted the little girl, quite uselessly, on the back. 'There, there, you'll soon be home.' She loved Grace, but children were a bit of a mystery to her. Still, she was learning, she hoped.

'Want to go home,' Grace had sniffled. 'Now please.'

So they'd gone. It was Friday night and Cori and Simon were coming up tomorrow. And she had to admit, part of her was looking forward to Stef being there as well. Only a very little part, mind you – but still a part of her was quite desperately wanting to see him. Lissy stared out at the sea, lost in her thoughts. A mermaid, he had said; she was like a mermaid to him. She wished she could sing. Then he really *would* be in trouble.

She saw a dark figure on the beach, walking along the edge of the sea and her heart began to beat a little faster. This was private land – no way should anyone be there. And, more importantly, how had they got there in the first place? They would have had to come along the little road that led past her house, which was also marked private, and she would have heard the car. Or they would have had to park up on the top and find their way down again, past the house – or possibly even walk from the town, and that wasn't exactly a five-minute stroll. The only other option was a boat. Not that she could see one. But that must have been it.

There had to be a little fishing boat or dinghy or something, bobbing around in the cove. They must have sailed over, found the beach and come ashore. Well – if the person didn't move soon it would be high tide and the beach would disappear. Lissy stood up and leaned over the terrace, ready to shout at the offender and tell them it was private land and they had to go. But then she realised she was a woman alone in a remote house. Whoever it was could probably see her silhouetted against the light from the French doors, and they'd know she was basically there in a skimpy pyjama set that didn't really cover much.

Lissy shivered and backed away from the edge. And then she had a thought. Perhaps it was Stef? Perhaps he had come around that way to surprise her and was going to climb up the dunes to the house. She wouldn't put it past him. She shivered again, but with a different sort of feeling that embarrassed her slightly. Her sunburnt face heated up even more from within as she blushed and tutted loudly. Bloody Stef; wandering on her land, stalking her almost, surprising her in such a way.

The ringing of her mobile made her jump and she swore. 'Yes?' she said, rather snappily into the mouthpiece.

'*Bella*.' His voice was warm and she could tell he was smiling. 'I wanted to call just to say how much I look forward to seeing you tomorrow. I would like to thank you for doing this. I know it has been difficult. I am very happy to be working with Jon.'

'Stef! How did you get my number? And why can't you just come up from the beach and tell me to my face?'

'What beach?' He genuinely sounded surprised. 'I am in my B & B, working on my photographs. Listen.'

He must have held the phone to the laptop. There were some clicking noises that sounded like random keystrokes and dance music in the background. It had always surprised Lissy that Stef had preferred that sort of modern day music over classic opera – which she had originally thought he would like. *Just because I am Italian, does not make me an opera singer*, he had said, laughing at the surprise on her face when she found out.

'But you're on the beach; outside my house. Aren't you?' she asked, knowing her voice didn't sound as sure as it had before.

'No, Elisabetta. I am not.' Then his voice hardened. 'Who is it? The land is private, *sì*? Who is it that walks your land? Will I come and chase them for you?'

'No! No. Of course not. They're not doing any harm. They're just ...' Lissy leaned forward, and her lungs constricted. The man was still there. She walked backwards into the house, keeping her eye on the stranger, and fumbled around behind her for the light switch. Her fingers finding it, she snapped the light off and padded back out to the terrace, the stone feeling somehow colder against her bare feet. The man couldn't see her now – but she could see him a bit better.

As if on cue, the few wispy clouds in the sky parted and the moon, bright as day, threw the whole scenario into stark, silvery relief.

'Dear Lord!' She began to shake from her feet up, and had to grab the phone with two hands to steady it. 'Stef?' Her voice wavered. 'Stef? Are you still there?'

'I am. What is it? You sound peculiar.' His voice managed to be warm, curious and full of concern, all at the same time. 'What can I do?'

'Oh God – Stef.' Her voice caught on a sob. 'He's got a gun. And he's looking up at my house.'

Stef let out such a loud exclamation of anger, Lissy automatically clamped her hand over the earpiece, frightened on some silly level that the man on the beach would hear it. She was certain he had a gun. He was walking along the beach, gazing out to sea, then alternately looking up at her house and staring at the cliffs. And in his hand as his arm hung loosely by the side of his body, was a shiny gun-shaped item.

'Then you cannot stay there!' shouted Stef. 'You call the police right now and tell them. And then I will come and fetch you. It will take me half an hour. In fact, I will meet you somewhere. I …' She could hear the tone of his voice change as he apparently stood up and moved rooms.

'No!' hissed Lissy. 'You're right. I'm not staying here any longer, not even to wait for you. I'm not calling the police because they'll want me to wait as well so they can talk to me.' She knew it wasn't exactly rational reasoning, but the sight of the shot gun or whatever it was had sent all common sense fleeing from her brain. She took a deep breath and closed her eyes. 'I'm getting in the car and I'm coming to your B & B. Text me the address. I'm going now to get my keys. I'll get your message when I'm in the car.' And with that, she hung up and ran back into the house.

Lissy didn't stop to pack anything. She shoved her feet into a pair of espadrilles, grabbed her handbag, phone, house keys and car keys, and ran out of the front door. Only when she was in the car and a good way down the road towards Whitby, did she stop in a lay by and check her messages.

As she had requested, Stef had sent her the address of his hotel. She knew Whitby well enough to realise it wasn't a standard Bed and Breakfast, and she knew whereabouts she would find it. She would worry about her own place tomorrow. Tonight, she just wanted to be out of that house and to have some company, and Stef would do just as well as anyone.

Chapter Eleven

Sea Scarr Hall, 1905

Florence looked rather wan and pathetic, huddled up on one of the white wrought iron seats Lorelei had ensured were arranged on the lawn behind the Hall.

'We shall try to ensure information about your punch incident goes no further than Whitby, darling,' Lorelei told her. The girl nodded miserably and a look of pain flitted across her face as she did so. Lorelei smiled and patted her knee. 'A cup of tea is just what you need, I think, before you head south. Archie and his family will not be long and you can huddle with him instead of on your own.'

'Oh, Lorelei!' moaned Florrie. Lorelei had long since told the girl not to call her Lady Scarsdale, much to Walter's disgust. 'I simply cannot recall anything about the latter part of the evening. I know that nice man from the Dower House arrived and then you both disappeared. After that, I am afraid much of it is a blur.'

'Then you need to remember that feeling in London, darling.' Lorelei smoothly skipped over the fact Julian had been referred to as a "nice man". 'Stay away from the punch or you shan't recall any of the lovely young men you meet there.'

Florrie's bottom lip trembled. 'I swear that I am dying.'

'I suspect not.' Lorelei smiled. She looked up and saw a maid coming across the lawn with a tea tray. 'Do you think you could manage a little cake with your tea?' There wasn't much that would stop Florrie's enjoyment of a piece of cake.

'I shall struggle with it, but I will try,' the debutante replied bravely.

'Good girl.' Almost as if she could sense him, Lorelei

suddenly turned the other way and saw a loping figure walking across the lawn. Julian had come, and he was carrying some kind of box which she realised was his camera. 'Oh, I say. I think this is the gentleman from the Dower House. I did extend an invitation to him to join us, as he had to leave very suddenly last night.'

She rose gracefully from the table, glad she had dressed in an ivory lawn dress this afternoon. She knew the style and the colour became her; and it was so very hot that she was grateful for anything that was cool. The dress was festooned with lace and had two tiers of frills, but it was light and pretty. She had added a large straw, cartwheel hat to the ensemble, and the lace scarf she had tied around the brim blew out gently behind her as she hurried across the lawn to meet Julian.

'Well, good afternoon,' Lorelei called as she approached him. A stray gust of wind appeared from the direction of the coast and almost lifted her hat off. She raised her arm and held onto it as she smiled up at Julian. 'I'm so pleased you could come. Florrie is suffering horribly still, but I am feeding her cake and that usually cheers her up.'

Julian laughed and looked across at the girl. Lorelei followed his gaze. Florrie was now seemingly on to her second slice and was munching steadily through it with a third one lined up on her plate, and her eyes fixed in the middle distance somewhere contemplatively. She looked a little like a cow and Lorelei smiled fondly. She would, however, never, *ever* tell the girl anything so mean. She was a delightful child, really, and Lorelei did love her.

'It's a shame to bother her,' remarked Julian. 'But this, I cannot resist.' He raised his camera and Lorelei realised he was taking a photograph of Florrie.

It was Lorelei's turn to laugh. 'Such a marvellous invention. And a wonderful way to record all these moments that we might otherwise forget.'

'My aim is to record you this summer.' Julian turned his attention back to her and smiled. 'I gave the matter some thought after our wee chat this morning, and I decided if Mrs Cameron can't take your photograph in the style you want, then I can.'

'Truly?' asked Lorelei. 'You can do that?'

'Why do you look as if you find that difficult to believe?' asked Julian. 'You've just said what a marvellous invention the camera is, and that it was perfect to record moments we might otherwise forget. I don't really want to forget this summer.' *Or you.*

The last words were silent, yet Lorelei thought she understood, simply by the look in the man's eyes.

'No, I don't suppose I want to forget it either,' she replied. 'Is there anything you had in mind for the photograph?' It was like a layer of Lady Scarsdale had melted away; once more the consummate professional model, Lorelei was ready to be guided by the artist.

'I did have something in mind. It came to me when I saw you on that rock and I christened you my Siren of the Sea. And then to hear your name is Lorelei – well! It is truly a gift. You are aware, of course, of the legend of the Lorelei Rock in the Danube?'

'I am,' replied Lorelei. 'I believe I was named after it. My parents lived there for some time. I've been told I was conceived within view of it.'

'Oh, my! I couldn't imagine my parents discussing that sort of thing with me!'

'My parents were very young when I was born. My mother had eloped with my father and I don't even know if they were married. I don't believe they *are* married, come to think of it.' She laughed and shook her head, making the loose ends of the scarf on her hat drift with the motion. 'They live quite comfortably wherever they please – and that is Cornwall at the moment, I think. But they don't stay in one place for very long, so who knows how long they will be there? I swear there is some Gypsy in at least one of them.'

'The Gypsy would be where you get your colouring from, then,' said Julian.

'Perhaps,' replied Lorelei, 'but tell me more about this marvellous photograph you have envisioned.'

'Ah, yes. I would like you to be seated on the rock with your hair plaited as it was when I saw you emerge from the water. And I think, for the sake of modesty, you should be clothed.'

'Mermaids do not have extensive wardrobes.' Lorelei smiled and raised her eyebrows at him. 'Perhaps I should simply be naked?'

Julian grinned and leaned forward, lowering his voice. 'Much as that appeals to me as an artist and as a man, I think we had better maintain *some* propriety, don't you?'

He was deliciously close to her and his warm breath and his spicy cologne made her stomach do odd, fizzy things. Lorelei wondered why she didn't feel that sort of attraction to her husband. And, she realised, without even feeling guilty, she was as good as sinning in her head. She could sin very easily with this man, given half the chance; and, she also thought, she had the perfect outfit for the photograph.

'Would something rather medieval encompass what you are envisaging for my photograph?' asked Lorelei.

She looked stunning standing there in front of him. Her face was upturned and her eyes were alight with excitement. And he adored the way she had already claimed the photograph – "my photograph". She was, clearly, a little vain; but, having said that, when you looked at her and you knew the circles she had moved in and the work she had done, one shouldn't really be surprised at such a revelation. In fact, Julian thought, it endeared her to him even more.

'Medieval would work very well, I should think,' he replied. 'It did Mrs Cameron no harm to clothe her models as such.'

'Marvellous.' Lorelei clapped her hands. 'I have just the thing. We had a fancy-dress ball here one Christmas and I dressed as The Lady of Shalott. Well, to be precise, Waterhouse's *Lady of Shalott*.' A shadow flitted across her face. 'Walter was supposed to be my Sir Lancelot, but he decided to come as a Sea Captain instead. We were hardly the unified Lord and Lady of the Manor as I had hoped.'

'"*The mirror crack'd from side to side*",' quoted Julian. 'From Tennyson's original poem. Did you go as the Lady who had seen life through her mirror or did you go as the suicidal maiden in the boat?'

'The suicidal maiden,' replied Lorelei. 'Only I didn't have a boat.' Then she smiled ruefully. 'I had a Sea Captain though, I suppose. By default, if by nothing else.'

'Well I am pleased to hear that – the dress is much more medieval in the suicidal maiden portrait – although I must confess you look more like the model in the mirror portrait.'

'Thank you. I do feel more of an affinity with her – trapped as she is in her gilded cage. Never mind. You are not here to discuss my marital disharmonies. Allow me to seek the dress out and we can see if it is suitable.' She looked across at Florrie, who had perked up considerably after demolishing the cake. 'We must go and see my other guests. Archie will be here soon, and the ladies are leaving at about seven to catch the sleeper train. Will you be able to suffer our company that long? I wish I could get away sooner to find the dress.' She frowned.

'There's no real hurry,' said Julian. 'But I think it's maybe best if I don't outstay my welcome with the ladies? Your husband may return and you don't want me to monopolise you if that happens. Because I would monopolise you. Without a doubt.' He couldn't quite believe he had spoken the words out loud.

'I wouldn't mind being monopolised.' Lorelei smiled. Her voice seemed to lose some of its upper-class polish and suddenly she was just a girl from Yorkshire who was a little out of her depth in this Society nonsense. 'It would make a nice change.' She dipped her head and turned away from him, walking across the lawn back towards the tea party. She raised her arm and waved at Florrie and her mother. 'Allow me to introduce our summer visitor,' she called. 'Mr Cooper is a famous photographer and he is extremely interesting. I invited him to meet you all before you leave. After all, Florrie, you may need to appoint a wedding photographer should you ensnare a man in London.' Lady Scarsdale was back. But Julian had had a little glimpse of who she really was and he liked it very much.

The tinkle of feminine laughter made Julian smile. Or it might have been the sight of Lorelei Scarsdale walking in front of him and the way her dress hung in perfect folds from her gently swaying hips. Either way, the smile was refusing to leave his face.

In the event, Julian remained at the house for a good couple of hours. Lorelei was torn between smiling at poor Archie who was staring lustfully after the young, curvaceous Florrie as his parents practically dragged him away, or watching Julian MacDonald Cooper as he sat easily in the garden chairs and sipped tea, fielding all the questions the other guests put to him, then seeming to unfold himself, stretch, and take his leave.

Lord Scarsdale himself was notable by his absence, which was most certainly a blessed relief to her.

Lorelei couldn't tell anybody where Walter was. She supposed he would make the excuse that he was at the sailing club or some other place only men frequented. Lorelei and Walter did not spend a great deal of time together, which she was quite grateful for. If he wasn't around, she wasn't on edge. She wasn't playing a part and trying to behave, fearful of whatever punishment he would come up with next, for her latest misdemeanour.

It was just as the servants were carrying the travelling trunks to the front door, and Lorelei was moving around her bedroom looking for the leaving gift she had prepared for Florrie, that she caught sight of herself in the mirror. Honestly, what a fright she looked. She had removed that hat and her hair was desperately flattened to her head, not to mention that the bulk of her tresses had come undone and had tightened themselves into little ringlets with the sea air. It was getting damp out there. There was a definite hint of a summer storm coming over from the sea and she hoped the ladies would make it to London safely.

Roughly, she pulled the pins out of her hair, determining to smarten herself up a little. She hated looking ruffled and told herself that she wanted to give Florrie nice memories as she left the Hall, rather than the child looking back at a terrifying scarecrow. Given Florrie's behaviour over these few days, London was going to be frightening enough for her. Such an innocent.

Lorelei dragged the silver-backed brush through her hair, feeling the wild, salty, tangled curls stretch out and pull into the soft waves she was more accustomed to. As she did so, she looked around the prim, perfectly neat room and longed to be outside, rather than trapped in this gilded cage; she yearned to feel the sea breeze on her face and the sand crushing beneath her bare feet. She didn't belong here, with Walter, but she knew she had to stay, at least a little while longer.

Then she hurried down the stairs, not bothering to pin her hair up again, and was gratified to see Florrie stare at her in awe.

'You really are very beautiful,' said the girl. 'I feel such a frump next to you.'

'You're not a frump. You are a stunning young girl who is going to set London alight. Here. This is for you. It's a little clasp for your hair. I've got one the same. You can wear it and remember I am thinking of you and wishing you all the luck in the world.'

'Oh, thank you!' cried Florrie. She flung her arms around Lorelei. 'I hope that by wearing it, it will make me as pretty as you.'

'Prettier.' Lorelei smiled. 'Or is it more pretty? I was never good at grammar.'

'I will truly settle for *as* pretty.' Florrie hugged Lorelei again and went to stand by her luggage. 'Mother will be here soon. Then we shall have to go.' She sighed. 'I did like Mr Cooper. He said I would make a marvellous study for a portrait photograph. Although I do so wish I looked like that red-headed lady in that big painting in your ballroom. Who is she?'

'Oh,' said Lorelei, selfishly grateful for the fact she could avoid mention of Julian or agreeing how nice he was or how marvellous Florrie would look in a photograph, 'the tale will appeal to your youthful romantic side, I suspect. The story is that one of the Scarsdales' poor relations was an art tutor at the time of the Pre-Raphaelites. He always refused to be parted from this picture so we do not know whether it was his lover or just a painting he was particularly fond of. He lived here for a few years teaching the children of the family, and the picture came with him. It stayed here after he died.'

'Maybe one day someone will paint me like that,' said Florrie. 'Would you wish to be painted again, Lorelei?'

'I would indeed.' Lorelei smiled.

She didn't tell Florrie that a photograph taken by the right photographer would be even better. It would absolutely make her feel appreciated again as a woman.

Chapter Twelve

Whitby, Present Day

Stef had been standing on the pavement outside the apartment for fifteen minutes when he saw Lissy's little MG speed up the road. He stepped forward and waved as she approached and flinched as she skidded to a halt centimetres from him and wound the window down.

'Where can I park it?'

Stef blinked in astonishment. She had escaped from a gun-wielding maniac and was worried about where she could park her car?

'Err. I guess around the back with my hire vehicle?' He gestured to an entrance at the end of the terrace. 'You will see the sign.'

'Good. Thank you. Car parking is terrible in this town. I'm fed up of ...' Then her pretty, elfin face kind of crumpled. She clambered out of the car and slammed the door shut behind her. 'Oh, Stef. It was horrible!' She collapsed into him, and he automatically brought his arms up and around her. He closed his eyes and leaned his chin on the top of her head, remembering how well they had always fitted together.

'You are shivering.' He held her closer and felt her tremble. 'You have silly shorts and a strappy vest on. It is not so warm now.'

'It's my pyjamas. I'm sorry. It was warmer before and I wasn't planning on going anywhere.'

'Look, you are really shaking now. Do you trust me to park your car? Then you can go inside and wait for me whilst I do it.'

'Yes. Thank you.' She moved away from him and handed

over her car keys. 'It's quite a fast car. Watch it when you pull away.'

'I will be careful,' he said, amused. 'My rooms are on the first floor. The door is open. Just go in and I will be with you shortly. I make you some *cioccolata calda*, yes? I always know how much you like hot chocolate. It will help you sleep. But you must talk to me first, okay?'

'Okay. But just so we're clear, I wouldn't have raced up here to see you under normal circumstances. You know that, don't you?'

Even as she said it and challenged him with those bejewelled eyes, he laughed. 'I know. But I have no gun and no reason to hurt you. Hey, could you not have gone to the studio? I am sure you must possess a key?'

'I ... I *do*.' Lissy's eyes slid away from him then back, as if she was quickly coming up with a reason for not going to the studio. 'But it's a mess. Grace's toys are all over the place and it's very much Becky's office in there as well so I don't like disturbing anything. So, no. I wouldn't have gone. Plus, you were on the phone to me and I panicked.' She shrugged her thin shoulders. 'So I came here.'

'I see.' He felt the urge to smile but suppressed it. He knew she would deny everything. 'Well, I shall move the car and as I said to you, please go in and make yourself at home for the evening. There are two bedrooms so please understand I will not take advantage of you. The second room has my workstation in. We'll have to move things for you to access the bed, but it will be fine.' He pointed towards the door of the building. 'Go. It's cold and you're freezing I think.'

Lissy looked down at his feet and shook her head. 'You tell me that when you're not even wearing shoes? I don't know how I put up with your bare feet all summer – it's like you had an aversion to footwear.'

He stood still and there was a beat. 'Maybe,' he said quietly, 'it was because you loved me.'

Lissy was silent for a moment. She ducked her head and turned towards the house. 'Maybe,' she said equally quietly. 'Maybe I did love you, once upon a time. Before I saw you with her.'

Stef watched her disappear into the house and sighed. He jangled the car keys against his hip, thinking. He wondered how tonight would go.

Stef parked the car, rather skilfully, he thought, and bounded up the stairs to his apartment. When he reached the door, he hurried in and saw Lissy sitting on the sofa. Her hands were clasped on her lap and her legs crossed at the ankles. She looked all folded up, as if she didn't really want to take up much space.

'Did you see your room?' Stef nodded across the lounge to the bedroom which contained his makeshift studio equipment. A faint glow and the steady whirr of a computer fan came through the open door, dance music still thumping bass notes in the background.

'I haven't been in it yet. It looked as if you were working. I didn't want to disturb anything.'

'Oh, you won't disturb anything. Go, go.' He indicated the door. 'Take a look at your room while I heat the milk for your chocolate.'

'If you microwave it, it only takes seconds,' Lissy pointed out.

'Ahhhh, I do not microwave the milk.' He pulled a face, as if the very thought disgusted him, because it did. That would be sacrilege. 'It's much nicer heated in the pan. That's the way I always made it for you, and I never had any complaints.'

Lissy stayed where she was and didn't answer, and he didn't pursue it. Instead, he bustled around in the tiny galley kitchen and found what he needed in the orderly little cupboards. 'I think this may still be your favourite, yes?' he asked, holding up a tin. 'Fortnum and Mason, Rose and Violet hot chocolate. To me, it tastes like a bouquet of flowers. To you,' he said, giving a little bow, 'it tastes divine.'

Lissy whipped her head around, her eyes and mouth making three astonished little 'o' shapes in her perfect face. 'Rose and Violet? You remembered?'

'I did.'

Then her face and her voice hardened. 'Why the hell did you come pre-packed with my favourite drinking chocolate?'

'It slipped into my suitcase unnoticed. And why the hell *not*?' he answered. 'Now. You want some, yes?' He flipped the lid off and turned to the kitchen bench, busying himself with making the drink. 'Go, Lissy. Go and see your room whilst I work. You put me off.'

The vibes coming from the woman were palpable, but she remained seated. 'What are you working on? I don't want to walk in there and see thumbnails of hundreds of naked blonde women on the computer screen. It's embarrassing for us both.'

Stef sighed. 'Why are you still like this, Lissy? Seven years have passed. Seven years!'

'You hurt me. I didn't like being hurt.'

'You hurt me too. That cut on my foot did not heal for days,' he replied.

She was silent for a moment, maybe remembering their time together. 'I suppose I should apologise for that,' she said finally. 'I wouldn't normally want to draw blood.'

'I still have the scar. I will show you. It is a constant reminder of my Elisabetta and our summer in Cornwall.'

'I don't want to see it, but thanks for offering.' He heard the sofa creak as she stood up; felt the warmth of her body as she came up just behind him in the kitchen. 'What do you think that man was doing on my beach? It was horrid. I swear he had a gun.'

'I don't know.' He stirred the chocolate into the warm milk. The sweet, floral scent drifted out of the mug and tickled his nose. He passed the mug to Lissy and she wrapped both hands around it, hunching her shoulders in that way he remembered, inhaling the scent before drinking the stuff.

'I do think you need to speak to the police. Maybe they will have evidence?'

'Whatever evidence he left will have washed away with the tide.' She shivered. 'I'll just have to see what happens tomorrow.'

'Well, if you want me to spend some time with you and watch the shoreline, I shall do so.' He put up his hands in a gesture of surrender. 'No strings attached, I promise. Now, is the chocolate good?'

'Very good,' she answered.

'Excellent. So – forget the man on your beach and think about your room. Believe me, there are no naked women on the laptop screen. Come. Let me show you what I have been working on. You will like it. You will see why your brother contacted me to come to England. This is, as you said, an important opportunity for him.' Stef shrugged. 'How many photographers would be able to get wall space in a Mayfair gallery?'

'Not many. He's done well.'

'He has done *very* well.'

'Are you going to include some of your prints in the exhibition?' asked Lissy.

'Why would I do that?' He was surprised at the question. 'I don't need to build my name. The work you will see here is for my own private amusement. Your brother asked me to come because he thought I might enjoy the process. *Dio*! I have enough success of my own without trying to steal his. I am on holiday and relaxing.'

'Good. It matters a lot to him – and to me – that this

exhibition works. He deserves so much more recognition. All right then. Let me see the computer – in *my* bedroom.'

'Excellent.' Stef bowed again and indicated that she should leave the room first.

Lissy had kicked off her espadrilles by the sofa and her feet slapped across the polished oak floorboards into the bedroom. That room, she was pleased to note, had carpet down. She liked the look and feel of wooden floors in living areas, but preferred a soft carpet on the bedroom floor.

Her apartment in London had the most gorgeous, deep carpet in the bedrooms. She imagined for a moment how Stef would enjoy stretching his bare toes out of her bed and feeling the soft pile beneath his skin; then she quickly chased the thought away. She had to try and remember why she had binned him in the first place. That naked woman in the cove had been the reason. She tried to harden her heart – she was alarmed to find it had been melting a little with the hot chocolate fix – and realised she was failing at the hard-hearted thing quite miserably.

She was also horribly aware of Stef behind her; knew exactly at what angle she would have to tilt her head up in order to meet his dark, almost-black eyes; knew how his hair would feel if she took one of his curls and crushed it between her fingertips; knew exactly how his lips would feel pressed against hers ...

'This room is a mess,' she said. 'How is anyone supposed to have a night's sleep here?' Her voice had a too-posh, ringing tone to it; clipped, sharp and altogether not very nice, but it was deliberate. God forbid Stef should think she'd been thinking of naughty things with him at the centre of them. Those barriers were too precarious as it was.

'It will soon tidy up. I need space to work. Look, you can squeeze through the gap here and sit on the bed. I will sit next to you and turn the machine around and you can see some pictures.'

'I'm not sitting on the bed with you.' Lissy knew that was one step away from him reaching one of those long, sensitive fingers out and stroking the back of her hand, and her responding by reaching up and touching his face. She could almost hear her latest brick fall down. If she sat too close to him it would be a landslide and she'd be lost. 'You can show me them as I stand here.'

'If you wish. Here. This is my own Pre-Raphaelite collection. I am sure that you know Jon will be working like the marvellous Julia Margaret Cameron. He is going to use traditional methods of developing the pictures and recreate the Cameron shots that *she* recreated in the style of the Pre-Raphaelites. Do you see? One photographer paying, what is it – *omaggio* – homage to another. Myself, my work is different.' He wiggled the mouse around and the laptop flashed into life.

Lissy gasped. There was a picture of little Grace on the screen – Grace, sitting on a seat, with her hands clasped in her lap and her eyes trained on the photographer – Stef, she presumed – but the image appeared as if the real-life Grace had been inserted into the picture. The only thing that looked truly photographic about it was indeed the figure of Grace herself. Everything else was like a traditionally painted background.

'That's so clever!' Lissy leaned forward. 'It's like you've dropped her into a painting.'

'I was unsure as to whether to make the whole thing painted,' mused Stef, his gaze travelling critically over the screen, 'or to make her the focal point and paint in the rest. I have been using what is called combination art, as well as digitally painting the background myself. Cameron used the combination technique, but it is much easier to do it digitally. One can paste layers together and make a kind of collage. Look. See this picture?' He clicked a file and another image appeared on the screen. 'This is Waterhouse's painting called *The Easy Chair*. See how I have based our girl on that picture? It is difficult to explain.' He moved the picture up the screen so the two images were side by side. 'I have done a whole series of Waterhouse's whilst I have been here. This was the first one I attempted.'

The girl in the real Waterhouse stared out at the painter in the same way as Grace had stared at Stef. Even her hair was similar, although it was quite apparent that the colours in Grace's eyes had been enhanced somehow, making them sparkle with a sort of mischief.

Lissy smiled at the picture. 'It looks fabulous the way it is. It's so odd how you could put either one of those girls in the other's time frame and they'd still look like they belonged. That child,' she said, pointing at Grace, 'has been in this world before. I swear it. So, what else have you done?'

'Oh, I have done a few.' Stef looked across at Lissy and smiled. 'Are you sure you want to see them? You don't feel the need to report the gunman at all yet?'

Lissy shuddered. 'No. I'm trying to forget about him. Show me the next picture, please, it's taking my mind off him.'

'Good. It's making your mind relax, yes? That and the floral chocolate.'

'Yes.' Lissy felt her shoulders relax a little as well as her mind, and took the chance of sitting next to him. She definitely felt a lot better. It was probably a fishing rod the man had. Yes, that was it – a fishing rod. No matter. She wanted to see more of Stef's work, anyway, so she pushed the thought away. She was getting good at that. That was the effect he'd always had on her – he had made real life seem, well, insignificant, somehow. All that mattered had been the two of them. A little sigh escaped her lips and Stef shot a glance her way, frowning slightly.

'Are you all right?' he asked.

'Fine. Fine and dandy as they say. Come on,' she nudged him with her elbow and nodded at the screen. It was a mistake; a little tingle zipped up her arm as their bodies connected. She shifted on the bed, moving away from him. They were too close; much too close. 'Show me another one.'

'Okay.' He smiled at her. 'How about this one. Do you recognise the person?'

Stef clicked an icon and Lissy laughed. 'That's Becky. It's another Waterhouse, isn't it? *The Mermaid*. Gosh, I'm pleased she's clothed in your shot ...' She shut her mouth as she realised what she had said, images of that day in Cornwall popping unbidden into her mind.

'Yes.' Stef seemed oblivious to the comment as he skimmed the mouse around and brought up the original. 'See, in the Waterhouse, she sits naked – except for her fishy tail of course – and brushes her hair. She turns to someone out of sight to her left and is distracted by them. In our picture, Becky is also sitting on the beach. She turns to her left, and her left hand is up at the right side of her face, but her right hand is holding out a bucket full of shells – for the child, I presume.'

'That's so her!' said Lissy with a smile. 'She's always fiddling with that thing in her ear and she can't hear out of the left one anyway, so it makes sense that she's looking around at that angle because someone must be talking to her!'

'Ah. And the child? I did not like to ask,' said Stef, frowning.

'Grace? Oh, she's fine. No problems there, thank goodness. They took a risk, but they knew that when they decided to have her.'

'Risks are good. Some risks, anyway.'

'That one was.' Lissy nodded. 'Grace is wonderful. I don't think I show it all the time, but I do love her. Have you done lots of these pictures then?'

'A few, as I say. I might show you them another time. There are some I am still working on.' He turned his attention to the laptop. His black eyelashes brushed his high cheekbones as he looked down at the keyboard and began pressing buttons. Those lashes were unbelievably long and when they framed his eyes as he looked at you ...

Lissy cleared her throat as Stef closed the last picture down and made to switch the machine off. 'Wait!' She laid her hand on his forearm. He was like a magnet. She clearly hadn't shifted far enough away from him. The dark hairs tickled the palm of her hand and his skin was warm.

'What is it?' He seemed surprised at the physical contact. And by the look of him, now he wasn't distracted by his photos, he had felt the same jolt she had done when those few square centimetres of their bodies connected.

'What about that picture of me? In the studio?' She felt her face colour and cursed herself. Cori was the one who blushed all the time – that pretty redhead in London who knew more about Pre-Raphaelite muses than was probably healthy. 'When you turned up that day. You said something about me being like the Lady of Shalott looking at Lancelot.'

'And so I did.' Stef grinned and closed the laptop lid, knocking the thing into sleep mode. 'But I liked that one as it was. You looked too beautiful and I didn't want to change anything. Not even the Pre-Raphaelites could compare to you that day, Lissy.'

Lissy felt herself blush again. She'd never been referred to in those terms before. And he'd called her Lissy and it still sounded so sweet and lovely.

But then – in her mind's eye, there was the spectre of that naked woman wrapping herself around him to contend with. And the memory of *her* wasn't going to go away any time soon.

Chapter Thirteen

Sea Scarr Hall, 1905

Walter sent a curt telegram from Whitby, advising Lorelei that he was spending the night in the town. She had already fobbed Florrie and her mother off with a story about him being delayed by estate business, so it didn't matter much in that respect and now they had left, but it was still damned irritating of Walter. She threw the telegram into the fire and walked to the front window, taking a deep breath. Actually, her main emotion on reading it had been one of immense relief. She was spared his presence for a while longer. Good.

From here, she could see that the sea was just starting to creep up across the sand, and she felt a yearning to be out there, swimming across the ocean, all the way to her rock and maybe, one day, beyond – all the way to the horizon.

Escape. That was the thing. She wanted to escape.

It made no sense to Lorelei to sit in the Hall and waste the evening. Once the beach was swallowed up, she would lose her chance of feeling the sand between her toes for yet another day – so it was obvious to her what she should do. And if she was quick enough, she'd miss the storm. It was still warm – and really, if it began to rain when she was swimming, she'd be wet anyway, so what would it matter?

She dared to hope she would have a willing conspirator in the matter and her lips curled upwards into a smile as she thought about that conspirator and what could happen.

Walter was away, after all. Who could stop her? She left the room, pausing only to pull a fresh bathing dress and a clean towel out of the linen press, then headed outside, down towards the Dower House and the beach.

She wondered for a brief moment whether she should knock on the door of the Dower House and announce her presence, but then thought that simply the best thing to do was to discard her clothing on the dunes and go straight into the sea. She would swim out as far and as fast as she dared – and if anybody should care to join her, then that was all to the good.

Julian had developed his most recent photographs and was especially proud of one in particular which showed an artist at work on the beach, his dog by his easel and the imposing cliffs behind him. He desperately needed fresh air after being cooped up in his makeshift darkroom, and stepped out onto the terrace, away from the overpowering smell of chemicals. He was still thinking about the tea party and Lorelei looking up at him, the ribbons on her hat lifted by the breeze.

So far, he had very little to complain about as far as this job was concerned – he had, after all, met Lorelei Scarsdale through it. Why—

'Good Lord.' He walked out further, to the edge of the terrace, and saw her again; a living, breathing mermaid, her dark hair plaited with a red ribbon, streaming behind her as she headed towards the Siren's Rock. She was, he could tell, determinedly looking straight ahead, not taking any notice of the Dower House at all, sticking her chin out of the water in a haughty fashion even as she swam.

It amused him greatly. 'Well now, Madame Mermaid,' he said to nobody in particular. 'I think I might just go for a swim myself.'

He stripped off his outerwear there and then, dumping it all on the terrace and running down the steps towards the beach. The tide was coming in, but there were still a couple of hundred yards of warm sand to cover before he hit the water and splashed out as far as he could, then plunged full length into the sea. The water was deliciously cold and he gasped as it took his breath away; yet it wasn't long before he was ploughing after the mermaid, his hair soaked, dripping stinging saltwater into his eyes as he focussed up ahead of him.

'Fancy meeting you here!' he called, as he approached Lorelei. 'Such a big ocean and we happen to find each other right here, in this tiny cove. Good evening, Lady Scarsdale!'

Lorelei stopped swimming and turned around, treading water. 'Mr Cooper! How peculiar indeed. I never expected to see you here. How fortuitous.'

'It is indeed. I thought for one moment that I had spotted a mermaid, and I decided to come out here and investigate.' He sighed, also treading water, so they faced each other, bobbing up and down with the motion of the waves. Lorelei's sea-green eyes were mischievous and Julian couldn't help but grin. 'I see now that it is *not* a mermaid, but a true Siren. A temptress, drawing me into her web. Or is that a spider? Do Sirens possess webs?'

Lorelei laughed. 'No. I don't have a web, but I have a rock, and a necklace made of shells, and you are more than welcome to join me on my rock if you wish.'

'A necklace made of shells? Why, I'm afraid you are mistaken, my lady. It appears to have become undone. Perhaps it is beneath our feet, floating in the ocean.' He dived under the surface and grabbed Lorelei's legs, giving her a quick tug downwards.

He surfaced and she was laughing out loud. 'Oh, Julian! What a shock. You made me scream out! How embarrassing.'

'I'm sorry.' Julian grinned. 'It was too much to resist. Or—' He pointed a finger at her. 'It may have been the tentacles of a sea-monster grabbing you. Wait there. I'll have to check again.'

He made to dive down again and she shrieked, kicking her legs out and backing away from him laughing. 'No! No, it's not a sea-monster, I promise! I'm heading to the rock. You can check again after I've gone.' She turned and kicked out, streaking away like a seal.

'You can't escape me that quickly!' Julian shouted and swam after her as fast as he could.

To his shame, Lorelei was the far better swimmer and she was already on the rock, squeezing her plait out and laughing at him by the time he scrambled up to sit beside her. The surface of the rock was rough on the bare skin of his legs, the late evening sun warm on his shoulders.

He shook his wet hair out of his eyes and smiled at her. 'The sea-monster disappeared. Odd, that. I'm only left with a mermaid.'

'A mermaid who'll have to go back to dry land soon.' Lorelei sighed. 'I wish I could stay here. It's much nicer.'

'I'll build you a castle on this rock,' promised Julian. He reached out and lifted her plait, weighing it in his palm, then letting it drop gently onto her shoulders. 'And you can live in it forever. I'll build it out of seashells for you, and I'll decorate it with pirate gold and rubies.'

'There *are* supposed to be some shipwrecks hereabout,' said Lorelei. 'Maybe there are treasure chests galore beneath the waves. Maybe, one day, something will turn up on the beach and I'll see it and I'll know it to be something wonderful.'

'I've already had that happen to me.' Julian traced his finger down her neck to her shoulders and let his hand drop away as it caught the edge of the stiff fabric of her bathing dress. 'You're shivering,' he murmured, leaning very close to her ear. 'Why's that, Mermaid?'

'I'm not shivering,' whispered Lorelei. 'I'm not cold. It's not – that – sort of shivering.' She dropped her gaze and studied her hands. 'I should go.'

Julian drew away from her and sighed. 'Yes, you probably should. There are pirates hereabouts, as well as shipwrecks.

Pirates are better than Sea Captains. But some of those pirates are contemptible fellows who would take advantage of a mermaid if they were left alone with her for too long.'

'I've never met a pirate who I found contemptible.' Lorelei looked up at him and their eyes locked.

There was a beat and Julian leaned in again, inches away from her, their lips so close he could almost taste the saltwater on hers.

Then he suddenly pulled away, jumped up and dived into the sea. 'You probably *should* go,' he called from his position a little way away from the rock. 'You probably should.'

Lorelei paused only for a moment, until she too stood up. She reached up and fiddled with her plait, then stretched her arms above her head and made a perfect dive of her own.

She emerged, shaking the loose strands of hair from her face and smiled. 'Race you!' she cried and started off for the shore.

Julian laughed and began to follow her. He paused, however, to change direction and rescue the red ribbon that was floating off, away from the rock and out to sea. Purposefully, he stayed out in the water and let her reach the shore, pick up her towel and discarded clothing from the dunes and run off, barefoot, towards the house.

Julian smiled as he watched her go, then came to the shore himself. He wound the ribbon around his wrist and walked back to the Dower House whistling. He had the perfect excuse to return the ribbon to her later.

It was almost as if she had loosened it deliberately.

The Road to the Cove, Present Day

Lissy drove back to the Dower House in her little MG. She'd spent the night in the spare bedroom, but she had barely slept, far too conscious of the man in the next room to her. It was bad enough that she'd had to borrow one of his shirts to wear over her pyjamas this morning and all she could smell was his aftershave. Surreptitiously, she kept dipping her nose inside the shirt and inhaling his scent. The owner of the shirt was following behind her in his own "hire vehicle" as he called it, and they pulled up, one after the other, on the verge at the turn-off for the private road.

Lissy was just going to head down to the house and leave Stef to make his own way down, but as they reached the cove, she saw a couple waiting there, outside a small sports car. The girl's hair was glinting red in the sunlight, the man's shining golden beside her. The redhead was sitting down on the path, the man leaning on the vehicle.

Lissy parked up and climbed out of the car. Stef was beside her in an instant.

'Cori and Simon made it then,' said Lissy.

'Your London friends?' replied Stef. 'You're right. She has the perfect looks for a model. And you say you have known her a while?'

'Yes. We studied art history together. Then we lost touch and I found her in London again. Well. Simon found her and I just helped things along.' Lissy looked at the pair of them – yet another success story. Why couldn't she sort her own love life out as well as she could other people's?

'She's very beautiful. She reminds me of Lizzie Siddal, Dante Gabriel Rossetti's muse. She was a real 'stunner' as they used to say.' Stef half-smiled, his eyes on Cori.

Lissy cast a sidelong glance at him, that old jealousy striking her like a punch to the stomach. 'She's put some weight on since I last saw her,' she said, and immediately regretted how horrid that sounded. Poor Cori – there was no way she should be mean to her beautiful friend, just because Stef had a habit of going off with his models. She flushed and turned, slamming her car door shut so she didn't have to look at him.

Cori stood up, and held her arms out to Lissy. 'We thought you were on the beach. We saw a girl down there and wondered if it was you. I told Simon your hair wasn't that long, and he said had I never heard of hair extensions.' Cori shook her head. 'But it doesn't matter. You're up here. And you're late!'

'Yes, I'm up here,' agreed Lissy. 'I had some issues last night and I – well – I didn't spend the night in the Dower House.'

Cori smiled, her gaze taking in the makeshift outfit and then sliding unbidden to Stef.

'No!' said Lissy, more sharply than was strictly necessary. 'It was *not* like that. I thought I saw someone on the beach and ...' her voice trailed off. 'I had to borrow this shirt; I wasn't decent. I just had pyjamas on.'

'Elisabetta was scared,' said Stef, 'but I think she is all right now. It is good to meet you. I'm Stefano Ricci.' His voice was mellow and sexy and heavily accented, and Cori blushed to the roots of her hair as he took her hand and shook it.

'Oh,' said Cori.

'No *oh*-ing, please,' snapped Lissy, seeing how her friend's eyes were roving around Stef's person appreciatively – from the top of his curly, dark hair to the tips of his, thankfully covered, toes. 'It wasn't like that. It was scary. I thought I saw a man down there and it's a private beach.'

'Well, as Cori said, there was a woman down there before – that's why we thought you were here,' Simon put in. 'Clearly it's not that private. It's good to meet you, Stefano. I've heard about you.'

'Simon!' Lissy was horrified. Curses that she'd ever mentioned the man to him. Hurriedly, she turned to Cori. 'Stef is a friend of Jon's.'

'I was a friend of Elisabetta's first.' Stef smiled. 'How are you guys? Simon and Cori? Yes?' He looked at Cori and Lissy knew he was measuring up her red hair. 'That is a beautiful name.'

'No, it's not.' Cori pulled a face. 'I hate it.'

'Is it short for anything?'

'Corisande. It's an old family name.'

'Ah. My name is a family name as well. My friends call me Stef.' He smiled down at Lissy and Lissy felt herself colour. It should be impossible that his smiles could still have that effect on her. 'I am a photographer. I am also a friend of Jon's, truly, but Lissy and I go back a very long way.'

'Please!' Lissy turned to Cori, worrying that this was leading into dangerous territory. 'It was a long time ago. Oh – goodness me, are you all right?' She put her hand out as the colour suddenly drained out of Cori's face.

Cori blinked. 'Sorry, the heat's getting to me. Do you mind if I just …?' She pointed to the ground and sat down again.

'Oh, no, it's all my fault. Really. I'm sorry you've had to wait out here for me,' said Lissy. 'Come on. Let's get to the house. I'll let Becky and Jon know you're here, and we can get started.' She suddenly smiled. 'And I need some clothes. It's so nice for us all to be together again, isn't it?'

'It has been good for me to see you again,' murmured Stef, so quietly that Lissy knew he had meant it for her ears only.

The Cove

Stef thought it looked like a Laura Knight painting. They were all on that private little beach of Lissy's and, if you were an outsider looking at the golden and blue canvas, there were studies of people dotted around the cove.

Becky was sitting under a candy-striped umbrella on the beach with a very drawn-looking Cori and a much more cheerful Grace. Grace was digging holes enthusiastically, filling up her bucket and dumping piles of sand around the excavation area. Closer to the sea, Jon and Simon were pointing at the rocks, composing some sort of picture between them.

Stef had left them there, clapped Jon on the back and was now striding over to the beach hut barefoot and long-legged, a portfolio under his arm. Lissy was drifting here and there with a tray of cold drinks, her toe-nails flashing scarlet in the sand. She was wearing the tiniest pair of shorts known to man, the widest brimmed straw hat he had ever seen and a classic white *broderie anglaise* camisole top.

Stef voiced his thoughts to Lissy as he caught up with her. 'It's like a painting. It's all the colours blending together and the people in it – I feel like it's a Laura Knight come to life. It's like Lamorna Cove.'

'But it's not Lamorna Cove. We can never go back to how it was at Lamorna Cove.'

'I wish we could,' said Stef with a sigh. 'Although I would definitely change a few things.'

'Would you now?' For a moment, Lissy's mask of perfection and veneer of disdain slipped and she seemed vulnerable – she looked like a young woman who had dealt with the biggest blow to her confidence she had ever anticipated; and he knew he was the one who had dealt that blow to her. It was nothing to be proud of.

He wanted to be able to take her in his arms and apologise for it all over again. He wanted it all to have been different. He had suffered the consequences of that afternoon for years. He had no excuse. He should have tried harder to dissuade Kerensa, not let her play her little games or go so far. It wasn't her he wanted and he'd known it then as he did now.

Damn it.

'I have to go and see what Grace is doing,' said Lissy, before he could say anything further.

Stef looked across at the umbrella and saw that Grace was digging holes industriously, emptying the resulting buckets of sand over Becky's feet. 'She looks fine to me.'

'Becky needs my help.' Lissy turned away and headed purposefully over to the little girl.

Stef let her go. What else could he do? He sighed. He was far too good at letting her go; and that as well was nothing to be proud of. It was always too easy to let her walk away. He was no fool – he knew it was going to be harder to get her – if that was even possible – and keep her this time. Last time, he hadn't fought hard enough. It had been easier to just give up and go away with Kerensa – who was, it had to be said, a more than willing companion.

However, the fact that he was at least here with Lissy, breathing the same air, and close enough to touch her was a start. It was a very good start. And the warmth of the day was incredible; he couldn't remember it being this warm in England for many a year. Of course, it couldn't compare with that summer in Cornwall. Nothing could. He looked at Lissy playing Lady Bountiful with her tray of drinks and her burst of speed as she hurried across to Grace made him smile.

Jon and Simon were so enthusiastic about what they were planning that he couldn't help feeling enthusiastic with them, and his smile widened as he continued over to the beach hut. He turned the handle on the door to enter it and wasn't surprised to see that it moved smoothly and without creaking; yet another sign that no expense had been spared on this little holiday home.

The hut was fractionally cooler inside, but pretty stuffy. The door needed to be wedged open to let some air circulate, and, looking through the beach hut, he saw a back door which opened up onto the square patio garden area. He couldn't risk leaving the front door open, just in case of prying eyes, so he took the few long strides he needed to cross the ground floor through a tiny kitchenette of sorts and threw the back door open. Then he turned to survey the place and a slow smile spread across his face.

It was *perfezione* – perfection. There was a little seating area downstairs, a tiny lean-to at the back which he guessed was maybe a bathroom and the lovely garden area behind him. The hut even had a mezzanine floor, reached by a set of ten low, white winding stairs. The owners had thoughtfully added a double bed and a tiny bedside table to that floor, and it looked inviting up there – all white and crisp, with windows in the roof so they could lie there and look at the stars ... They? He quickly brought himself back to reality. That was a little premature, perhaps. He had to win her back first. It might be a difficult task, but after that, he dreamed that he would be able to lie on the bed with her here and watch the stars.

Having said that, he would forego the star-watching and settle for daylight, so long as he got her back. Having her so close to him last night had reminded him of how much he wanted to have her next to him forever.

Chapter Fourteen

Sea Scar Hall, 1905

Lorelei had a clear view across the cove and the sky was certainly more threatening than it had been earlier. There were huge, black clouds rolling in now and they seemed to be sinking into the sea. It was only just after eight o'clock and she just wished the storm would come, blow over as they usually did and then she could stop peeking out of the window and go to bed, even if it was ridiculously early. She knew now what they meant by a 'sea-change' – this was very different to the warm weather she had experienced a little earlier.

In fact, no. She wouldn't go to bed. She would paint. That's what she would do. She was still fizzing from her swim with Julian and she knew there was no way she could settle.

She was putting the finishing touches to a little seascape she had been working on over the past few weeks. Walter did not encourage her art, so she seized every chance she had when he was away or otherwise engaged to work on it. Her painting and drawing skills were getting rusty and she didn't like that feeling.

Just as she was about to pull the curtains closed and shut out the impending storm, Lorelei saw a figure coming up towards the house. She pressed her face closer to the window. Cursing under her breath, she hoped that her husband hadn't decided to come home after all.

Then she recognised the loping gait and the too long hair. The figure was wearing a loose white shirt and had his hands in his pockets and Lorelei's heart gave a little skip.

'Julian!' She hurried across the room and ran out into the

hallway and down the stairs. She pulled the heavy front door open and greeted him. 'Julian! What a wonderful surprise. Do come in.' She cast a glance at the sky. 'It does look rather ominous out there and I'm sure you will be warmer and drier inside if the worst happens.'

'You forget that I'm from Scotland.' Julian laughed. 'I'm quite used to a wee bit o' rain. And shouldn't I be introduced by a butler or somebody? I'm sure it's not the done thing for the lady of the manor to open the door to waifs and strays.'

'Nor was it the done thing to bring you champagne last night.' Lorelei smiled and held the door wider so he could step inside the hallway. 'Or perhaps to talk of shipwrecks and pirates on a rock. Florrie also pointed out that I shouldn't have taken the champagne over to a guest. I told her exactly the same as I am telling you now. I am the hostess and what I say goes.'

'Very pleased to hear it.' He walked past her and she was deliciously aware of his warm body as he came close to her and stepped inside.

'I think there *is* a storm coming,' she said, for want of something better to say as he stood in the hall waiting for her. He seemed to fill the huge room with his presence, much more than Walter did. Unless Walter's temper was in evidence, then there was no space for anything else.

'I think you could be right,' he replied. 'Let's hope your guests make it to London safely. I can't imagine they'll get a restful night in a moving metal box when a thunderstorm is going on outside.'

'Well my husband has decided it is too risky for him to travel and he is only in Whitby.'

'More fool him for staying away. I know where I would rather be,' said Julian. Lorelei had a feeling that he wasn't just referring to Sea Scarr Hall and she felt herself colour a little with pleasure.

'In fact, that's why I came back tonight,' he continued. 'I couldn't bear to stay away. I was trying to think of an excuse when I was walking up here and I really can't. Oh, yes – here's one. I decided to take another photograph of Florrie. Oh, dear. What's that, you say? She left at seven?' He shook his head. 'I suppose I had better leave then.'

'Well. Walter will be away all night, so I am abandoned.' Lorelei tried to keep her voice even. 'So I'm more than happy for you to tarry here a little, Julian. And don't you have a better excuse to be here?' She glanced meaningfully at his wrist, where he had threaded a red ribbon through the buttons on his cuff.

'Your husband's abandoned you? Why, that is a terrible thing to do.' Julian stepped to one side, ignoring the fact he had the ribbon on his wrist, and allowed Lorelei to lead the way into the drawing room. 'I trust he will make it up to you when he returns.'

'I doubt it. Please. Have a seat.' She indicated a chair next to the window. 'I'm quite happy to be abandoned. I have some work I need to do and I can't work when he's around.'

'Oh! Well, if you're busy, I'll just—'

Julian made to stand up again, but Lorelei waved him back into the seat. 'No!' The retort was sharper than she had meant it to be. 'I mean to say, it's perfectly all right for you to be here. The work I wanted to do was simply some artwork, and it can wait. I'd much rather have your company.'

'You can have both,' said Julian reasonably. 'Oh – and you can have your ribbon back as well. See? You're right. I had an excuse all along.' He carefully unthreaded the ribbon and let it dangle enticingly, looped around his forefinger until Lorelei gave in, laughed and snatched it away. 'If you want to work on something, I can sit with you. I'm no expert, but if you need a second opinion, I may be able to help with composition and so forth. I do have an eye for things. Especially beautiful things.'

Lorelei felt a little flame of heat shimmy up her body. 'Beautiful things? What do you mean?'

'I think you know what I mean, Lady Scarsdale. Now, are you going to tell me what you are working on at all?'

'No,' she said. His face registered surprise; then she smiled mischievously. 'I'm going to show you. Please – come with me? If you don't mind accompanying a lady upstairs? Just to my sitting room, I hasten to add. It's where I paint. There's a wonderful view of the sea and the cove from the window. I can see the Dower House from there as well. So, effectively, I could spy on you, Mr Cooper.'

'Ah! Intriguing. Yes, of course I'd like to see it. Lead the way, my lady.' Julian stood up and bowed.

Lorelei laughed. 'Very well, then. This way.'

She took Julian back through the foyer and towards the main staircase. More than a little aware that he was very close behind her, she began to ascend the staircase.

She was wearing the ivory tea dress, and she was conscious of the skirts dragging up the stairs behind her. They seemed heavier, as if she couldn't climb the steps quickly enough and she cringed as she remembered discarding her petticoats in Walter's arms after that swim. It all seemed a lifetime ago now. She'd been lucky he hadn't reacted more severely.

'Aren't you concerned that the servants might see you taking a strange man upstairs?' Julian's voice, sounding amused, broke into her thoughts.

'Not at all.' She paused and turned, looking back at Julian. They were almost the same height, as she stood up above him on the staircase, just like when she'd been at the Dower House with her programmes. 'As I said, I make the rules.' Her sharp eyes caught sight of a shadow pressing itself into the stairwell below and she raised her voice slightly. 'And anybody who questions what I do, where I go or who I do it with, knows where the door is. I shall have no hesitation in dismissing people should rumours begin to circulate.'

'Very much the mistress,' murmured Julian, as the shadow peeled away from the wall and hurried into a nearby room. 'Remind me never to cross you in any way.'

'I don't think you *could* cross me.' It was Lorelei's turn to sound amused. 'I'm ever so glad my husband let the Dower House out to you this year.' She caught the twang of Yorkshire in her voice and recovered herself. 'It's not long since it was renovated and I do feel he is trying to recoup the costs. Nobody has lived in it for years. Tell me, did you see the sconces in the window?'

'Sconces?' Julian frowned. 'Well, I cannot say I have taken much notice of the interior of the house. The exterior and the things one finds to admire on the beach are far more interesting than a dull old interior.'

'Hmmm. Indeed. Well, let me show you what I have in my sitting room; then we will see if the sconces at the Dower House are not more interesting after that.'

She turned away again, hitched up her skirts and ran up the last few steps.

The Cove, Present Day

Lissy flopped down beside Becky; if she was over here, under the umbrella, away from Stef, it might make it easier for her to control her emotions as far as he was concerned.

'Antissy!' The child was there in an instant. 'I sand you as well.'

'She wants to tip sand on your feet,' Becky explained. 'It's easier not to argue.'

Lissy sighed and, stretching her legs out, gave herself up to Grace's ministrations. 'So, what do you think he's doing in the beach hut?' she asked as the first bucket load was upended on her feet. 'Ouch!' That, as Grace managed to stick the sharp edge of her spade into Lissy's ankle, trying to poke a pure white shell out of the sand.

'Ah. Got it. Thank you,' said Grace politely; then she handed the shell to Becky and went back to digging.

'Does she ever stop?' asked Lissy, astonished.

'No,' replied Becky. 'And back to your question – I don't know what he's doing. Did he not tell you?'

'No.' Lissy looked at Cori. 'Do you know? He had a portfolio with him.'

Cori shook her head. 'Sorry. Maybe he's setting something up?'

'Maybe. The hut's to be used as a changing room for these pictures. Jon's been carrying equipment back and forwards all morning. I just worry that Stef might wander in and find one of us in there, naked or something ...' She shut up as she felt herself colouring.

'Naked or something, naked or something,' chanted Grace, hitting the top of the sand in the bucket with the spade.

'Grace!' cried Becky. 'Anyway, Stef would have seen we were all here before he went in there. So your argument holds no water.'

'I don't even know why he came back,' said Lissy. 'If I'd have known, I would have told Jon not to bother.' Grace emptied the next bucket of sand on Lissy's knees. Lissy brushed the stuff away mechanically and folded her arms. 'No. Not on the legs, Grace.'

'On your feet then.' Grace was undaunted. She started to brush the sand down towards Lissy's ankles. The stuff was like glass being dragged across her hot skin and Lissy flinched.

'Oh! Can I go to the little white house and play?' Grace suddenly asked.

Becky shook her head, beginning to protest but Lissy waved her arm, cutting her off. 'Oh, why not. I'll take you, Grace. Let's go there now. You can see inside it. It's like a giant doll's house.' She scrambled to her feet and held her hand out. Grace threw her spade down and put her hand in Lissy's, and Lissy began to walk over to the beach hut, Grace running along beside her to keep pace.

'You're only taking her now because he's in there!' called Becky. 'And you want to see what he's up to!'

Lissy stuck her chin in the air and ignored Becky. That wasn't the reason at all. Of course it wasn't.

Stef was hunkered on the patio area, packing a few things back into his portfolio when he heard the slap, slap of pink jelly-sandals on the little path that surrounded the beach hut.

'Hallo Stef!' Grace was in the process of trying to scramble over the low fence, and Stef leaned over to pick her up. He stood her up in the middle of the yard and she clapped her hands. 'Now, doll's house.' She turned and jogged into the beach hut. 'Oh, wow!'

Stef couldn't help but laugh. 'It is rather fine, is it not? But maybe you shouldn't be here, no?'

'Antissy's here too,' said Grace. 'She's coming. I ran away.'

Lissy walked around the corner. 'She did. She let go of my hand. She's uncontrollable. Stef, it's no good. I have to ask. What are you doing at the back door of my beach hut?'

'I was investigating it.' Stef grinned. 'No, *Grazia*!' he shouted as he peered into the hut. 'Stay downstairs, there's a good girl.'

'Okay!' Grace shouted back. There was a soft *flumf* as she apparently threw herself onto the small couch, followed by an expression that sounded very much like a delighted, '*Ooh*!'

'I wouldn't have thought it was big enough to investigate.' Lissy frowned.

'Have you been in?' asked Stef.

'Yes, when I first got here. It's quite quaint, I think. I suggested Jon and Simon could store their costumes and equipment here if they didn't want them on the beach when they were working.'

'Ah, and that is what I am doing.' Stef smiled. 'Storing equipment. Yes. That's it. For Jon and Simon.' He nodded.

'Jon must have filled it up by now. Surely to goodness it's not that big inside.' She reached across him and took hold of the edge of the door, but Stef held it tight and she couldn't open it any further.

'*Wheeeeee*!' came Grace's voice.

'Oh God, she's probably making a slide out of the couch cushions.' Lissy shook the door and glared at Stef. 'Leave go. She could hurt herself and then Becky would kill me.'

'Nope.' Stef smiled at her again and stepped a little to the side. 'She's fine. I will bring you back sometime and we can explore together, once the equipment has been packed away.'

'Explore what?' asked Lissy. She shook the door again.

Again, Stef held it tight. 'The huge expanse of beach house.' Stef shrugged. 'We shall come back tonight. I want to see the moon rise above the sea.'

'Does the moon rise from the east?' she asked. 'Because that's the only way you'd see it rise over this part of the sea.'

'I believe it does. Let's come back later and find out.'

'No,' said Lissy. 'You won't be here later.'

'Will I not? We shall see. Now.' He poked his head into the house. '*Grazia*, come out. Time for some paddling in the water.'

Grace appeared at the door. 'Paddling? With you?' She smiled up at Stef in that trusting way a well-loved and confident child has, sure that any adult they meet will defer to them.

'Well. Yes. Why not?' said Stef. 'I shall leave my belongings here. My bag of special things – my *sacchetto di cose speciali*. Can you say that?' She repeated the words in a good imitation of his accent. 'Good girl. We shall have you speaking Italian like a *bambina* from Portofino soon. Why does your Antissy not speak Italian to you? It is a good time to learn when you are so tiny.'

'That's all right.' Grace took Stef's hand. 'You can talk it to me when you live with Antissy.'

The little girl looked quite shocked when Stef burst out laughing and Lissy simply stared at the pair of them.

Much later on, when the day was drawing to a close, Stef was sitting with Simon and Cori, flicking through some of Simon's sketches. He laughed when he saw a few quick strokes depicting him and Lissy, with Grace between them, playing in the sea.

'You three all looked great together.' Simon said. 'The composition worked perfectly.'

Stef smiled, remembering the afternoon. Grace had had a short nap, then rallied after a picnic tea and demanded 'Stefandantissy' take her out into the water yet again before she had to go home. Jon had been busy in the beach hut and Becky had been helping Cori brush the salt and the tangles out of her long, red hair. Cori, still in her loose, white dress from whatever picture she'd posed for last, had yelped each time the comb caught on a knot and Becky had been blissfully oblivious to her protests.

Stef and Lissy had taken a hand each and lifted Grace up and over each wave as it licked onto the beach. Then they'd carried her, dangling between them, shrieking with laughter, back up to the beach and dumped her on the sand near the rest of the adults. Stef was laughing with her, and was pleased to see that even Lissy was smiling – and it was a long, long time since he had seen that smile. It gave him hope.

'That little girl is a perfect subject for a painting,' mused Simon. Grace had been racing around after a football and had finally tumbled into an exhausted heap beside Becky. 'I wonder whether I can borrow her when I've done this exhibition? I know it's not exactly the sort of Pre-Raphaelite art I create, but I'm thinking of Millais?'

He looked at Stef questioningly and Stef nodded. 'Indeed. Millais would be an excellent choice.'

'You weren't thinking about that horrible *Bubbles* picture, were you?' interjected Cori. 'I hate that awful Little Lord Fauntleroy style.'

'You know that I hate it too,' said Simon with a laugh, 'but it's a fabulous piece of art. No. I was thinking more about *Cherry Ripe* or *Meditation*. The ones with the little dark-haired girls in them. Grace would be perfect.'

'Oh! Yes. So she would. I'd forgotten about those ones.' Cori patted him on the knee. 'Good idea.'

Stef looked at the two of them, so well-matched and so in tune with one another. He smiled, his eyes holding Cori's as she glanced at him.

'Yes,' he said. 'A child can be the perfect addition to anything.'

Cori dropped her gaze and began to gather her belongings towards her. 'Well, whatever you decide to do about Grace, I'm glad Jon doesn't want any more photographs out of me. I've had enough. I'm not sure if I'm *Maud* or *Echo* or plain old Cori. I just feel sorry for Becky, wearing that awful heavy medieval stuff. She said she just wanted to write some articles about the exhibition. At least I got this thing to wear.' She tugged at the white gown and pulled a face. 'I'm just going to leave it on, I think. It's comfy and I can't be bothered to change just to drive up to my gran's. It's been so bloody hot today as well. I can't cope anymore. I'm pleased it's cooling down a bit.'

'And at least I've managed to produce one or two sketches to go alongside Jon's photographs,' Simon told Stef. 'They'll complement your work too, I should think. Would you be prepared to let me use a couple of your photos? I know you keep telling us no, but I'm trying one more time. I spoke to Jon and he said he would be honoured if you'd consider it.'

Stef picked the sketch book up again and flicked a few pages back and forth as he frowned, considering it.

Eventually, he nodded. 'I *did* say no. I want people to go and admire *your* work and Jon's, not mine. But you are right. It is clear you are a great artist and that you have an eye for all of this. I think, now, it will be *good* to see some of your quick pieces of work and our photographs depicting the same moment together; so yes – I shall agree. But only a couple. It's not my moment – it's you guys that need to shine here. It's incredible that one instant can be captured so many different ways. Little Grace will probably forget most of it, but at least there will be a record of her father's first London show. We shall all have a summer to remember, I think.' Stef smiled as he handed the book back to Simon. A summer to remember. He hoped they would remember it for the right reasons this time.

Chapter Fifteen

Julian was much more interested in the small, dark figure a few steps ahead of him than he was in the sumptuous red carpet that covered the corridor, or the stern oil paintings of ancient Scarsdales that seemed to track their progress with dead eyes. He thought the cabinets full of stuffed animals and birds that lined the walls hideous, and wondered how someone like Lorelei could live in such a stifling environment.

The woman led him along this corridor with an air of excitement and he admired the way the white lace frothed around her elbows and how the square neck of that beautiful dress made her look far more modest than he thought she really was, deep down.

'Let us hope *he* stays away tonight, anyway.' Lorelei hurried along the corridor to the room at the very end. 'I don't need him turning his nose up at my painting.'

Julian did not need to be reminded that "he" was Lorelei's husband.

'And here we are,' she said triumphantly. 'Now let us see whether we can change your mind about those sconces.'

Lorelei threw the door of her sitting room open and walked inside. Julian followed her and saw an easel at the window and a wooden box of watercolours open on a small table next to it. On the easel was a small seascape, half-finished and depicting a much sunnier, cheerful day than he saw out of the window that night.

'So you see, I really do have an ivory tower,' she said. 'Well. The fireplace is marble so maybe not ivory. But I too can see the world pass by from my window. Poor Lady of Shalott. I sincerely sympathise with her.'

'No wonder you went to the party dressed as she.' Julian should have felt awkward in Lady Scarsdale's sitting room – he was the summer visitor renting her property for a start – but he felt oddly comfortable in that little room with its bright, floral wallpaper and its collection of – yes – brass sconces. 'Aha!' He moved over towards the sconce in the window. 'So this is what you were telling me about. But I am torn, my lady. Do I admire your painting or your brasses? I truly don't know which one to be appreciative of first. Or even,' he said, looking up at the walls, 'the plasterwork. It's wonderful.'

'Oh, Julian!' Lorelei laughed. 'Stop teasing me. Call me Lorelei. Please. Not "my lady" or Lady Scarsdale. That's an old woman's name and I'm nowhere near matronly yet.'

'Very well. Lorelei it is. So – what is it that you want me to see in the sconces?'

She brightened even more and it was like the sun had burst through the storm clouds outside.

'Well, the pattern, intriguing though it is, is modern and not the most interesting part of the fixture. I had them remould the decoration on them when I took over this room. I tried to put my own stamp on things.' Lorelei pointed to one of the sconces on the wall and Julian leaned forward, seeing the delicate filigree pattern carved into the brass. Leaves and flowers and what looked like tiny waves were cresting over the surface, and a lamp was attached to the sconce itself.

'Beautiful workmanship,' he murmured, looking closely at it. He trained his camera on it and took a photograph.

'It is. But once again, it isn't the workmanship I want to show you.'

Julian looked up, surprised to see Lorelei blushing. He tucked his camera away again and she met his eyes for a second, then moved over to the window.

'This is what I want you to see.' She ran her finger over another sconce, exactly the same as the one Julian had just been admiring.

He looked at her curiously. 'What is so different about this one?'

'The difference is that, if I light the lamp attached to *this* one, you should be able to see it from the Dower House.'

'Oh?' He was, as she had suggested, intrigued.

'And,' she continued, 'if you light the one in your upstairs room at the Dower House, I am supposed to be able to see it from here. It's a tiny pinprick, or so I've been led to believe, but it shines through the night.

'I've done some reading of the old legends, and people suggest that the twin lamps – or candles, in those days, I suppose – were supposed to guide smugglers' ships in to the cove. Allegedly, there is a cave somewhere around the cove where the smugglers used to store their goods. I don't really know what happened after they came ashore. As you can imagine, the history books are somewhat hazy, as too many people would be implicated by the stories.

'There are, however, tales of wreckers and ne'er-do-wells abounding around this coastline. One of my dreams is to see one of those shipwrecks I told you about. There are some that lie just off our coast. In the late eighteenth century, barrels of rum were washed ashore from one of the wrecks, and they were stolen by looters – just about the same time that a previous Scarsdale had to sell off another property to raise some funds. It's all conjecture, of course, and his lack of money possibly wasn't even related to the fact he'd lost money through the theft. But isn't it delightful?'

Julian had ceased truly following what she was saying at some point. He heard the words but most of his attention was caught up by this vision in white before him, talking about the romantic legends of the coast. He imagined that she had not been so animated for quite some time.

He realised he was leaning against the windowsill as she spoke, his arms folded, a smile playing around his lips. It was, he felt, some sort of defining moment and thought that, in years to come, the emotion, the underlying excitement and the sheer attraction he felt for her right then would somehow be indelibly marked on the fabric of the building.

'Incredible.' He shook his head gently, his gaze still fixed on her. 'You astound me more and more, every moment I know you.'

He straightened up and suddenly, he had no words. The woman was staring at him, her voice now silent in the room. But they were saying more with the silence than they could ever say with words. They took a step towards one another. Then another step. His face was inches from hers as she looked up at him. Her lips parted slightly and their hands met, reaching for one another in some sort of final acknowledgement that they were being swept away by something they couldn't harness. Call it a riptide, call it a tidal wave – who knew?

'Lorelei—' he began.

Then the thunder came; a crack so loud it seemed to have ripped the storm open and released it, giving it permission to attack right above the house.

Lorelei screamed and jumped, letting go of Julian's hands and grabbing hold of his arm as the lightning split the sky and the rain drops began to pelt against the window pane.

'I'm so sorry!' she said as she seemed to realise what she had done. 'Did I hurt you at all? What a shock.'

'No. I'm not hurt. But *I'm* the one who should be sorry.' He stepped away from her and gently released her grip. 'I shouldn't have done that. If the thunder clap hadn't happened, I couldn't have been held responsible for my actions.'

'But Julian—' She gazed up at him, confused. 'What's to apologise for?'

'You're a married woman. I shouldn't be feeling like this about you. I barely know you and I'm a tenant of your husband—'

'My husband be damned!' snapped Lorelei. 'Do you really believe he's staying at Whitby because of this storm?' She waved her arm at the window. 'Truly? Because I'll tell you where he is. He's with his mistress. I caught them at the fancy-dress ball I talked to you about before. He was in the billiard room with her, and I walked in on them.

'The fool of a man hadn't even locked the door. She was sitting on the table and he was in front of her and he was practically naked and her skirts were up around her hips. I've had a *lot* of experience in my life – so don't for one minute think I'm a prude or even was a virgin when I married. I'm not and I wasn't. And when he found that out, he practically discarded me there and then. He hates me and what I was and whatever he thinks I am, and that doesn't always make sense either. For the sake of propriety, I'm still here and I'm still mistress of this Hall. But he has no compunction about being with another woman – she was dressed as a serving wench, that evening – and he didn't seem to care that he was sullying the woman's marriage prospects by rutting with her like a damned animal.'

Lorelei sobbed, and suddenly seemed to run out of strength. She flung herself onto a day bed, and for the first time Julian realised that not only did she paint here, she probably slept here on occasion as well.

'The woman lives near Whitby, but further south. She's engaged to be married apparently, and I believe Walter is spending as much time as possible with her before her husband takes her away. She's called Harriet. And I tell you ...' She raised her tear-stained face to him and he felt his heart break just a little. '... that if he ever asked me for a divorce, I would gladly give it to him and I wouldn't care about my reputation being ruined. He's ruined me anyway. I'm not the same person I used to be, not at all. But what's that quote from *The Duchess of Malfi*? Something like "*I have youth and a little beauty*". Well I do, I *do*! And I would be perfectly all right. I just wonder whether that woman's husband will overreact when he thinks *he* has a snow-white virgin to take down the aisle and finds he hasn't.' She wiped her eye with the back of her hand and laughed humourlessly. 'To hell with the pair of them anyway.'

'Lorelei – I had no idea.' Julian strode across the room and dropped to his knees before her. He took her hands in his and clasped them tight.

'You wouldn't have any idea,' she said on a sob. 'You wouldn't be expected to. I know it still doesn't make what I feel for you right, but I can't help it, Julian, and I don't feel guilty. Does that make me a bad person?'

'Not at all,' he said quietly. He brought her hand to his lips and kissed it.

'I would have done exactly what you wanted and more, had that damned thunder not happened.' She choked out another laugh. 'I suppose that makes me no better than the harlot. Harriet the Harlot. She suits it.' This time, her laughter was hysterical and Julian pulled her closer to him, burying her face in his shoulder and stroking her dark hair until she subsided.

'I've never told anybody this before,' she said eventually. Her voice was muffled and he had to hold her gently away from him so she could speak more clearly. 'My parents don't live by the normal rules of society, so why would they expect me to? They'd probably tell me to accept it, and that it was my fault for committing myself to someone. And I don't have any proper friends anymore. So I'm rather stuck.' And there, once again, was the voice of the old Lorelei. She took a deep breath and Julian could see the effort she was making to calm down and act more appropriately, as supposedly befitted her station in life. 'I'm sorry you had to hear all of that. As you said, you are simply a summer visitor.'

Julian opened his mouth to respond. But what could he say? He had basically told her the same, that he was just a summer visitor, just a short while beforehand. As if in agreement, there was another clap of thunder and another strike of lightning.

But there was one thing he knew he had to do and it wouldn't be much fun going back out in this, but what choice did he have?

'Lorelei, I'm going to leave now,' he said, standing up.

Lorelei held onto his hand and looked up at him, horrified. 'Why? Has my history disgusted you as well? Do you think I'm just as bad as she is?'

'No. Nothing like that.' He smiled at her and raised her hand again to his lips. 'If I stay here tonight, I know exactly what I'm going to do and that will be no good in the cold light of day. Tomorrow, we would throw accusations against each other and I would feel I had taken advantage of you.

'You need to find that dress and you need to come to the cove tomorrow evening. I'm going into Staithes to meet an associate for work and I shall be busy all day. But I'll be back in the evening, and I want to see you. You can change in that awful little shack you have down there if you need to and this storm will have passed over by then. So we can take your photograph. And then I shall develop it and you will see what a true Siren of the sea you are and we will comment on how idiotic your husband is.' He grasped her hand tightly and pulled her to her feet. 'Now. Come and see me to the door safely. Then you have all night to paint. I suggest you do some more work on that seascape. It shows a definite promise. Do you swear to me?'

Lorelei nodded mutely and Julian smiled. 'Good girl. Let us

go.' He opened the door to the room and ushered Lorelei out in front of him. To give the woman credit, she held her head up high and despite a slight puffiness and redness around her eyes, there was no sign of the fact she had bared her soul to him.

God, had that storm not broken at that moment ... Julian felt the colour creep into his own cheeks as he followed Lorelei out of the door. He really, truly, would *not* have been responsible for his actions.

Chapter Sixteen

The Cove, Present Day

'Are you sure you won't stay?' asked Lissy, watching Jon pack up his camera gear later that evening. 'Have you got everything? I thought you had more?'

He stood up and shook his head. 'No, this is it. I have to try and get these developed tomorrow. I need to make sure Simon and Stef see them, so they have to be done quickly. We'll see Simon when they're heading back from Northumberland, and Stef – well, he'll be around for a little while longer anyway. I've got an appointment first thing in the studio as well, so I need to be on site early. No offence, Lissy, but you'll just delay me if I stay here tonight.'

'Oh.' She felt deflated. Such a lovely day with everybody around her and now they all had to go. Lissy was independent and confident and nothing seemed to faze her – on the outside, anyway. Inside, she wanted to be as confident as she appeared on the outside. She'd been burned by Stef's betrayal, and part of her still wanted to resist that pull he'd always had for her. But part of her wanted to run to him and thank the Lord that he'd come back into her life. She had missed him; God, how she had missed him. And she hadn't mentioned that to anyone; not even Becky. She was far too confused and, truly, didn't want to be alone with her thoughts.

Lissy knew they all had good reason to leave her tonight, though. She wasn't stupid and, although some people might think she was, not selfish either. Jon and Becky lived just a few miles away and she knew her brother spoke the truth. His studio was important and he'd already lost a day's trade by coming here in the first place. He didn't have an assistant he could call on, so he literally was the only person who ran that place, apart from when Becky put a couple of hours in to help him out between her writing sessions.

But then, Becky needed to build up her freelancing as well – she hadn't really talked about it, but Lissy knew what little hearing her sister-in-law had left was fading. So Becky was using the time now to build up her portfolio and her contacts, making sure she had a steady stream of buyers in case it affected her fieldwork in the future. She was adamant that it wouldn't – and knowing Becky, she would probably only admit defeat when she was on her deathbed. But Becky wasn't stupid either, and Lissy knew that she just wanted to plan for the worst; then anything else was a bonus.

And as for Cori and Simon – they lived in London, and they were travelling up to Cori's grandmother's in Northumberland tonight. They would have to call into Whitby on their way back to see Jon, then get back to London mid-week. They'd waved as they left her and Cori had blown kisses, and Lissy had felt Stef's arm snake around her waist as they stood, as if he understood how she felt. For a moment she'd allowed herself to lean into him, but then she stepped away. That way lay danger, possibly more heartache. She couldn't risk it.

So that left Lissy quite alone and with the prospect of thinking far too much and far too deeply tonight.

'Don't worry.' Jon seemed to read her mind as he always did. 'Stef'll come out and play. You just need to ask him.' Then he laughed and she felt as if she wanted to cry.

'What am I missing?' Becky came across the lawn towards them. She had been strapping Grace into the car seat, ready for the off. 'She's asleep, by the way. This fresh air's worn her out. It's been a lovely day, Lissy. Thank you so much.'

'You're welcome,' replied Lissy.

'And promise me you'll get things sorted with Stef, Lissy. Life's too short. Please – we've all had a lovely day and I know as soon as we go you'll boot him out back to town again and spend the night cursing him. Don't do it.' Becky reached out and took Jon's hand. 'When you find your soulmate you just have to ride with it – that's all I'm saying.'

Lissy saw the affection that passed between them as they looked at each other and felt her don't-care façade begin to slide away.

Quickly, she stood straighter and gave herself a mental shake before anyone caught her drooping. 'Yes, like that's going to be the thing between me and bloody Iago over there.' She nodded to the beach where Stef was scrambling about on the rocks barefoot, looking for a fresh angle for his photographs. Or maybe he was looking for a mermaid. Who knew?

'Iago?' Becky stared at her. 'I know I don't hear stuff properly but even your lips there – it looked like you said Iago?'

'Ah, the perfect Shakespearian villain,' commented Jon. 'I do wonder why Othello was so taken in by him at times.'

'Iagos always take people in,' Lissy pointed out darkly. 'The reason I called him that was because I've been doing my research – don't look at me like that Becky, you know I enjoy it – and I saw a simply amazing photograph by Cameron. It's an Italian man.' Here, she felt her cheeks colour but continued regardless, hoping nobody would have noticed. 'He reminds me of Stef. He's not looking at the camera and he's just *seething* with hidden depths. He's the only paid model she used, the rest of them were people she knew. And they think he's either Angelo Colarossi or Alessandro di Marco.' She frowned. 'See how he's taken people in all these years? He's always been "Iago" but nobody knows who he really is, except Cameron and the model himself; but if he's

Colarossi, he's quite short in real life as he was only about five feet tall I think.' She raised her hand and brought it level to the top of her head. 'About my height.'

'And Stef is taller and better looking?' asked Becky.

'Yes. No. I mean, yes he's taller but …'

'Why are you blushing?' Becky sent her a teasing smile.

'Oh, shut up! I'm just saying he reminds me of Iago.'

'You've done some pretty extensive research then.' Becky's stare drilled into Lissy as if she too could read her mind.

'It's interesting, all right?' snapped Lissy. She folded her arms. 'I like research.'

'You like more than that,' said Becky. 'Look, we have to go.' She broke free of Jon and embraced her sister-in-law. Then she stood back, her hands dropping down to grasp Lissy's and squeezing them. 'Just think about what I said okay? If there's going to be a wedding, I'd quite like Grace to be bridesmaid before she outgrows the cute stage.'

'There will be no bloody wedding between me and him!' The cut-glass version of Lissy's accent shattered the air around her. 'I'll tell you that now, darling!'

'"The lady doth protest too much",' said Jon. 'Sorry – wrong play. That's *Hamlet*, I know. But it's true.' He leaned over and kissed Lissy, then picked up his camera equipment. 'See you soon, little sis.'

Lissy watched them disappear across the grounds towards the car and climb in. A few moments later, they were off with a toot of the horn, two hands waving out of the windows as if the car had somehow developed antennae. She raised her hand and waved back, then folded her arms again.

She cast a glance over to the house and sighed. She didn't want the day to end just yet; she felt too fizzy somehow to go indoors. Down at the cove she saw Stef balanced on a rock, his legs bare and brown from the calves down, the point where his cut-off jeans stopped. His white shirt was open all the way down, flapping around in the breeze and exposing his rather pleasant midriff. Okay, more than pleasant – pretty spectacular actually, Lissy grudgingly acknowledged to herself with a little sigh. She'd loved to run her fingers over it and ... No, she wouldn't think about that now. He lifted his arms up, pointing the camera to the cliffs that surrounded the cove and Lissy got a quick glance of his biceps hardening as he curled his arms up.

The fizziness bubbled over and she realised it was probably nervous energy – and seeing Stef like that didn't help at all. God, he was beautiful.

So she had two choices – she could go back in and sit in the house by herself and mope and think and do all those horrible things she didn't want to do; or she could head down to the beach and try to work off some of that nervous energy.

She chose the latter.

'*Cara mia*.' Stef knew she was there, before she had even spoken. He could smell her perfume drifting across the evening and cutting through the salty tang of the ocean.

'You freak me out, you know that, don't you?' she said.

He turned to see her picking her way across the rocks. She had changed out of her shorts after Grace had tipped a bucket of water on her, and was now wearing a little shift dress. The aquamarine material skimmed her knees and had silver and white squiggles all over it.

'You are truly a mermaid now. Look at your beautiful fishy costume.'

'You called me a mermaid at Lamorna Cove.' Her expression was pensive. 'I can remember.'

'And as I recall you were not insulted then, were you?'

'No. I wasn't.' She stooped and tugged her flimsy little sandals off, throwing them back onto the beach so they bounced on the sand and landed in a heap.

'I have bare feet for a reason when I scramble. Come.' Stef smiled and held out his hand. Lissy hesitated for just a moment then took it. She allowed him to guide her over the rocks and help her onto the one where he stood. He pulled her to him, waiting for the inevitable flinch or step away. But she didn't move.

It felt good to have her standing next to him, fitting together as they always had done. She stared out to sea, the breeze lifting a tangle of dark hair away from her face and Stef dared to smooth her wayward fringe back, remembering the softness of it even after so long. Of course, it hadn't had pink and purple streaks in it then, but he ran his finger lightly down the colours and was pleased to feel a little shiver going through Lissy's body. He didn't push it though. He moved his hand and let her stand on her own as he raised the camera again.

'What are you taking a picture of?' Lissy asked.

'I see a ruined house over there.' He nodded to the green and brown tumble of rocks and a little clearing in amongst them. 'I'm trying to get a close-up picture of it. It looks very interesting. I do not think we can get close to it ourselves, which is a pity.'

'What – that ruin up there?' Lissy pointed to the clearing.

'The very same.'

'Well of course we can get close to it.' Lissy sounded surprised. 'It used to be the main house for this land, until it burned down. That's Sea Scarr Hall. My cottage is the Dower House. If you want to go there we can. I mean …'

Stef looked sidelong at her. She was red and flustered and he smiled. It was out of character for her to be so un-poised as it were. Yet oddly it made a nice change; like you could be confident she wasn't going to attack you and claw your eyes out. Or throw things at you.

'Sssssh. Yes. I accept your offer, Elisabetta.' He bowed slightly. 'I would very much like to go there. If you will escort me? Right now? Tonight? It is still warm. We can easily walk there I think, and you will not be too chilly, will you? I know your friend Cori was pleased it had cooled down. She is not handling the heat well, it seems.' He shrugged. 'It happens like that sometimes.'

'What happens like that?' Lissy's voice was like a gunshot. 'What do you mean?'

'You do not know?' He widened his eyes. 'It is blatantly obvious to all. Corisande is pregnant. Surely you knew?'

'How the bloody hell …'

'Ah, ah,' he said, shaking his head and cutting her off. 'No swearing. Think of *Grazia*.'

'*Grazia* has gone home!' Then she swore very roundly in Italian. Stef was impressed. 'How did *you* know?' she continued. 'Did they tell you? They never said anything to me.'

'Nobody told me. It's obvious. Just watch her. Look at the way she moves so carefully like it is a chore; the way she droops around, the way her hand hovers around her stomach when she does not realise. Her face – it's all pale and drawn. No. She does not bloom, poor woman. But she will.' He nodded sagely. 'My cousin has four children, my sisters have a brood each, I know the signs. I would say she is having a girl – that makes the mothers more sickly in the beginning. But fortunately, the Cameron pictures that Jon is emulating have miserable models on as well. They had to hold a miserable face, you know, due to the exposure time. So she is perfect. Her hair looks wild as well. Knotty. It is so obvious. Well – obvious to me, anyway. What? What's wrong?'

'Well that explains it then.' Lissy sat down on the rock and put her chin in her hands. She sighed, her temper blazing and subsiding as usual. 'I thought you were looking far too interested in her. That was it, wasn't it? You were looking out for her.'

'Perhaps,' said Stef with a grin. 'There *was* that, but then there was also her beautiful hair, and some very nice curves. You said yourself that she had put weight on. I would say, as an outside observer, that she has put it on in the right places. Are you upset that you did not guess? I don't think they're ready to tell anyone yet.'

Lissy nodded. 'Yep. Yes. I am upset. God that is so *me*. I'm so wrapped up in everything else going on, I'm missing the most obvious signals. I should have *known*. I bet they're off to tell her granny and then we'll find out later. Incredible.'

'Missing signals, hmm? Well now. Some you just choose to ignore. That is how I see it.'

'I know very well what signals you're hinting at.'

'Seven years is a long time,' Stef pointed out. 'People deserve a chance to admit how much of a mistake they made, all that time ago. I'd like to clear the air, talk to you properly.'

Lissy stood up and brushed the sand and seaweed away from her skirt. 'I don't know if I'm ready for that yet. One step at a time. Do you want to go to the ruin then? Or not.'

'I do.' Stef looked at her and tilted his head on one side. 'Just wait there. I will go from the rocks first. I would like to take a photograph of you.'

'Oh, God, what vision do you have of me this time?' asked Lissy, scowling.

'Well, if you are nice you can be Miranda. And if you continue to scowl, you can be the wicked Circe, poisoning the sea for the sake of jealous love. Your choice.'

They both knew there was an undercurrent there that had nothing to do with Waterhouse's seaside art. There was a brief stand-off, where they stared each other out. *Locking horns* was a good phrase to use at that moment. It felt as if they were exactly doing that.

Then Lissy eventually looked away. 'Miranda,' was all she said. It was a start.

'Thank you,' said Stef. And he took the photograph.

Despite the fact that she was only wearing her flimsy sandals – having put them back on – the path leading up to the ruin was quite easy to walk on. It had obviously once been a long, wide driveway, and even though there were weeds growing through the cracks in the paving stones and what used to be neat borders were well overgrown, it was more or less even – so that was a bonus.

Sea Scarr Hall, which faced the sea side on, was like something out of a Gothic horror movie when they got up to it, though.

'All we need is a thunderstorm,' said Lissy, looking at the place, 'and a couple of vampires floating around.' She moved closer to Stef, as she stared around her. It felt safer, somehow.

'There is a skeleton in Italy which has a brick jammed between its teeth.' Stef waited for her and took her hand before picking his way across some piles of rubble, long overgrown with ivy. She didn't pull away. She entwined her fingers in his and let him guide her through what was probably some sort of formal garden. 'It was thought to be a shroud-eater – one of your vampires – and they put a brick there to stop it feeding and feasting on the plague victims of Venice, in 1576. I know that date is so, because the very talented artist known as Titian died in the plague. Very sad.'

'That is disgusting!' Lissy stumbled on some fallen stonework. She looked incredulously at Stef, so serene in the face of such vile thoughts. 'A brick!'

'Not very pleasant but the woman was dead. What did it matter to her? So!' They were eventually standing in front of the house. 'This is the place. I am astounded.'

'It was rather grand in its heyday. They were important

landowners with a suggestion of smuggling and rumoured links to legal piracy – vehemently denied, of course.'

'Of course,' said Stef. 'Yet a very grand house.'

'*Ideally* situated for smuggling. You see the window on the second floor, just where the balcony is?'

Stef nodded. He let go of her hand and raised his camera. He snapped a picture and Lissy wondered if he'd take her hand again afterwards. He didn't.

'They say a light used to burn in that window on stormy nights.' She tried not to think about how empty her hand felt now. 'It was meant to guide the smugglers through to the cove. There was a light supposed to burn in the Dower House as well. The skilled sailors knew they could aim between the two lights and they would be safe. There's a folder in the Dower House with some information inside it and some old plans as well. It's all very interesting.'

'Fascinating. Do you think we can go inside?' Stef walked over to the staircase at the front of the house and stared up at the doorway. A few planks of blackened, charred wood rested against the stone archway; Lissy saw there was enough space for her, at least, to squeeze past them and get inside the hall. She wasn't too sure about Stef and his camera making it through the gap though. She strategically ignored a lopsided sign with hand-painted words on it that may or may not have said *Keep Out*.

'I'll go first,' she said. 'If there's anything interesting, I'll tell you.'

'When you go inside, *bella*, there will be something very interesting in there.'

'Yes, well something that isn't me that's interesting.' Lissy ducked her head and fought against a smile. He had always been a charmer. Nothing had changed there. But now was not the time. That ship had sailed with a naked blonde at the prow, and perhaps if she kept telling herself that, she might believe it.

Regardless, she walked up the stone steps, marvelling at how they dipped in the centre through three hundred or so years of use, and squeezed through the gap in the doorway.

Once inside the hall, she stood on what had clearly been a grand, chequer-board patterned hallway and looked around her. The tiles on the floor were dirty and cracked, but she could envisage what they had looked like when they were cared for. Standing here, in this cold, blank house, she shivered. She understood now what Becky had meant, when she said she had a sense of the past all around her the first time she had visited Carrick Park – a hotel out on the moors she had discovered just before she met Jon.

Lissy imagined that, if she closed her eyes, the sounds of parties and laughter and glasses clinking would come from that room to the back of the hallway, which she knew had once been the grand dining room. Beyond that was a terrace leading down to what had been a walled garden.

She walked over to the dining room and looked down the corridor. Just along there was a cantilevered staircase that looked horribly dangerous; some of the banisters were missing and she wondered whether the things would hold *her* weight, never mind Stef's. But she had a terrible urge to go upstairs and poke around up there – try to see the room where the candle had burned in the window for the smugglers and look out of the window to see what the view was like and whether you could see the small vessels coming in and heading towards the cove.

She peered along the corridor a little more and saw rows and rows of rooms, some with their doors shut, some with no doors at all. She wished she had brought a torch – it might not have illuminated much, but it would have enabled her to see into some of the dark corners.

There was a creak and a bang behind her and she swung around, just in time to see Stef emerge from a cloud of dust and tread across the doorway plank he had obviously managed to break down. She was awfully glad to see him.

'It is the maid's day off,' he announced. 'Quite so.'

'Maid's century off! This place has been abandoned since 1905.'

'Is that when the fire was?'

'Yes,' said Lissy. 'I don't think many people would have come here after that. Well, not legally, anyway.'

'It is definitely off the beaten track.'

Lissy nodded. 'The only people really to have access would be people from the Dower House. And as that's only been restored and used as a holiday let for the last few months, it's still quite a hidden gem. I don't suppose that there's much to do here once you've seen it.'

'Unless they creep in like you and I have.' Stef grinned. 'Are we criminals?'

'Possibly. But you know what?' Lissy found herself turning to Stef and smiling. 'I quite like the idea of trespassing in here. Don't you?'

'I do. What's upstairs?' Stef came over to her. 'Shall we?' He offered his arm, in a very gentlemanly fashion.

Lissy surprised herself by taking it without hesitation. It felt right, and not just because she'd loved being so close to him outside. She frowned as a bizarre image of the two of them walking up the stairs took a strange turn in her imagination and she had a fleeting image of them hurrying up the stairs and entering a bed chamber at twilight.

She caught her breath and looked at Stef. As their bodies connected and their eyes met, he made the same sort of noise and they stared at each other, surprise registering on his face. Her own face, she knew, would be mirroring his.

'If only,' said Stef quietly.

Lissy kept staring at him, wondering quite how much of the image they had shared.

She had a feeling it would have been quite a lot.

'It's creepy,' was her response. Stef merely nodded.

The stairs now seemed to take on a different aspect – instead of the blackened stonework, Lissy blinked and saw them as sturdy and pale and smooth, a red carpet running up the middle of them. She knew for a fact they would take her weight. They would take both their weights.

'Come with me,' she said to Stef. Her voice seemed to be coming from somewhere else, but he didn't seem to think it sounded unusual.

'As you wish,' he replied.

And they walked forward, linked together, towards the staircase.

Chapter Seventeen

Sea Scarr Hall, 1905

Lorelei watched Julian walk away down the path, his figure occasionally lit up by lightning, and she felt as if her chest had been cut open and her heart laid out bare for all to see. She had told him things she had not mentioned to another living soul tonight and felt a tear slip down her cheek.

She would never see him again, would she? She had terrified him into leaving and he was as disgusted by her past as Walter was. Julian would be gone by the time she trailed down to the cove tomorrow night and she'd just be another pathetic lonely person who had nobody; only she would be the wretched one trying to cling onto the past by clutching a dated satin dress. Well. On the bright side, the thing was probably heavy enough to drown her á la Ophelia, if nothing else. It was a possibility, anyway.

The idea of what Julian might think of her made her ashamed of who she was and what she had done in her Other Life. Why was it one rule for men and another for women? Oh, if she could only have met Julian MacDonald Cooper at that exhibition. How different her life might have been. He would have been a kind husband, and he might – just might – have forgiven her for her past transgressions. But what was the point of dreams and wishes? No point at all.

She went back upstairs when she finally realised that Julian had been completely swallowed up by the evening, and, despite herself, she sent a little prayer up that he had reached the Dower House safely. It was still bad out there, but the storm seemed to be passing over and moving inland.

She sat in her sitting room for a few minutes trying to

collect her thoughts. If she closed her eyes, she could still see him leaning against the windowsill as if he belonged there. She could still feel his lips on her hand, albeit that the sensation had lasted only briefly, and she could sense the contact between their bodies as their fingers touched ...

Oh, dear Lord.

She opened her eyes and glared at the easel and the window. Then she stood up and stalked towards them, meaning to finally pull the heavy curtains closed and shut out the night and all thoughts of Julian Macdonald Cooper.

Just as Lorelei grabbed hold of the edges of the fabric, a flicker in the distance caught her attention. She narrowed her eyes and peered out into the darkness.

The rain was streaming in rivulets down the glass and she couldn't see properly, so she let go of the curtains and opened the window wide. She caught her breath as a gust of salty wind blew in and made the flames in the fireplace flicker wildly. Then she leaned out as far as she dared and stared into the distance.

There was definitely a light there. Every so often, the wind blew and branches of trees obscured it ever so slightly; but it was still there when they settled again.

Lorelei realised it was coming from the cove.

Indeed, it was coming from the Dower House.

'Julian?' she whispered, hardly daring to believe it. Then the trees parted again and she saw it, seemingly glowing even stronger than before. '*Julian*!' she cried, as loudly as she could. Her voice was whipped away on the wind, but she didn't care. She laughed out loud in delight and withdrew her head. Then she hurried to the fireplace and unhooked one of the glowing lamps from the sconces there.

She ran back to the windowsill and hooked the thing on the fixture next to the window. The lamp swung in the breeze, and she shut the window firmly.

The light stopped swaying and settled down in the corner as if it had always been there.

And who knew, she thought delightedly, leaning on her elbows and staring out across the cove, watching the light in the Dower House flicker as if in acknowledgment; it might always have been meant to be there.

Sea Scarr Hall, Present Day

Lissy felt as if she was floating up the staircase. If she closed her eyes, she could almost swear she could hear the swish of fabric around her ankles and feel the starchiness of frills around her elbows. She knew there would be a satin ribbon tied around her waist and there was the fizzing warmth of the man beside her. Her hand rested on his arm, and there was, she knew, a hint of danger with it.

They had to hurry. Her husband might be back soon and …

'We're here.' Stef's voice woke her from her trance. She realised they were at the top of the stairs and new, exciting corridors led off in both directions. She stared at Stef, disorientated. He was looking down at her, something unreadable in his eyes.

'Stef, did you feel anything strange when you walked up those stairs?' she asked him cautiously; yet part of her wondered if it was just the fact that she was so close to a man who, clearly, still had the power to attract her and haunt her every waking moment. Seven years had not been long enough to make her forget – not at all.

And looking back at those stairs, she saw with horror that they must have been utterly mad to even consider walking up them – they looked even worse from this angle.

'I was there yet I wasn't,' he replied. 'It felt very dangerous, but I was glad you were by my side.' Lissy saw a reddening under his olive skin. 'But hey! We are talking crazy talk, are we not?' He laughed, embarrassed.

'Crazy talk,' she repeated. 'I would agree there.' She hesitated on the landing and cleared her throat, trying to buy herself some time. 'I think, if we get the orientation correct, the room with the lamp in the window should be this way.' She pointed to the right.

Lissy was aware that she was still arm in arm with him and she considered carefully extricating herself, but decided against it. However odd this place was, however it made her feel, Stef at least was solid and real.

A gust of wind rattled down the corridor, scattering leaves and debris in its wake and Lissy jumped. Stef felt her flinch and squeezed her arm again. She seemed very edgy. She was looking along each corridor in turn, hesitating, as if she didn't really want to go down any of them. Yet she had been so eager to find that room with the light.

'Maybe a storm is blowing up,' he said, by way of calming her down. 'I would not like to have been out on the sea in this sort of weather.'

'But it's been simply gorgeous today!' Lissy turned and looked at him, her mismatched eyes wide.

'That is no guarantee that the weather will hold.' He shook his head. 'Pah! Listen to me!'

'What?'

'I talk about the weather! The *weather*!' He swore spectacularly in Italian. 'I have a beautiful, terrified woman on my arm. She and I are in an empty building, unlikely to be disturbed any time soon – by the living at least – and I talk about the weather.' He shook his head and laughed. 'This is where I should become some sort of hero and rescue you, sweep you up into my arms and run through the fires of hell with you, just to save your life.'

'I'm not terrified! And I don't need rescuing! And what do you mean by not being disturbed by the living?' Lissy looked along the corridors again, still standing on the wide landing at the top of the stairs.

'I don't know. Do you not get the feeling there is something else here, *spiriti*, perhaps?'

'Ghosts?' Lissy almost shouted the word, then laughed, mirthlessly. 'No. I don't do ghosts. I know people who *do*, but I'm not one of them.'

'I disagree. I think the more you dabble in the otherworld, or know people who have seen into it, the more open you become.'

'Stef, shut up. You're just doing this to scare me. Stop it.' His words had the desired effect. Lissy shook herself free from his arm and headed off along the corridor.

'Excellent,' Stef murmured. 'Action as opposed to inaction. I win this one.' He followed her along the corridor, his hands in his pockets, eyes scanning the skeletal rooms as they passed them, wondering what was behind the closed doors.

Stef had a friend whose passion was to break into old, abandoned buildings and take photographs. It was something he was very strongly attracted to himself. But at this present moment in time, he was much more attracted to the small, dark figure a few steps ahead of him.

An image flashed into his mind of her leading him along this corridor once before. The walls lost their grim appearance and the colour came back. That same red carpet he had imagined on the steps continued along where he walked. There were oil paintings on the walls, cabinets of stuffed birds and animals – hideous. The figure in front of him was dressed in white lace which frothed around her elbows, a further two layers of lace swishing around the bottom of her skirt. A square neck that made her look far more modest than she normally was.

Let us hope he stays away tonight …

'I think this might be it,' said the figure, jolting Stef back to reality. He blinked and stopped just behind her. The room they were standing in front of was the furthest one down the corridor. He couldn't help it, but he moved closer to Lissy, so they were almost touching. He needed some sort of contact with her, as if someone was going to try to pull him away – which was, as Lissy would say, utterly ridiculous.

Lissy didn't complain. Instead, she put her hand on the door handle and turned it slightly to the right. The door popped open and she stepped inside.

'Yes,' she said after a moment. 'This is it. Look.' She walked over to the window, reaching out and drawing her hand along the marble mantelpiece as she passed the fireplace. This room looked as if it had escaped the worst of the fire. There was still faded wallpaper on the walls – some sort of regular floral pattern – and brass sconces where lamps must have once been fitted. There was one of these sconces still attached to the corner of the windowpane, and this was what Lissy had wandered over to. She touched the delicate filigree pattern carved into the brass and Stef saw her lean into it and rub her fingertip over a section of the brass.

'This looks …' She didn't finish the statement, but instead shook her head. 'No. Utterly ridiculous and frankly impossible.'

'What is it?' Stef asked, reluctantly leaving a section of beautifully moulded plaster border he had discovered. He peered at the sconce and saw, in the filigree, leaves and flowers and what looked like tiny waves cresting over the decorations. 'A floral effect. Beautiful craftsmanship, and a common theme in Edwardian décor.'

'Oh. Thank goodness.' Lissy laughed, and Stef was surprised to see that she seemed embarrassed. 'I'm glad it's common.' She wrinkled her nose. 'It would just be a bit peculiar, otherwise. I've seen it before, that's all.'

'It reminds me a little of that Cornish ring you ran away from,' said Stef. 'Just a little.'

'That ring?' Lissy jerked away from the sconce as if it still held a lamp and the flame had burnt her. She stared up at Stef, her eyes narrowing. 'You still remember the ring?'

'Every detail,' nodded Stef. 'I still don't know why you did not buy it.'

'It was too expensive.' She wrapped her arms around herself as if she had suddenly become chilled. 'And it just seemed like it was wrong somehow. I don't know – no, the *ring* wasn't wrong. I loved the ring. It was – oh God, I'm going to sound like I'm mad – but it was as though it didn't belong to me. As if it was possessed. Crazy. Becky and Cori swear they've seen things, but I've never seen a ghost. As far as I'm aware, anyway.'

'Ghosts?' said Stef. 'How interesting. You see – as I tried to explain, if your two closest friends experience things, then it is possible that you may also experience things.'

'I don't know about that, but yes, those two say they're real.'

Stef laughed. 'So they love their ghost-friends. So what? I'm more interested in the ring you talk about.'

'Oh. Yes.' Lissy dropped her gaze. 'It was just the wrong timing for the ring. I loved it. I wanted it. I could have had it. But it was the wrong *time* and it wasn't for me. And yet now I kick myself because I didn't get it.' She turned and looked at the sconce again. 'I guess that pattern just brought it all back for a moment.'

'Still. It was a good summer. Even if you didn't buy the ring.' Stef sighed. 'Most of it was good anyway, although at the end I was very stupid and I curse my Italian temper. And now I have to come grovelling back. For me, it all went downhill after you walked away, and yes, I take full responsibility for that. I haven't had a decent summer since. Although this year hasn't been too bad, so far.'

Lissy didn't answer him. Her gaze travelled from the sconce to the wall behind him. She looked as if she was going to say something, and Stef's heart began to beat faster. Now, here, would they finally be able to discuss it? Could they come full circle?

And then her eyes widened again. 'Oh, look. An old cupboard!' The moment was lost. She darted around him and headed over to the cupboard which was built into the wall. 'I just love old cupboards and hidey-holes. You never know what you might find inside them.'

Frustrated, Stef watched her, knowing she was shying away from it again. 'I suspect you will not find very much in here,' he said. Damn the fact they still hadn't opened a dialogue about Kerensa and what a disaster it had all been, and how, if Lissy had given him a chance, he wouldn't have been so irresponsible and picked up with Kerensa, just to hurt the keeper of his heart. Well – it had backfired and backfired big time. He'd only succeeded in wrecking his own life and Kerensa's for six years. It hadn't achieved anything after all. It was his own fault for being too impetuous and stupid. But that's not what Lissy wanted to discuss right now. She wanted to talk about cupboards. *Cupboards!* Of all things. 'The place has been empty for so long,' he commented, 'it will have given up all of its secrets by now.'

'Don't be too sure. There are *always* secrets to discover, no matter how long things have been abandoned or how many hands they have passed through. That's what I love about antiques and old books, that sort of thing. Always something new. And I know people mock me about it, I know Simon calls me the Junk Shop Junkie and Becky just generally thinks I'm a pain in the arse if I present her with anything new, but I just have a feel for these things.'

'I'm sure that old things can be very interesting,' Stef said, 'but would you like me to help you at all? You seem to be struggling.'

The whole time Lissy had been speaking, she'd been poking around the edges of the cupboard, which looked like it hadn't been opened in decades. The old wood had swollen and jammed so tightly into the rectangular spaces that she was going to have a fair old time trying to open them. But, knowing her, she wouldn't give up. Neither, it seemed, would she accept any assistance.

'No thank you, I'm fine.'

Stef saw one of her vicious-looking, perfectly manicured nails dig into the gap and he turned away. The nails would either act as daggers and slice through the wood or she'd break the damn thing. Either way, it was easier to let her get on with it. He meandered to the window and studied the brass sconce again.

She'd call him if she needed him, and the more he looked at her, the more he was remembering, again, how those nails had felt when they'd dug into his back. And how her lips had tasted and how her body had responded to his over and over again. He was very much in danger of losing himself to her once more; and this time, if it didn't work out, and if he messed it up again, he knew he would never get a third chance. He would not, he acknowledged, even *deserve* a third chance. And so, for now, he must think of other things.

It was very interesting how similar the pattern on the sconce was to that ring. He smiled to himself, remembering the little man who looked like a clotted cream scone. One day, if she ever forgave him, he would like to take Elisabetta back and they would see more of Lamorna Cove and Newlyn. He would see if Jon and Becky wanted to come as well. He didn't think Jon had been to Cornwall since the Fran incident. Stef thought Jon might like to wipe out the bad memories of that time; heaven knew he, Stef, needed to eradicate the memories of the end of *his* time there. And little *Grazia* would love Tintagel Castle. She ...

'Got it! The damn and bloody blasted damn bloody thing!'

There was a massive crack and a hideous squeak, and that combined with Lissy's voice made Stef turn around. The door of the cupboard was hanging open and there was a horrible smell of mildew and mould and charred wood coming out of the opening.

Stef wrinkled his nose. 'Are you satisfied, *bella*? Now you have damaged private property along with trespassing?'

'Yes, I'm satisfied for now.' She smiled and inspected the nail she had used. 'Bloody good, these gel manicures. Look – not a chip on it. Worth every penny. Now. Let's see what we have in here.'

And it was almost as if someone up above had ordained it. Lissy reached into the cupboard and the sky turned black in an instant. The room was plunged into darkness and the loudest crack of thunder Stef had ever heard seemed to shake the old building to its foundations. He spun around and stared at the window as an extraordinarily bright flash of lightning lit up the opening. Lissy screamed.

'It's all right,' he said. She rushed up to his side and grabbed his arm. He could hear the sob catching in her throat. 'It is only that pesky storm coming in. I did not think you were this scared of thunder.' He reached out to take her hand, wanting to reassure her; but his fingers closed on nothing.

Then: 'What are you flailing around over there for?' Lissy asked, surprise clear in her voice. 'I'm over here.'

And Lissy was behind him – standing in the exact same spot she had been before the thunderclap.

Chapter Eighteen

The next day, in the mid-afternoon, Lorelei stood before her seascape, admiring it.

The thing was finally finished. She had rushed it a little, just to get it done and she had already decided that she would be framing it herself. Even now, she had the perfect frame lying on the day bed. She hadn't slept in the day bed last night. She had used the marital bed, safe in the knowledge that her husband would not be returning, and the marital bed was far more comfortable anyway; at least it was when Walter wasn't in it.

Lorelei often wondered if she should simply get a proper bed brought into her sitting room. She would be very happy to do so, but sadly that was a decision her husband had to make. He hated her sleeping in there – but after an argument, being next to him was horrendous. She barely closed her eyes, for fear of what he might do to her. She could be stabbed or suffocated, and who would come in to save her, if indeed anyone even heard the commotion?

She pushed the unpleasant thoughts of Walter out of her head and, instead, smiled at the painting. She took the colourful rectangle from the easel, and laid it on the day bed next to the frame. The gilt frame contained an old picture of an ancient pig that was ridiculously large and fat. It was a stupid looking picture and a stupid looking pig and she had taken the painting from one of the overly decorated guest suites, quite sure that nobody would really miss an ancient porcine depiction.

She cracked open the frame carefully, and the pig was

removed and placed securely between the leaves of a book, which Lorelei had liberated from the library earlier. Then, she reasoned, if anyone did query its disappearance, she would replace the damn thing. But really – was anyone that observant? And by anyone, she meant Walter, of course. His name was gall to her very thoughts, but that could not be helped.

There would be no room for the damn pig in that frame by the time she had finished, anyway.

Once the pig was hidden away, Lorelei picked up the seascape and laid it into the frame. It was a very good fit. Then she took it out again and went over to the easel.

Hidden behind a blank sheet of paper was the painting she *really* wanted to frame. This hadn't taken her long at all, and was, even if she said so herself, a very good likeness. She moved the blank sheet and picked up the portrait she had done last night as the lamp had burned in the window and she had known that Walter wouldn't reappear.

Considering she had done it from memory, it really was a nice picture of Julian. She had captured that freedom he had about him: his too-long hair and his open shirt as he had leaned on the window sill studying her, his attitude that of a young Lord Byron – before the scandal about that worthy poet had broken, of course.

Julian's dark brown eyes burned in the painting, staring directly out at her and she shivered a little, congratulating herself on how the eyes were quite possibly the best part of the portrait. She didn't think that she would ever have the courage to show him the likeness.

But if Fate intervened and he went away at the end of the summer, and they never saw each other again – God, how could she even *bear* that – then she would at least have his picture. She would put it on the wall for now and that meant she could look at him any time she pleased. All she had to do was take the frame to pieces, remove the seascape – and there he was.

Lorelei glanced at the clock. Time was creeping up on her and she still needed to find that damn dress. Last time she had seen it, it was in a large hatbox in the built-in cupboard, thrust there in a fit of pique because she had ripped it off and hidden it as best she could in the time she had available before anybody came to find her and coax her to rejoin the party. She had meant to burn it, but then thought it was such a waste, and it wasn't really the costume's fault that her husband had been with his mistress – so she had left it there, crumpled and abandoned.

She cast another look at the small, framed seascape, and decided to hide that as well as her paints – just for now.

Lorelei locked the little watercolour box, turned and walked over to the wall with the cupboard and laid the items on her day bed. Then she dragged a stool over and climbed up so she could open the door and hence reach the high little shelf inside it, just behind the door. It was a fearsomely annoying little shelf, but it was another secret and not the easiest of things to find, which was something to be grateful for – just until she got the picture hung.

She leaned on the door frame and peered into the recess. It wasn't a huge space, but it was big enough to hide things in. And sure enough, there was the hat box. The lid wasn't on it properly and some white silk spilled out. She tutted and wrestled the box out, throwing it onto the day bed.

Then she clambered down, picked up the paint box and the seascape, and climbed back up to push them into the cupboard. She felt around blindly for the little shelf and guided the things onto it. There was a tiny rattle – probably the key from the watercolour box falling out again – and she shook her head in exasperation.

Unfortunately, she managed to bump her head on the shelf

with that action, and she swore as the paint box slid off the shelf and landed with a thud in the bottom of the cupboard. Losing patience, she shoved the thing onto a shelf lower down at the back, just to get rid of it.

And that was it. She climbed down, pulled the stool back to the corner of the room and moved across to the day bed to unpack the dress. The fabric would be rather wrinkled, but she didn't care that much. The best part of the whole escapade was that she would see Julian again.

The Cove, 1905

As the late afternoon crept in, Julian wondered whether she would actually come down to the Dower House or whether she would have decided against it. He felt, deep down, that perhaps he hadn't made himself clear last night. He was immensely attracted to the woman, but it wasn't the right situation to take it further. Not in her own home when her husband – terrible as he seemed to be – was away. She would obviously have been feeling fragile and unloved and who was he, a summer visitor, to take advantage of that?

Julian leaned on the railing of the terrace at the Dower House and watched the path which led down from the Hall. His camera equipment was all ready and he had checked the tide earlier. It was going out, which would make it easier for them to get to the rock.

It was as he was staring at the rock, imagining what she would be like actually naked on the thing, that he suddenly felt his skin prickle and senses become alert. Sure enough, he turned and saw her walking carefully down the path, a bundle of cloth in her arms.

Julian didn't wait for her to reach the house; he vaulted over the railing onto the scrubby dunes and ran across to meet her. The sand was hot against his bare feet and he was vaguely aware of a stabbing sensation as those sharp blades of grass scratched against his ankles – but all he could really focus on was her and getting to her quickly.

Lorelei stopped when she saw him coming, and he ran faster, waving at her like an idiot – *whit a dunderhead, ye look, laddie*, said his grandfather's voice in his head – but it didn't make him slow down.

'Lorelei!' He reached her, barely out of breath, and felt his face split into a huge smile. 'You came.'

'Of course I did. Why wouldn't I? I saw the light last night. I hope you saw mine.' She looked up at him, her cheeks rosy and her emerald eyes sparkling and he grinned at her.

'I did see it. Indeed yes. Indeed, I did see it.' He nodded wildly. Then realising how stupid he sounded he laughed and shook his head then held his hands out. 'You have no idea how much I want to hold you right now, but I will have to be a gentleman and take the clothing from you, I think. It looks heavy.'

'It's not really,' said Lorelei, but she handed the white satin dress to him regardless. 'I wanted to wear it to walk down here but then I thought someone might see me and ask questions. Or have me committed for dressing up during the day.'

It was on the tip of Julian's tongue to offer to help her undress and prepare for the picture in that case, but he pressed his lips firmly together and simply smiled. 'Probably a wise decision.'

'Probably,' she agreed. 'I'm ridiculously excited about this little game, anyway. It's been so long since I had any fun posing at all, that I'm quite afraid I shall be rather rusty. I hope you will guide me.'

'Every step of the way,' replied Julian. 'Come now, let us make a start. The tide is out and the rock is easy to get to.'

'Where will I get changed?' she asked as she fell into step beside him and they began to walk down to the Dower House. 'I have the bathing hut, I suppose.'

'You have. Or you have the house,' said Julian. The satin was warm and slippery, almost a living thing as it spilled over his arms and bumped against his knees through the linen of his trousers.

'I do like the idea of the house, but I think I shall use the hut. At least to put the dress on.' She looked up at him from under her eyelids. 'That's the time-critical part of the exercise, isn't it? It doesn't matter how long it takes to remove the thing afterwards or how long it takes for me to put my own clothes back on. So maybe *that*, I could do in the house? Perhaps?'

Julian swore that his heart missed a beat at that point. He wondered if he was interpreting the words too literally – or whether there was some sort of subtext there. He cast a glance down towards her and there was something in her eyes that told him the answer.

There was a subtext there; definitely.

Sea Scarr Hall, Present Day

Stef did look like an idiot standing there with his hand sticking out and nobody attached to it.

'I need you here,' repeated Lissy. 'You're no good over there.'

'But Elisabetta – you came over here. Just after you screamed and I ...'

'I didn't scream. It would take rather more than a bit of thunder to make me do that. No, I want you here because I wonder if you would be kind enough to lean into the cupboard and see what's in the back. You're taller than I am.'

'You are saying then that you are too short,' said Stef, a little distantly. He looked around him as he spoke as if he'd lost something. 'Very strange. Very strange indeed. Hmm.'

'Stef. Please.' Lissy was much too short to reach in and she thought that there was something on a shelf way back, something that had perhaps been overlooked when the house had been emptied – but she needed Stef to have a look and confirm it for her.

'Very well.' Stef stared around a moment longer and raked his fingers through his hair. Lissy watched the movement, remembering all too well how that hair had felt, wanting to reach out and touch it herself, just one more time. 'Okay. I will help you.' He covered the room in a couple of those long strides and stood beside Lissy. 'Where is it? Or what is it?'

Lissy took a wobbly breath, trying not to think about the way his hair fell back into place and looked just as wild and unruly as it always had done. 'At the back. There's something in the corner like a box. It's a bit flat, so I'm not too sure ...'

'I have it.' Stef leaned in, moving even closer to Lissy and she could smell that spicy aftershave he always wore, the aftershave that had clung to his shirt when she had worn it to travel back to the Dower House. He apparently hadn't changed the brand in the seven years they had been apart. She breathed in quite deeply – she had always liked that scent. 'It is almost stuck to the shelf. It is ... ah! I have it.'

There was a cracking sound, the sound you get when something has been stuck in the same place for too long, and Stef drew his hand out.

He was holding a dust-covered rectangular box, which looked as if it was made of wood. Without waiting to be asked, he handed it straight over to Lissy, his dark eyes connecting with hers, amused.

'Thank you.' Lissy felt that flutter of excitement in

her stomach she always got when she discovered a new, interesting artefact. Well – that's what she told herself the flutter was for. It had nothing to do with his scent and his proximity and those eyes looking into hers.

'What do you think it is?' asked Stef, his voice low and curious.

'I would say it's a box,' she replied, trying to make a joke to distract herself from the idea of falling into his arms, right there and then. She wiped a thick layer of dust off the box and read the faded, gold writing on the top. *G Rowney & Co.* 'I think it's a paint box. This is a brand of watercolour that was really popular in the Victorian and Edwardian era. I'm sure you can still get Daler and Rowney paints but — oh!' She suddenly made a connection. 'You know the Staithes Group of artists? They were *plein air* Impressionists and a lot of them trained in Paris and Antwerp during the Impressionist movement.' Lissy rubbed at the gold lettering again. 'If we think about the time of the fire here, in 1905, the Staithes Group were just starting to break up, but they were still working in and around here. So – it makes sense that we have a box of paints. They obviously inspired someone.' Lissy smiled at the box. 'Oh, what stories you could tell!'

Then: 'Oh, buggeration! There's a bloody keyhole, no key in it and the damn thing is locked.' Lissy shook the box angrily as if that would open it up. An enticing rattle came from inside. 'Probably the cakes of paint. Oh, Stef, I have to get into this thing – I have to!' She held it out to him. 'Can you do anything? I don't think my nails will pick a lock! Can you see anything else in the cupboard?'

Stef sighed. 'Not from here. I may have to get up higher to check right at the back. What can I stand on?' He looked around the room as if something would materialise which he could use. 'Nothing.' He folded his arms. Then he eyed her speculatively 'Ah. Elisabetta.'

'What? What are you looking at me like that for?'

'You're small.' He unfolded his arm and brought his forefinger and thumb together in a small circle. 'So small that I can maybe lift you up? Then you can stretch inside and you can have a look. Deal?'

Lissy looked back at Stef, equally speculatively. She was conscious of the fact she was wearing a dress that only skimmed her knees and he would have to lift her up by at least placing those strong hands around her waist.

'All right.' Her heart was pounding. She placed the paint box on the floor and Stef moved to the side, bowing low and sweeping his arm around as if inviting her into the space. She stood in front of him and waited, took a deep breath and closed her eyes. It wouldn't take much for her to give herself up to him once again. Perhaps his soft breath on the back of her neck, or his warm touch on her waist.

She felt his hands rest lightly on her shoulders and her heart began beating in double-quick time.

And suddenly it was seven years ago, and it was Lamorna Cove and Newlyn and Cornwall in the summer. It was the antiques dealer with the clotted cream scone demeanour and the ring she wished she had bought. It was her and Stef together again.

His hands slipped down her arms, as soft and gentle as she remembered them. They paused at her wrists and drifted over her hands. Then they moved to her hips and his arms came around her waist. She could hear the catch in his breath as their bodies connected and she inhaled deeply, trying to find that spicy scent again; but it wasn't quite there. Instead, there was the scent of rain and salt and the sea air.

A chill wafted across her body and her eyelids flew open. 'Stef?'

'Are you ready yet?' he asked. 'Just give me the word and I'll lift you up.'

Lissy spun around. Stef was standing a little way from her, his hands in his pockets.

He grinned at her apologetically. 'Ready when you are. Just tell me when you want me to lift you up. I do not want to rush at you and scare you. You need to be sure you get your balance.'

Lissy, quite uncharacteristically, was speechless.

Chapter Nineteen

Sea Scarr Hall, Present Day

There were a couple of beats where nothing happened. 'Are you okay, Lissy?' asked Stef.

She just stared at him. 'I thought ...' she started. Then she shook her head. 'No. My mistake. Yes. I'm ready.' She turned back to the cupboard, and he noticed her cheeks were slightly flushed.

He hoisted her up in one easy motion and heard her catch her breath, but at least she didn't flinch or stiffen under his hold. And she smelled very, very good as well; that combination of sun-tan lotion and the ocean he had loved so much in Cornwall. 'Do you see anything?' he asked.

'It's too dark and it smells horrible.' Her voice sounded echoey and dulled. The weight of her lessened as she rested her hands on the frame of the cupboard and pushed herself up a little further. She must have brushed against the inside as a shower of plaster came tumbling down.

'Oh, my God, it's disgusting!' Lissy coughed and shook her hair to get rid of the plaster dust. She shifted position, moving her hands further along the frame. 'Ouch!'

'Let me bring you down!'

'No!' The answer was quick. 'No. I've got something.' Lissy leaned in a little further and her weight shifted, so he held her tighter. 'I'm leaning on it. Hang on ...' She shuffled to the right a bit and lifted up her hand. 'Ha! I have you. I do think I've got the key!'

'Okay, I will bring you down.' Stef lowered her to the ground and thought she had never looked so lovely – all plaster-dust covered and flushed with happiness.

'Yes. I have the key.' Her mismatched eyes were sparkling. 'Here it is. That dust shower must have brought it down.'

Stef leaned backwards into the cupboard and raised his hand, stretching up as far as he could.

He felt around, checking the space with his fingertips. 'There's a shelf of some kind, just behind the top of the frame. The key must have been on that – when you bumped it, you probably dislodged it.' His sensitive fingers felt around a little more and fastened on a small, rectangular shape, half hanging off the ledge. 'Oh, and we have something else as well.'

'What is it?'

'I don't know – let me get it,' he replied.

A quick flick of his fingers and the object fell into his waiting palm. He eased his way out of the cupboard and presented Lissy with a small, dirty rectangle. She took it from him, wiping it down her dress, obviously too caught up in the excitement of the moment to care about her clothing, and he saw a gilt frame show through the grime.

'Oh!' She exhaled on a long breath. 'Thank you. I think it's ...yes. Look.' She rubbed her fingertip on the front and drew a line through years of filth to reveal a glass fronted watercolour. She kept rubbing until she'd uncovered the whole picture. It was a small seascape, the colours as fresh as the day they had been painted. Lissy looked at it and then up at the window which faced out to the cove. 'It's the view from here. How lovely!'

'Painted with those watercolours, I suspect.' Stef nodded to the box on the floor.

'Yes! And now we can open it!' Lissy thrust the seascape at Stef and dropped down onto her knees. She began to fit the key into the lock. 'It's rusty or something. It's ... ah! Got it!'

Stef hunkered down next to her, holding the painting. 'Is there anything exciting in there?'

Lissy cracked the lid and the box opened with a painful

creak. 'Oh.' Her face fell. 'Just loose cakes of paint, like we thought. Two brushes. One pencil. Well used. Look, the paints are all worn away, see the blue and the yellow? She must have liked painting the sea and the cove. The brushes are well-cared for, and the pencil is blunt.' She looked at the corner of the tray which contained the paints and pencils and picked at it with one of those long nails.

'You said "she",' said Stef. 'You said "she" must have liked painting. What makes you think it was a woman?'

'I don't know.' Lissy looked up at him. 'I just think hiding things away – it's secretive, isn't it? Women are more secretive than men. Or at least I think so.' She looked back at the box, then studied the corner. 'It looks as if this is a tray. Let's see if there's another layer.' She lifted the corner and took it out of the box, laying it on the floor. 'There are a couple of sketches. Nothing exciting. A boat. The cove again. Look – this is the Dower House, isn't it? So that's my little beach.' She smiled, yet seemed disappointed.

'Why so sad?' asked Stef gently. He laid his hand on hers. 'Is this not a nice discovery?'

'Well, yes. It's *nice*. But that's all. It's not very *interesting*, is it? Just pictures of scenery. And a teeny tiny figure in the boat. But they used to just put random people in pictures for the sake of it, rustic peasants and fishermen and the like.' She shrugged and sighed. 'Nothing exciting. Nothing personal.'

'I don't understand.' Stef sat down and crossed his legs, facing Lissy. 'Nobody has seen inside this box for one hundred years. You're the first person to handle ... *her* ... items. I find that exciting, no?'

'I think I just feel cheated,' said Lissy flatly. 'With Becky, I found an amazing writing slope and it had a photograph in it. We found out who she was, you know; she was called Ella. And with Cori, I found her a diary. And Daisy, who wrote the diary, had a fantastic relationship with the Pre-Raphaelite

Brotherhood! She wrote all about it. Yet me – my story, if you like,' she said, looking up at him, her mouth turned upside down, 'boils down to a seascape, a few sketches and a blunt pencil.'

'Hmmm. One cannot measure excitement by what other people discover, you know.'

'I know.' Lissy looked at the little box and replaced the tray with a little sigh. 'But it would have been nice.'

'Okay.' Stef wrapped his arms around his knees. 'What was the lady called who lived here in 1905?'

'Lorelei. Lorelei Scarsdale. Isn't that a wonderful name? The house was in her husband's family for generations apparently.'

'Lorelei. Like a mermaid, yes? I like that. Okay. So we have a lady who lived here with a mermaid's name. Why don't we, then, attribute this beautiful little paintbox to *Signora* Lorelei Scarsdale?'

'Yes. Why don't we?' Lissy sighed again and her eyes drifted to the window. 'We've got nothing else to go on.'

Stef couldn't resist. He rocked forward and dropped a kiss on her hair. Despite the remnants of plaster dust that clung to it, it was still soft and smelled of that shampoo he had always liked – he closed his eyes briefly as he remembered and felt that old pang of regret. How utterly stupid he had been. A complete idiot. One positive thing, at least, was that Lissy didn't shout at him or tell him to back off; or slash at him with those vicious nails. Progress indeed.

'Nope. We have nothing to work with,' he said sadly, drawing away, 'except the name of the lady.' He picked up the watercolour. 'Yet this is very beautiful.' He studied it and then looked more closely. 'Oh.' He held it up. 'Do you mind if I break into the casing?'

'What? No, not at all. It's not mine anyway,' said Lissy.

Stef nodded and began to work at the casing. 'Aha!' He

managed to ease the picture out of the frame and held it up. He looked at Lissy and pointed to the edges. 'Do you see this? There are two edges to the paper.'

'So has it not just been mounted?'

'No. It looks different to a mounting. You know, I don't want to get your hopes up, but I think there may be something hidden under here.'

'What?' Lissy leaned forward. 'What do you mean?'

'All I'm saying is that Laura Knight hid a painting of Alfred Munnings behind one of her own pieces of work. The work was *Carnaval* from 1915. The hidden work was *Alfred Munnings Reading* – by her husband, Harold Knight. It was only discovered recently and it's a mystery as to why she hid it.'

'Yes, I know all about that, but —'

'Well, I'm wondering if this is a similar situation. Only it would predate Laura Knight, would it not? Hey, perhaps Lorelei had the idea first?' He laughed, and examined the picture again. 'Oh, my. Do you know, I think we might be right. Your nails, *mia cara*. I need demon talons on the case. Please – get the picture off the backing board and let us see what we shall find.'

'How wonderful!' Lissy took the picture from Stef and slowly picked at the side of the picture so it was loosened from the backing. 'You're right!' She looked up at him, her face glowing. 'There's something underneath it.'

'Why is your hand shaking, Elisabetta? Surely you are not worried about what you might find?'

'I'm not worried – I'm excited!' Lissy laughed. 'Maybe my story isn't over!'

And ever-so-carefully, Lissy peeled back the seascape watercolour. And ever-so-slowly, the picture beneath unveiled itself.

A man. A head and shoulders watercolour of a man, wearing

a white, open-necked shirt, looking to his right. Behind him, the vast sea. His hair was longish and dark, curling at the base of his neck, his eyes a deep, chocolate brown.

'Oh, my God,' Lissy breathed.

Her hands began to shake even more and Stef leaned forwards, putting his hands on hers, trying to steady her. 'What is it, *mia cara*?'

'This man. I'm pretty sure he's the one I saw on my beach that night.' She looked at Stef, her face white. 'He's the one who had the gun.'

The Cove, 1905

Lorelei pulled open the door of the bathing hut and looked down at Julian from the top of the steps. 'Will I loosen my hair for you?' she asked. 'Like the suicidal maiden?'

'No. I don't want anything obscuring your face.' He handed the satin gown to her and smiled. She reached out, then seemed to change her mind and pushed his hair out of his face instead.

Then she let her fingertips slide down his jawline. 'But your face is obscured and I want to see it.'

'Then we are in agreement,' Julian replied. He raised the costume and Lorelei took it from him.

'What shall I do with it then?' she asked.

'Plait it,' Julian said. 'Haven't I already told you I wanted it plaited? Just like when I saw you swimming – or, more to the point – when I saw you sitting on the rock that first day.'

Lorelei smiled. 'Very well. Allow me to change, and I shall plait my hair for you.'

'Wonderful. I'll just wait for you here, then.' Julian seemed to fold up and all of a sudden he was sitting on the sand cross-legged; all without taking his eyes off her.

Lorelei laughed and stepped inside the bathing machine. 'I shan't be a moment.' She put the dress down on the chair and closed the door.

Julian's amused voice drifted through the cracks: 'Let me know if you require any help dressing, Lady Scarsdale.'

'I think I can manage, Mr Cooper,' she shouted back, and began to undo the fastenings on her modern-day clothing.

'That's a shame,' he replied. Lorelei smiled into the shadows, noticing the little drifts of sand in the corner of the room, and wriggled into the medieval costume. It was the work of a moment to shake her hair loose from its chignon and swiftly plait it, tying it up with the red ribbon, and then she was ready. She took a deep breath and pushed open the door.

Lorelei was rewarded by Julian's face altering as he saw her. The man was, quite clearly, taken aback.

He scrambled to his feet and held his hand out to her. 'You are the very vision of a Siren,' he told her, helping her out of the bathing machine.

'A vision?' She laughed as she came down the steps onto the sand and stared up into his dark brown eyes. 'Well now, that's a very good start. Shall we head straight out onto the rock?' She nodded towards it. It had a silvery sheen in the late afternoon light and shimmered deliciously, calling to her.

'I think so,' replied Julian.

Lorelei let go of his hand and picked up her skirt. Her own feet were bare and she began to walk through the sand to the edge of the sea.

'Allow me.' Julian swooped down on her as soon as her toe touched the water, and suddenly she was aloft in his arms.

She gave a shout of glee and laughed as she clung to his neck. 'I'm perfectly capable of wading out to the rock!' she cried. 'Put me down!'

'No. I shan't put you down, at least not willingly. But I might drop you!' He loosened his grip for a second and she slipped down a few inches before his strong hands clasped together again and caught her.

Lorelei shrieked and kicked her legs as Julian began to wade through the shallows towards the rock.

'I don't trust you at *all*, Mr Cooper!' she said – but there was amusement in her voice and they both knew she was joking.

'You'll learn to,' he said.

They reached the rock, the water well over Julian's knees, and he placed her carefully on top of it, still in the same position she had been in when he had carried her. Lorelei shifted slightly and made herself more comfortable, then turned to look at him. He was wading back towards the shore, looking down and fiddling with the camera he had slung around his neck. She hoped she hadn't crushed it when she was in his arms.

Lorelei wrapped her arms around her legs, and watched him as he stood on the shore. He was turning around and holding the camera up, spending a while doing something with it, framing the shot no doubt. She would just wait for her cue. All she had to do was sit there and he would tell her exactly when …

CLICK!

'Perfect!' Julian looked up from the camera and grinned. 'Got you.'

'Excuse me?' Lorelei squirmed on the rock, the dress hampering her movements somewhat, and kneeled up, her fists planted on the rock either side of her. 'Was that it? Have you done it? Oh.' She was horribly disappointed. That was it? All that build up? For that?

'Sadly, yes. It's a little different to posing for a sketch or a painting, isn't it? Much faster for all concerned. But regardless, I truly wanted a candid picture of you so I could remember you like this – no airs and graces, no Lady

172

Bountiful. Just you. On a rock. In the summer. With me.' He smiled at her, a little shyly, Lorelei thought.

'Really? Am I very interesting when I'm just – me?' she asked, blinking like a rather stupid sort of owl. She was utterly confused. The speed of him taking that photograph had thrown her.

'You are more interesting like that than you will ever know.' There was the briefest of pauses, when the look Julian gave her told her more than she felt he would ever be able to vocalise.

She tried to match his look, wanting to tell him the same thing.

Then his face split into a smile. 'I know,' was all he said in response. 'I know.'

'Well then!' Lorelei shook herself a little. 'You could have at least taken one of me smiling. Let me try again.'

'No need,' replied Julian. 'You *were* smiling on that one. Believe me. I don't know what you were thinking or what you were planning, but you were very definitely smiling. Now. Let me be content with my work. In fact – I think I shall come out there and join you shortly.'

'No. I insist you take some proper photographs!' pleaded Lorelei, not knowing whether to laugh or cry. 'I want to at least enjoy my time in the spotlight for more than a few seconds!'

Julian laughed and shook his head. 'Imperious Lady Scarsdale. All right. But just two more. I can't be wasting my plates when I know the first picture was perfect.'

'Two more will be lovely,' said Lorelei. 'Now – tell me what I should do.'

'Very well, then,' replied Julian. And, as she requested, he proceeded to take two more photographs, posing her and advising her and finally lowering the camera and smiling out at her. 'That is it. Truly. One cannot improve on perfection.'

And all of a sudden he was simply Julian again – no longer a professional and clearly just a man wanting to feel the freedom of the seaside. Lorelei didn't know what his plans were for the photographs and she really didn't care. On the surface of it all at least, there was nothing to discredit either herself or Julian.

Below the surface, however, there was an undercurrent that she feared was sweeping her mercilessly along – for the first time in her life, she was caught in a riptide she didn't want to fight against.

Chapter Twenty

'So what do you want to do about him?' asked Stef. The empty frame lay between them on the dusty floor, the seascape curled up and abandoned somewhere towards Lissy's left ankle, the portrait of the young man between them.

Lissy stared at the picture, her elbows on her knees, her head resting on her hands. 'I don't know. Is he a bad guy? Is he dangerous? Or rather – *was* he dangerous?'

'Do *you* think he looks dangerous?' Stef raised his eyebrows at her.

'I don't know.' She shifted and leaned forward, then picked up the painting and held it up in front of her face. She stared at it with such concentration that her wonderful, beautiful eyes did not blink for oh so many minutes. 'His eyes are the same colour as yours. I don't get the feeling that he *was* bad. He was protecting something. I have a suspicion that Lorelei hid his portrait for some reason. But the way this is painted ...' She ran her fingertips down the picture and Stef could tell she was tracing the profile of the man from forehead to chin. 'She loved him. Actually,' she said, 'you know what this picture reminds me of? It looks like that really famous Byron one. The Thomas Phillips one? Where he sort of looks off to the distance.'

'Byron the poet was a construct of popular appeal,' observed Stef. 'Nobody really knew *what* the man was like.'

'Exactly.' Lissy nodded. 'Hence all the glorified images of him. He was a Romantic hero to so many women – and this chap looks like he was a Romantic hero to Lorelei. Maybe he was a smuggler after all. Maybe that's how she knew him. Maybe she was helping him!'

She looked at Stef hopefully and he laughed. 'You have such a wonderful imagination, Elisabetta. Maybe he was her lover? Her secret lover and she was scared to let him out of her bedroom and into the real world.' He looked around him at the bare walls and the rotten wood. 'Okay, maybe she could have kept him in a better place, but it must have been nice one hundred years ago.'

'It was. Can't you see it? This was her room, and her bed would be about there.' She stood up and walked over to a wall. 'Just here. So she could sit in it and turn her head and look out of the window. And she would have had her easel here.' She moved over to the window and stood staring out at sea. 'So she could watch for him coming, but look as if she was working if anyone found her.'

Stef stood up and walked over to join her. He stopped next to her and dared to put one arm around her waist. He pointed at the view with his other hand, joining in the game. 'You are correct. The light here. It would have been perfect. This was her sacred area. Her husband was not allowed in here without a damn good reason. It was not the marital bedroom.'

'Nope. No way.' Lissy shook her head and leaned on the crumbling window sill, looking out at the storm-washed vista. There was still a big cluster of black clouds just passing over the cove and heading out to sea, taking the rain with it. 'The marital bedroom thing died a long time ago. They'd had separate rooms for so long, she was living an absolute lie.'

'All for the sake of propriety,' murmured Stef. 'How sad.'

'But there was more to it than that.' Lissy turned so she half sat on the window sill, looking up at Stef and resting her weight on her hands. 'But I'm damned if I know what it was. And anyway, this is all conjecture. How can I find out so much for other people and so little for myself?' Her gaze slipped over his shoulder so she was looking at the cupboard they had broken into, the door of which was still hanging open.

'Sometimes, one cannot see what is staring one right in the face.' Stef held his hand out to her. She took it and he pulled her gently up from the windowsill and drew her towards him so she was in his arms. The movements were so smooth, it was as if they were choreographed.

And perhaps tomorrow he would be able to show her what he had travelled all this way to bring to her attention. He just had to persuade her to come back to the beach hut with him. Which might be easier than he had anticipated, judging by the fact she had come into his arms so willingly – and also, thanks to the fact that, in this room, he got the oddest feeling that he had persuaded her to go back down to the beach a thousand times before.

Which was, in itself, incredible; because trying to tame Lissy was like trying to tame the sea itself, and persuading her into anything was a feat few people were capable of.

Lissy was quite unaware that she was moving towards Stef so naturally. The whole thing was slowed down, softly-focused; dreamlike. She was wearing that white dress and he was standing there with his hand out, asking her to go with him, down to the beach, to their special place. He was half in shadow, and his hair was like the man's in the picture and his shirt was open at the neck, just in the same way. His eyes too were definitely similar; dark brown, intense, as if they saw magic that nobody else was aware of.

She came to a stop, fitting into his arms perfectly, staring into his eyes as if she could read every thought he possessed; knowing that she was at the heart of everything he held dear.

'Oh, Lissy ...' His voice was soft.

Lissy looked around her and saw the place for what it really was: a slightly damp, cold, bare room with vestiges of grandeur. It was such a shame. She looked at the sconce by the window and imagined it lit with a flame, glowing into the night for the smugglers to see. She wondered whether it had guided people into the cove, even as Lorelei painted her seascapes and her secret lovers in her ivory tower.

At the thought, a chill crept across Lissy's shoulders and goosebumps prickled her flesh, despite the warmth of Stef's arms around her.

'Do you feel it too?' whispered Stef, pulling her closer. 'You're shivering. There is something different about the room. I get the sense that the house wants us out, now we have delved into its secrets.'

Lissy looked around, her eyes catching every shadow, noticing every nook and cranny. It felt as if something was drawing closer to them, the heartbeat of the house increasing.

Stef followed her gaze and smiled a little. '*But to what sound her listening ear stoops she? What netherworld gulf-whispers doth she hear,*' he murmured as he turned his attention back to her. 'Rossetti's *Sea Spell*. It seems appropriate, somehow. There are echoes in here, for sure.'

Lissy nodded, hardly daring to breathe, not wanting to leave his arms. 'I can feel it too.'

Stef lifted a hand and drew his finger down the side of Lissy's face. It felt as if sparks were flashing off his fingertips and igniting her skin. His dark eyes were staring right into hers, only a few centimetres away and her heart beat a little faster.

'Do you?'

A movement in the corner caught her attention, something detaching itself from the shadows; then it was gone again.

'Come on, Stef,' she said suddenly. She pulled herself away from him, leaving him looking a little startled, his finger still crooked where it had been resting against her chin, his mouth slightly open as if he had just about been ready to brush her lips with his. 'We have to go.' Her voice came out all wavery and shaky and she didn't like the way it sounded. She was one heartbeat away from throwing herself at him and begging him to take her, right there in the middle of the floor, but she knew they couldn't stay there.

'Your pictures.' He anchored her with his grip of her hand. 'What of the pictures and the paint box? What of Lorelei's treasures?'

'We don't even know that they're hers. Come on. We have to go.' Her heart was beating fast again, and she could feel sweat trickling between her shoulder blades. Sea Scarr Hall was pushing down on Lissy and she couldn't wait to be out of the place. She squeezed her eyes shut, feeling like she was suffocating and the only way to stop the horrible claustrophobic energy was to leave.

There was a slight delay as she felt Stef dip down and she forced her eyes open to see him bending over and picking up the paint box and the pictures. She cast a final glance around the room and froze. Her heart started hammering in her chest and she drew a deep, shuddering breath as she saw the faint shadow of the dark-haired, dark-eyed man leaning against the windowsill where she had just been, watching them both with his arms folded.

Stef flinched as Lissy twisted out of his grasp and practically flew out of the room.

'Elisabetta!' he called, straightening up with the box and pictures in his hand. 'Wait for me! That staircase is dangerous!' He hurried out after her, not bothering to shut the door behind him. He was half way along the corridor, jogging to catch her up, when he heard the unmistakeable sound of a door clashing shut.

The sound served to give wings to his feet more than anything else he had ever encountered – and he refused to turn around and see which door had slammed. Eyes forwards, arms and legs powering through the chilly air, he came to the top of the staircase. 'Elisabetta!' he called again.

'I'm going outside!' The faint voice came at him through the darkness of the corridors down below and he knew somehow she had managed to get down that horrible staircase. He heard her cursing as she clambered over the wreckage of the door panels and then he realised he was alone in that dangerous ruin of a house.

There was a sound, very close behind him of a footstep – which may, he reasoned, have been an echo – but then he heard a breath and the rustle of silk too close to him for comfort.

It was Stef's turn to curse and he made short work of that dratted staircase, running down the steps to where they ended in a giant hole, then hurdling over the banister to land in some weird crouching stance in the deserted hallway.

'I am also going outside!' he cried and raced through the building, climbing over the same panels Lissy had just cleared and escaping into the gloom of the coastal twilight. He saw Lissy, right at the far side of the overgrown gardens. And it wasn't long before he joined her.

'I hate that house!' Lissy shouted as Stef hurtled towards her. Her arms were wrapped around her body and she was genuinely terrified.

'It is not the best of places,' Stef agreed. He looked pretty dishevelled and Lissy's heart bounced around a bit more as she saw him open his arms. She ran into them, closing her eyes and leaning her face against his chest. She didn't want to look at that house anymore; all the excitement of exploring it had definitely dissipated with the emergence of the shadows and the strange feelings in that bedroom. Stef was real and he was safe and God he felt good.

'I don't think they wanted us there at the end. I felt like we were intruding,' she muttered into his body. It sounded stupid and she knew it; her cheeks concurred, burning with embarrassment.

'We are well out of it,' said Stef. 'I may not have done the right thing by rescuing the pictures, now I think about it. Maybe I should have left them there.'

'I'm not bloody going back in to replace them! No way.'

'Then they come with us,' he said decisively. 'And we do something with them later.'

'Whenever later is,' muttered Lissy. She looked up at the house and realised just how unnerved she had felt in Sea Scarr Hall. The image of that man leaning on the windowsill had shaken her up more than she cared to admit, but at least he hadn't had the wretched gun with him. 'It's his picture, isn't it? He's the one.'

'Who?'

'The man from the beach the other night. He was in that room. I saw him. Maybe we should have left the things there.'

'I don't know. Did he look angry?' Stef twisted around and looked at the Hall. 'If you want me to, I'll go back in for you. I'll put him back—'

'No! No, don't. Don't go back in. It's too dangerous. And he didn't look angry. He just looked – interested.' She shuddered, hardly believing she was defending the gunman who had terrified her the other day. 'Leave it for now.' She wanted to add that when the man's gaze had fixed on her, his eyes were like Stef's, but she didn't.

'As you wish,' said Stef softly. 'Shall we go back to the beach?' He took her hand and raised it up, kissing it. 'Will you come and see if the moon rises over the sea?'

Lissy's hand tingled where his lips had brushed it. 'I just

want to be away from here. It's all a bit grim and Gothic for me now. It's not a game anymore. Will you just walk me home, please, and I'll see you tomorrow?'

Stef looked a little deflated. But no. It was too soon and her emotions were all over the place. That man in the room – she'd felt a pull to him that she couldn't describe, gunman or no gunman. It was his eyes, definitely his eyes. And if she spent any longer with Stef, she'd fall into his eyes and never be able to climb back out.

'Come, then.' Stef took her hand properly and led her away from Sea Scarr Hall, back towards the beach and the Dower House and real life. The thrill of finding the treasures in the bedroom had also shrunk into nothingness, and she now felt vaguely disturbed by it all. She was very glad Stef had taken charge of them.

'Hey. May I make a suggestion?' he suddenly asked, pausing halfway down the pathway and turning towards her. He took both her hands in his and she didn't resist or try to pull away.

'You may,' she said carefully.

'May I suggest that tomorrow I come to collect you and we have a trip into Staithes? I would very much like to take some photographs. I have never been before and you have me intrigued with the artists you speak of. It is, I am sure, quite a different harbour town to Portofino. If you come with me, you can help me discover how that may be. I'm sure you would like to know more about your – what were they, *plein air* Impressionists? – as well.'

Lissy half-smiled, not knowing if she were relieved or disappointed that all he had suggested was an outing. 'I'd love to come.'

'Thank you. I shall be here around eleven. Then we can have lunch in the town.'

'Perfect,' she replied.

He squeezed her hands and recommenced walking down towards the Dower House.

He took her as far as the door and leaned in, very gently. 'Until tomorrow, *bella*,' he whispered and kissed her, very softly, before pulling away and smiling down at her. 'I shall take your treasures away with me as well; just in case you decide they are haunted objects or something.'

'Ha!' Lissy shook her head and smiled. 'Yes. Take them. I'm not sure I want them here at the minute.'

'Very well.' Stef smiled again and kissed her hand. '*Ciao*.' Then he walked away, back up to the road where he had left his car that morning.

Gosh, was it just this morning? Lissy watched him until he disappeared into the shadows and went back into the Dower House.

And she knew it was silly, but she made sure that all the doors were firmly locked – just in case anyone else decided to materialise on her beach that night.

Chapter Twenty-One

Sea Scarr Hall, 1905

Lorelei was handed the note by the maid who served her breakfast.

'Thank you,' she said in some surprise. 'Who delivered this?'

'The summer visitor, Madam. He came to the kitchens very early – said he was up to catch the light or something.' The girl blushed, clearly wondering if she'd said too much.

Lorelei smiled and nodded at her. 'He's a photographer, as you might know. That will be why he wants the light.'

'I see. Thank you.' The girl bobbed a curtsey, her red hair escaping from her cap, her cheeks beetroot.

'Oh – did he want an answer?' asked Lorelei, half-standing, wondering if he was still there, waiting for her. It had been a couple of days since she had posed for him and she was desperate to see him again. She had worried that she had done something to upset him, but then the reasonable side of her told her that the man had to work, and was quite probably busy with his photographs. Plus, Walter had returned and she understood that Julian wouldn't exactly want to risk seeing her if her husband was around.

'No, Madam. He said he would see you later.'

Lorelei's heart leapt. 'Thank you. You're excused.' The girl curtsied again and hurried away as Lorelei held the note, wondering if she dared open it in here. Walter was nowhere to be seen which was a blessing. But still – she didn't want to risk his wrath. Her shoulder was still aching where he had slammed her up against the wall and shouted at her last night. Her bodice was too low, he had raged, and he could see the tops of her breasts. The whole time he was shouting at her, though, he had been shouting at her breasts, which was rather astonishing. However. She would go to her sitting room and open the note there – in the window, looking out at the Dower House.

Breakfast was a rushed affair after that, but thank God Walter did not appear. He was probably sleeping off his whisky. But still, it seemed too long before she was eventually settled by the window, in her own room, carefully unfolding the note:

Lady Scarsdale.
I wonder if you would oblige me with your company this afternoon? I am intending to set up some scenic shots of the cove and surrounding area, and will be interested to see how a painter portrays the scene.
Should you be available, I look forward to your company around one o'clock.

Yours,
Cooper

Lorelei laughed. *How formal!* And of course, formal it had to be. If that letter were to fall into Walter's hands, it couldn't demonstrate anything but propriety and an interest in art. Although any mention of art might damn her in any case. Still … Her eyes drifted back to one word in it, though. *Yours.*

She wondered if he really meant it?

Julian was on the beach fifteen minutes early. He was prowling around, nervous, anxious that she wouldn't come.

He had kicked his shoes off and loosened his top button, his eyes scanning the pathway. Then he saw her, rounding the corner, running towards him, struggling with a portable easel and a paint box.

'Lorelei!' His heart rushed with love and he ran towards her waving. 'Lorelei! Wait! I'll help you!'

She saw him coming and stopped, dumping the things on the ground and waving back. 'Julian! I brought my painting materials!'

'I'm coming!' he called and took a few long strides up to her. Instead of reaching down for the paint things, he caught her by the waist and swung her round, setting her on her feet as she laughed delightedly.

'Do you even intend to do any work?' she asked, 'or was this all an elaborate ruse to get me here? Because it worked.'

'It's a little bit of both,' replied Julian. 'Come. I'll carry your things for you. I do need to do some work, and I suspect that you don't often get a chance to come down here and paint, so I thought I'd give you the opportunity.'

Lorelei put her hand up to her hair, pinning a dark strand back into place.

She winced a little as she raised her arm and Julian frowned. 'Are you all right?'

'I'm more than all right. I'm with you. I think I was sleeping in an odd position. My shoulder's a little stiff, that's all.' She fixed him with a smile that shone as brightly as the sun. 'Now, what exactly are we going to do this afternoon?'

'I'm going to set your things up next to mine,' said Julian, 'then we can try to tackle the same views in our different mediums. Later, we can compare the results.'

'That's rather unfair.' Lorelei followed him as he walked down to the beach. 'After all, you can take a photograph much quicker than I can paint a picture.'

'I can. But I can take lots of different pictures, develop

them, and perhaps make us a cup of tea whilst you work on your masterpiece.'

'It'll be a seascape,' said Lorelei wryly. 'But I like them.'

'Then play around with the seascape. Do something different with it. Add the cliffs at each side. Add the Dower House. Add two people sitting on a rock. Do whatever you want. This is your chance to express yourself, outside, in the fresh air, and nobody will tell you it's silly.'

'I do like that idea,' agreed Lorelei. 'Here?'

'Here on this piece of beach. Right here.'

'Good.' Lorelei looked up to her left, towards Sea Scarr.

Julian followed her gaze. 'Are we too overlooked here?'

'No.' Lorelei turned to him and smiled. 'Let him look. He can see this is perfectly innocent. He asked where I was going with my things and I told him I was painting *en plein air* today. He had no argument. Apart from suggesting I bring a maid with me.'

'And did you?'

'Yes. Phyllis is on her way – look.'

Julian looked over Lorelei's shoulder and saw a red-headed scrap of a maid coming around the corner, lugging a picnic hamper. 'Oh.' He felt deflated.

'It's all right. I've told her she doesn't have to sit near us. I've given her some books to look at – fairytales and what-not. *Little Women. Alice in Wonderland.* She loves reading, but she's quite slow at it, and she doesn't get the opportunity to do it very often, so that's my gift to her: a day off on the beach! She's got the books tucked in the hamper. I brought us all some food, anyway.'

Julian perked up and laughed. 'God bless you, Lady Bountiful. I'll go and help her bring them down. But, yes – Lord Scarsdale. I feared as much. I did see him return, which is why I have been keeping my distance. I hope you can forgive me? I didn't want to stay away, not really.'

'I know why you had to.' Lorelei smiled. 'It's all right.' She turned her back on the window and stretched. 'But this is just perfect. A perfect afternoon. He also said that I should keep my clothes on.'

Julian stared at her. 'Did he now?'

'Yes.'

'Oh, well. No swimming today then,' said Julian more flippantly than he felt.

'No swimming today,' she agreed. 'But it doesn't matter so much because I'm still with you.'

'That's good.' Julian knew he had a silly grin on his face. He couldn't take his eyes off Lorelei. 'I like you being with me.'

They were on the beach for several hours. There was nothing to complain about. It all looked very proper. Just as well he'd forced her to take that stupid little floozy with her – God knows what she might have done if she'd been alone. The thought of her flaunting her naked body in front of the summer visitor was abhorrent to him. It was disgusting. She was disgusting.

Walter moved away from the telescope, but he still wasn't satisfied.

It *did* look very proper. But looks were deceiving and he knew that better than most. He thought he'd married an angel and he'd shackled himself to a whore. He caught himself thinking of her peeling a sea-soaked gown off and dropping it at his feet, apologising because she'd fallen into the water and spoiled her clothes, and all she had fit to wear was her undergarments.

He looked back out of the telescope. She was dry. Bone dry. Nowhere near the water and packing up to come back to the Hall, by the looks of things.

The filthy whore. The disgusting, filthy whore.

Lissy was ready long before eleven the next day. It wasn't like her at all. She was usually a very careless kind of person – things in London ran on Lissy-time, and that was understood by everyone who knew her.

Here, though, it was different. She was peering out of the window, trying to spot Stef coming down the pathway. In her mind, just as he knocked, she would wait a couple of minutes, then saunter to the door and open it, all surprised that he had come: *Oh, Stef. You came? I didn't expect you to. I'm not quite ready.*

In reality, she waited until about quarter to eleven and decided to have a walk up to the parking area where her visitors had all left their cars yesterday. She had a better view up there and could watch for him properly.

Good grief, what was she becoming? She dipped her head and frowned at the ground as she walked up to the road. The Springtime Lissy wouldn't have given a damn if anyone was coming to see her or not, especially not him. They'd come and if she was there to greet them, she was there. If she wasn't, she wasn't. Her cheeks burned ferociously as she recalled the time Jon and Becky had driven down to London, poor Becky more than a little bit pregnant, to meet Cori and Simon. She'd been out when they arrived. She'd been shopping. Good Lord, what had she *become*? When had she polished up that brittle, unfeeling veneer, built up a don't-care attitude and expected everyone to dance to her tune?

Summertime Lissy looked up and was ashamed to feel a couple of tears sliding down her cheeks. She was an awful person; she truly was. But then—

She stuck her chin out and dabbed the tears away. She had bloody good reason. Stef had done that to her. Stef and – that other man. Her ex, who nobody was allowed to mention.

'Ugh.' She sniffed and composed herself, and clambered the last few feet onto the road.

He was there, just pulling up, and she drew up short as the engine stopped and he opened the door.

He smiled, a huge, genuine smile as he caught sight of her. 'Lissy! I'm so sorry – I'm early. Have I interrupted anything? A morning constitutional, perhaps?'

Lissy shook her head. 'No. I was swimming earlier. That was my constitutional. This was me just coming up to meet you.'

'I am privileged. Oh!' He was by now in front of her and he caught her face in his hands and tilted it up to study it. 'You are sad. What's happened? Shall I go? Do you not want to come to Staithes?' He dropped his hands and his brows knitted together. 'I understand. Perhaps I am being too quick. You maybe don't want to spend more time with me, just yet.'

'No! I mean yes! Yes, I do want to spend some more time with you!' Lissy was, uncharacteristically flustered. 'I was sad. But I'm not sad now. I'm happy now. Look – happy!' She smiled and pointed to her face. 'Happy.'

Stef laughed. 'I have been speaking your language long enough to understand the word, but nevertheless I am happy that you're happy.'

'Good.'

'But why were you sad?' he pressed, dipping down so he was eye to eye with her. 'Hmm?'

Lissy dropped her gaze and pushed her toe into a tuft of grass on the verge. 'I was just thinking of something.'

'Was I in that sad thought?' he asked, perceptively.

'Yes,' Lissy replied honestly. 'Yes, you were.' She lifted her gaze and stared directly into his eyes. 'Don't you ever dare make me feel sad again.'

'I suppose I deserve that.' He sighed and looked away over her shoulder, towards the sea. 'So are we going to Staithes or not?'

'Of course we are.' Lissy reached out and took his hand, surprising them both. She smiled again, properly. 'That's why I came up here so damned early.'

'Excellent.' Stef looked down at her and squeezed her hand, before lifting it and kissing it in that way which made her skin tingle. 'Come along, then. I have my camera with me. I shall try not to bore you with my work, but it's a good opportunity for me.'

'Oh, I won't be bored,' replied Lissy, letting him guide her to the car. He opened the door and helped her in. 'I've been doing some research and there are some very interesting things in the town. I'd quite like to see them for myself.'

Stef got in beside her and they pulled away. 'We have the rest of the day. We can do it all.'

Lissy watched the scenery melt, blue and green, into itself as she recalled some of the things she had wanted to see. 'I'd quite like to see the Captain Cook Museum, and, strangely enough, I really want to see Roraima House. It's a B & B now, so you wouldn't think it that exciting, but it used to be a private house. It was built in the 1890s by John Trattles, you know. He was a Sea Captain, and he named it after his boat. Apparently it has wonderful stained glass windows.'

'Stained glass would be colourful, and would probably make a very good photograph. I'm sure we could see it. I, myself, would like to see the Beck.'

'She's at Whitby today, I think.' Lissy risked a joke and peeked up at Stef to see if he was amused.

Stef nodded seriously. 'You would think so. But I have heard she runs into the sea at Staithes and is dotted with fishing boats. Fancy that.'

Lissy laughed. 'Let's not tell her that one! I've seen her paddle at Whitby and come into the water in the cove, but I don't know if she's ever been dotted with fishing boats.'

'I think Jon has made a very good choice with Becky. When

he was so broken without Fran, I did worry about him. He is happy. That's good.'

'I doubt he even thinks of Fran now,' Lissy replied. It was on the tip of her tongue to ask whether Stef gave much thought to Brigitte Bardot, but she thought better of it and stared out of the window before she could pursue it.

'He maybe thinks of her.' Stef indicated and pulled onto a road which would take them towards the town. It wasn't a long drive, but Lissy could understand it if he didn't want to lug camera equipment on such a walk. 'But I seriously doubt whether he thinks of her with love. Possibly with a great deal of embarrassment and also relief that he – what did you always used to say – binned her.'

'She binned him,' Lissy reminded him.

'Very true. There is a big difference and it is never pleasant being binned. Sometimes, people deserve it. Sometimes, they don't. Jon didn't deserve it. Ah – here we go.' He pulled into a parking space and pulled the handbrake on. 'It's not far is it?'

'Not far at all. But it looks quite nice. I love all the cottages – look, you can see them huddled down there.' She pointed to a collection of cottages and a ribbon of blue sea.

'It is a fine day to explore Staithes,' replied Stef. 'Come on – let's go!'

It was indeed a fine day to explore the town. Lissy delighted in finding all the alleyways she'd hoped for, and the little art galleries that she told Stef she could easily lose days in.

'When Laura and Harold Knight were here,' she commented as they had a cup of tea and some sandwiches in a little tea-shop in the old town, 'they had a studio. They'd walk three miles from Roxby down to Staithes every morning and three miles back. With all their equipment! Easels and paints and canvases. Gosh.' She shook her head and dusted the crumbs of a ham sandwich off her fingers. 'Imagine it.'

'It was quite a different time, then,' replied Stef. 'Imagine all the other artists, all doing the same thing. I wonder what the fisher folk thought of it.'

'I suppose they were all just too busy getting on with their jobs. But even now, you get so many artists here, it's not too hard to think of what it was like a century ago.' She looked out of the window and smiled. 'For instance, when we step out of here onto those cobbles, think about all of the feet that have done the same thing.' She leaned closer to the window and pointed. 'The road around *there*, for instance – imagine sitting here, so long ago and thinking "I'll just pop into the town for something" and heading that way. And people have done the same thing millions and millions of times. We must all leave a stamp on the world somehow. That's part of the charm of these little old towns. Apparently there are even shipwrecks in the water, not too far out.' She looked at Stef. 'Not quite like your Christ of the Abyss, but still part of another world. Fascinating.'

'Fascinating. Just like you.' Stef was leaning forwards, resting his chin in his hands, smiling at her. 'Oh – but that reminds me.' He sat upright again and rummaged in his camera bag. 'I have this for you. I printed it out this morning. I hope you like it – a token of my undying—' He stopped and coloured, looking instead further into his bag. Lissy had thought for a moment he was going to say the "L" word – his undying love. She shivered a little bit. She kind of knew where he was coming from; but he wasn't going to say it after all. The moment had passed and she released a breath she hadn't realised she was holding. '—respect and affection,' he finished, smiling at her.

'Respect and affection?' The words were out before she could stop them and she scowled. 'Oh.'

Stef looked at her curiously. 'What? Can I not respect and affect you?'

'Respect and *affect* me? I thought you'd been speaking English a long time.'

'So I have been.' He grinned. 'Do I not affect you? At all? Maybe not. I had hoped.' He shrugged. 'Here you are. For you.' His eyes sparked with mischief. 'With love.'

A gurgle of a laugh escaped Lissy. 'With love? Very well. Thank you. I shall receive this in the spirit of which it is intended.'

'That is a good start.' Stef handed an envelope over to her. 'I didn't have time to frame it, but you might want to discard it anyway.' He flapped his hand in the direction of the door. 'I think I will leave before you open it. I do not want to be here when you shout at me.'

'I won't shout! I promise. Wait – please. Just wait.'

Stef shook his head and grinned. 'No. I will pay, and I will head outside. Promise me you will count to fifty before you open it, then another fifty before you come to chase me so you can shout at me.'

'Stef!' But it was hopeless. He blew a kiss at her, winked and hurried away to the till. 'Count to fifty!' he shouted as he handed over the money. 'Promise me!

'I promise!' called Lissy, laughing and clutching the envelope. For a moment, there was just him and her in the world; she didn't care that other customers were staring at her curiously, noticing, perhaps, her odd eyes and the way they met Stef's and the way they connected, in some strange way, in that little old teashop.

It was the first time she'd been in it, but it certainly didn't feel like it. With Stef here, everything felt right – like they'd done it before and would most certainly do it again. She knew, also, that she had to count to fifty as he'd asked her – she simply had to.

She watched him disappear down the street and smiled again.

A couple of moments later and she tore open the envelope carefully. 'Oh! My goodness!' She looked at the photograph as if she'd never seen anything like it before. It was her, standing on the rock last night, her mermaid dress skimming her knees, matching almost perfectly the greenish blue of the sea and the vibrant hues of her eyes. He had digitally enhanced it all, of course he had. But it was stunning; absolutely stunning.

She turned it over, her hands shaking. On the back, he had written in his confident, scrawling handwriting: *Bella Miranda. Always.*

Lissy looked out of the window. He had, quite thoroughly, disappeared.

She dragged her chair back with a noisy scrape that had more of the customers stare at her, and hurried out of the tea shop onto the cobbled street. She looked left and right, and hazarded a guess – right. She would turn right and she'd find him up there.

Of course she would.

She dashed up the street and saw him outside a shop, not looking in the window, but instead on his mobile phone. He was running his fingers through his thick, springy curls and looking perplexed.

He turned as she walked towards him, and quickly finished the call.

He shoved the phone in his pocket and, switching on a smile, he began to walk towards her.

'Well?' he asked. 'Did you like it?'

'Who were you on the phone to?' There was more of an accusation in her voice than she had intended, but it was there. She couldn't help it.

'The phone? I was on the phone?'

'Of *course* you were on the phone.' Her voice was steel. 'Was it her?'

'Her? By "her" I assume you mean Kerensa.'

'Yes. I mean her.' Lissy couldn't even bring herself to say the woman's name. 'If that was the naked blonde you were amusing yourself with, I mean *her*.'

Stef rolled his eyes and raised his arms. 'No. It was not Kerensa.'

'You look guilty.'

'I am guilty of nothing, my love. Tell me, Miranda—'

'*Don't* call me Miranda. Who was it?'

'Lissy!'

'Who was it?'

Stef swore in Italian and ran his fingers through his hair again. 'Lissy. My love. Must it always be like this with us?'

'Stef! Tell me.'

'Jon! It was Jon, okay? I was on the phone to your brother!'

'Jon?'

'Yes! Oh, dear God. Here. Look here.' He pulled the phone out and thrust it at Lissy. 'Look. Look at the call list or whatever you call it.'

Lissy hesitated for a second, hating how she felt, hating how she wanted to look at the phone, but for her own sanity, she knew she had to check.

Sure enough, there on the call log were Jon's details.

'You can check it all,' said Stef. 'I have nothing to hide. Jon was contacting me with a question about our project. Would you like access to my emails as well?'

'No! No I don't! Oh, no. Here. Take it. Take your phone. I'm so sorry.' Lissy began to shake. 'I'm sorry – it's just …'

'I know, I know. And I must take the blame for some of the way you feel. But I swear, Kerensa is not in my life – nobody is. No woman, except, if you will allow it – you.'

'You mustn't take the blame for it. It's not all you.' Lissy laughed, mirthlessly. 'You are responsible for *some* of it – but not everything. Can we just forget it? Please?'

'I would like nothing more than to forget it!' cried Stef, right in the middle of the street. He flung his arms wide again, in a typically expansive gesture. 'I would much prefer to move on!'

'Me too!' responded Lissy. She moved into his arms and laid her head against his chest. 'I'm sorry. I'm awful. I love the photograph. I love it so much. Thank you. I promise I'll try my best not to be Circe, I'll be Miranda. But I just need to know I can *trust* you.'

'You can, I swear on my life I will be the most trustworthy person in history. I knew I'd have to convince you, and I hope that you'll see it's my heart speaking to you, and my heart does not lie. You're not awful. You've been hurt; but now I am back and I would like to look after you. I want to be Ferdinand to your beautiful Miranda. Ferdinand passed all of the tests in that play and proved he loved her always. Now—' He gently moved her away so he could look at her properly. 'There is a beautiful bookshop just up here. I believe it is called Tempest's Bookshop, or something similar. Ideal for my Miranda, yes? We can trawl it for books on local artists and some nice histories of Staithes. And then, after we have walked our socks off, and I have taken more pictures, we'll have a nice dinner and then I shall take you back to the Dower House. And perhaps we can walk along the beach for a little while and I will see the moon rise over the water tonight? How does that sound?'

'Perfect.' Lissy looked in his eyes and she knew he was telling the truth. She caught a glimpse of their reflections in the window of the shop they were in front of. A jewellers' – it reminded her of the one in Cornwall and she felt such a sense of loss for that summer; such a sense of loss over the Lissy she had been. She wanted to be herself again, that Summertime Lissy who knew how to laugh and love freely, who could give herself to the people she trusted fully.

It took her a moment until she realised that the reflections were a little distorted. The couple in the shadows of the old, pitted glass looked slightly different. Stef's hair wasn't quite so long in the reflection, and hers looked as it if was caught up under a hat. The couple in the window leaned in towards each other; he bent his head down and she tilted her head up to meet his lips.

Lissy was fascinated. She blinked. She and Stef hadn't yet moved in towards each other – but as she looked back at him and into his eyes, he bent his head down and she tilted her face up to meet his lips, and she didn't give those odd shadows another thought.

Chapter Twenty-Two

The Dower House, 1905

The pattern continued over the weeks, a little game they played to see, perhaps, how innocent the outings could look, should Walter take too much notice of them. Little notes were delivered to Lorelei inviting her to joint painting and photography sessions on the beach or walks along the cliff, or discussions over how Mr Cooper's project was progressing as she had expressed such an interest in the Staithes Group. Whenever they were within sight of the house, Lorelei ensured Phyllis tagged along with her books. It was a small price to pay to spend time together.

One day, however, when he had seen Walter drive off in the carriage, Julian hurriedly sent a note to the Hall and arranged a picnic – just for him and Lorelei; but unfortunately the weather had other ideas.

'Can't these damn clouds see I had everything prepared!' Julian shouted, standing on the terrace, shaking his fist at the skies as sudden rain pelted down in big, fat drops, drilling holes into the sand. He was soaked through, his shirt clinging to him, his hair plastered to his head.

'It doesn't have to stop us!' cried Lorelei, soaked through herself, but giggling despite it all. 'Look! We'll just take the picnic inside.'

'Marvellous idea!' They tumbled onto the plates and greaseproof-wrapped parcels and tossed everything back into the basket. Then Lorelei dashed into the house in front of Julian and grabbed a rug from the back of a sofa. She spread it out on the floor and sat down cross-legged as Julian placed the picnic basket in the middle of it.

They worked their way through sandwiches and slabs of cake and biscuits bought that very morning from Whitby.

Then, with a cry of delight, Lorelei recognised the rose-patterned teapot he brought out of the kitchen to top up their drinks with, as one that had belonged to the Hall. 'I wondered where that dear little thing was! They must have brought it down here for the guests to use. I always used to have my afternoon tea from it. They'd bring it to my room and I'd sit at my table and pretend I was a very grand lady indeed.'

'You *are* a very grand lady indeed,' Julian said with a smile. Just then, as the rays of sunlight broke through the glass and lit up the detritus of the picnic, he kneeled up and reached out to her across the rug. She mirrored his movement, going to him instinctively and forgetting all about the picnic and the teapot and crumbs between them.

She reached out to him and put her hands either side of his face, and stared into his eyes. 'Don't let this summer end, Julian,' she whispered. 'Don't ever leave me.'

'Never,' he promised. And he drew her closer and kissed her, so tenderly, she felt as if she'd be safe in his arms forever.

She would have let him take her there and then, had it not been for the soft chimes of the clock in the corner striking five. She could have cried.

She leaned her forehead on his and focussed on his open, still slightly damp collar and the warmth of his hands on her skin. 'I have to go. We're having a dinner party. I have to entertain a group of people I despise. I pray to God Walter is detained wherever he is and doesn't come back until late.'

'But we have tomorrow,' he murmured. He gently took her face in his hands and tilted it up so her lips were close to his. 'And the day after that and the day after that. We have all summer.'

'But I want forever.' There was a catch in her voice.

'We can have that too,' he promised her, 'but until then …'

He picked up the teapot, a twinkle in his eye. 'Take this back with you. Have a cup of tea and think of me down here, all alone, with nothing but my chemicals to keep me company.'

'Have you developed the photographs of me being a mermaid yet?' she asked in a small voice. 'I keep asking and you keep saying "not yet, not yet". Have you done it?'

'Of course.'

'Julian! Can I see them?'

'Eventually,' he teased.

'Awful man!' She tapped him playfully on the arm. 'Why not? I'm desperate!'

'Because the longer I string it out, the longer you keep coming here to see me.'

'Wicked, wicked man! How can you live with yourself?'

'Quite easily, thank you.' Reluctantly he stood up and held his hand out to her. 'You should go.'

The unspoken spectre of Walter was there between them again.

A thought suddenly struck Lorelei that made her go hot, then cold, and her heart bounce in her chest. 'Are we having an affair?' she asked bluntly. 'Am I as bad as Harriet?'

Julian considered her words carefully as he handed the teapot over; then he answered. 'No. We're not having an affair. Because affairs don't mean anything.'

'Well what are we doing?' she asked.

Julian fixed his dark eyes on her and she felt herself tumble, mesmerised, into their depths. 'We're falling in love,' he told her simply. 'At least I am.'

'Me too,' she whispered. 'Me too.'

She looked far too happy as she ran up the path to the Hall. Her cheeks were flushed and her damn hair was flying loose, damp and curling with the summer storm. Thank God he'd come back early, right in the middle of that rainstorm, and been able to catch her doing this. His suspicions were correct. She was a whore, through and through.

Revolting.

He had a good idea where she'd been. He just didn't know what she'd done, but he could imagine it.

He closed his eyes.

Oh, God. Yes. He could imagine it.

Lorelei smiled and chatted her way through the dinner party, her mind mulling over the events of the afternoon. She had put the little teapot in her sitting room, on the window sill, and now acted her part flawlessly as Lady Scarsdale.

Walter had excused himself at some point during the evening, leaving her alone with his business associates for a good twenty minutes or so. He returned, his face flushed and his brow furrowed and took his seat without a word. Lorelei did not particularly care. It was a shame he'd come home at all. If he was in one of his dark moods, then she would at least be safe from his company for the rest of the evening. He could sit in his own room and ponder the likelihood of smuggling ships through his damned telescope.

She was, however, not to be so lucky.

After the guests had left, Lorelei climbed the stairs to her room, desperate to get her evening gown off and brush her hair out. She would have had a million carpet picnics with Julian rather than even just one more of Walter's business ordeals, but ...

'What the hell is this?' Walter was at the top of the stairs, waiting for her.

'Walter? What is what?' asked Lorelei, startled. Instinctively, she moved away from the top of the stairs. Whatever it was, if he lashed out, she was liable to topple backwards and she had no intention of plunging to her doom in Sea Scarr Hall that night.

'This. This … *thing*.'

She realised he was holding something in his hand – no, *brandishing* something.

And she realised that the "thing" was her teapot. Her little rose-patterned teapot that Julian had returned to her this afternoon.

'It's my teapot!' She stared at Walter, wondering if he had gone mad.

'It's not *your* teapot,' he thundered. 'It's a piece of tat I had sent to the Dower House for the use of paying guests. It's not good enough to be in here. Like you!'

'Like *me*?' Lorelei was horrified, but she didn't know whether she felt more violated by his words or the fact that he had entered her sitting room and poked around to find something tenuously incriminating. 'Walter, what the *hell* do you mean by likening me to a *teapot*?' The words were out before she could stop them and Walter's face turned puce. His eyes were almost popping out of his head and spittle was forming in the corners of his mouth. If she hadn't been so terrified, she would have laughed.

'I'm pointing out that you can't hide what you are,' he growled. 'You're a filthy whore and you've been with that man Cooper or whatever he calls himself.'

'I'm not a whore!' cried Lorelei. 'I wish you would stop calling me one. Whatever I was before I was married doesn't even mean anything. And all I did was model! For artists!'

'You slept with men. You are diseased and disgusting and—'

'I'm *not*!' Lorelei was crying now.

'You *are*!' Walter suddenly turned and smashed the teapot against the wall. It shattered and he was left with a lethal looking shard in his hand.

Instantly, he brought it down onto her forearm, slashing her almost from elbow to wrist.

Lorelei cried out in pain and shock as blood beaded up to the surface of her skin.

'Next time, it's your face,' he hissed. He threw the shard at her and she managed to duck out of the way as it bounced off the wall, before she raced along the corridor and locked herself, shaking and sobbing, in the sitting room.

Down on the cove, a little light glowed in the window of the Dower House and Lorelei thought her heart would break.

It must have been around two o'clock in the morning when Julian was roused from his sleep by a smattering of pebbles against the window.

He'd lit the lamp for her to see after her dinner party, and had been disappointed that no answering light had appeared in the corner of her room. Hey ho. She must have been too busy entertaining the dinner guests.

But a second hail of pebbles had his heart racing, and he was up on his feet hurrying over to the window. He peered down into the darkness and saw a little yellow glow flickering. A white-draped shape was huddled into the wall and he squinted down.

The light flitted across the face of the person holding the light and he wasted no time in flinging the window open. 'Lorelei!'

'Let me in. Oh, let me in, Julian!' she hissed. 'Please!' She looked back at the path and the lamp flickered. She looked strained and tear-stained in the light.

'I'm coming.' He ran down the stairs.

She was in the door almost as soon as he had opened it and fell into his arms sobbing, the lamp discarded on the terrace. 'Oh, God, help me. Help me please. I have to get away from him.'

Julian held her away from him and stared at her. 'Who? From Walter?'

'Yes! Yes, from Walter. Look.'

She held out her arm and Julian saw the cut. 'What the hell? I'll kill him! What did he do?'

'It was the teapot.' She began to giggle, hysterically. 'The teapot. Oh, dear Lord, the teapot. He said it was tat and he smashed it and he did this to me. With my own teapot!'

'You can't stay there. You can't go back.' Julian started looking around him for his clothes. 'I'll go up there now.'

'No! No. It's all right. It's all right. He's gone. He's gone to his mistress's. Phyllis told me he'd gone. I waited to make sure. I thought he'd leave.' She clung onto his arms. 'He always goes there when he does something like this, he—'

'Stay here. Stay here tonight. Nobody can hurt you here and we'll worry about it tomorrow.'

'Yes, yes. I'll stay.' Her voice caught on a sob. 'Thank you.'

'Lorelei, my love—'

He picked her up in his arms and she clung onto him and there were no more words.

It ended in a flurry of bedding and discarded clothing. It ended with her in Julian's arms in the bedroom of the Dower House, feeling his fingers stroke her hair as she drowsed against him, her head on his chest, her arm draped across his warm body.

It ended with the smell of the ocean drifting in through the windows of the Dower House and no thoughts as to what would happen at the end of the summer. Or even what would happen when Walter came home.

It simply ended the way it was meant to – and the way she had dreamed it would end. *Oh, and if only this ending was a new beginning*, she thought in the gathering dawn. A new beginning, she had realised, was needed for them all.

Chapter Twenty-Three

The Beach Hut, Present Day

The beach hut was pale against the dark cliffs and the moon reflected in the high tide, turning the cove into molten silver. They had enjoyed a leisurely dinner in a truly romantic restaurant on the outskirts of Staithes and, perhaps mellowed by the wine she had consumed, Lissy had been happy to carry through Stef's suggestion of a walk on the beach before he headed back to Whitby. They were both barefoot – part of her dreams had now been realised and she thought it ironic to think it had happened here, and not in Cornwall.

'I didn't know how beautiful it was here of an evening.' Stef drew Lissy towards him and she didn't resist. 'You have a wonderful view from the house. And the beach hut. I think it looks very special tonight. There is just something about it. Shall we visit it and see if there is magic there?'

'Magic. That sounds lovely.' She moved closer to him. 'I hope I left our ghost at Sea Scarr. He wasn't scary, exactly, but I don't think he needs to bother us down here again, do you?'

Stef looked at her curiously. 'So you think he *was* a ghost then. I wasn't far behind you, and I too felt a presence.'

'Well, I don't want to dwell on it. Whatever it was up there, I'm glad we ran away.' Lissy shivered. 'I felt we were intruding. Come on, take my mind off it. Let's go and look for magic in the beach hut. Although I don't know what I'd expect to find in there that's magical. It's such a tiny little place.' They had arrived at the small white building, and Stef held her hand now, presumably so she didn't dash off ahead.

'I'll show you it all,' said Stef smiling. 'But you have to close your eyes.'

'Really?' She looked up at him. 'What for?'

'Because if you don't, it will simply spoil the magic.'

Lissy did as he'd asked and was aware of his rough hand on hers as the door clicked open. He guided her inside the little building, and she breathed in the faint salty smell of the beach mingled with the woody tones of the painted furniture. She was aware, also, of a fizzing that she hadn't felt for so long; the electricity that was sparking back into life through her body, through her skin, as she sensed how close he was to her.

There was a tiny *click* from somewhere to her left, then he spoke: 'There, *mia cara*. You may look.' His voice was a whisper in her ear, and she felt a tingling down the side of her cheek as his breath touched her. 'Your magic. All yours.'

She opened her eyes and was unable to move.

All around the place were twinkling lights – ropes and ropes of them, shining like little stars, draped over the picture rails and strung from the ceiling; running across the back of the couch and wound up between the banisters of the staircase, all the way up to the mezzanine floor and continuing along it.

'Pretty, yes?' asked Stef. Lissy turned towards him, astonished to see that he looked embarrassed and unsure. He was, almost, like a little boy shuffling from side to side, waiting for approval.

The idea was so incongruous that Lissy found herself half-laughing, half-crying. 'You did this for me?'

'I did,' replied Stef. 'But that isn't all. Come with me.' He took her hand and drew her into the tiny lounge. On the couch, the couch that Grace had been playing on, was a wicker hamper. 'Open it. Go on, It's for you also.'

'What is it?' asked Lissy.

'Only the very best. Fortnum and Mason's best. And it includes your favourite champagne and your floral hot chocolate – I asked them to make it up specially.'

'Stef!' Lissy was stunned. 'I can't believe you did this!'

Stef shrugged. 'I needed to do something.' He guided her gently to the seat, and produced two crystal glasses out of the hamper. The twinkly lights hit off the engravings on the glasses, and bounced sparkles around the room. 'I can't just follow you around and annoy you and hope you take the time to notice me.'

There was a satisfying *pop* as the cork came out of the champagne and Stef poured two drinks. He handed one to Lissy and she hesitated for a second before burying her nose in the glass, as she always did, enjoying the fizzy sound and the sensation of the bubbles bursting against her nose.

'Can I interest you in a chocolate truffle?' he asked, ever so politely, 'or a biscuit?'

Lissy giggled, shakily. 'Either would be perfect. I think I've walked off my dinner by now. But really. What have you done all of this for? What are you trying to prove?'

'I'm trying to prove that I still love you.' His eyes burned into hers, and she found she couldn't look away. The twinkly lights were reflected in his irises and she blinked, mesmerised. 'I never stopped loving you,' he continued, 'so I'm also trying to say that I'm sorry and I was very stupid and I have suffered from that stupidity for seven years. Kerensa and I are no longer together, as I told you. It was never meant to last, I could see that, and I realised very soon after she came to live with me that it was not right. But I was stubborn and I couldn't admit that to anybody properly; not even to myself. And in my heart, I was punishing you for ending it with me, for refusing to listen to me, but you had every right – every right on earth to do what you did. I behaved disgracefully and I've paid for it ever since.'

Lissy stiffened. 'Did you marry her? Because if you married her—'

'No!' Stef held his hands up in his defence, shaking his

head vehemently. 'No. I didn't marry her. We talked about marriage, and I kept making excuses not to get married. But it was when she began to mention children that I realised I couldn't go on with it. Elisabetta, it is embarrassing and I will forever hate myself, but it is done. It is finished.'

'So – when did you split up exactly?' asked Lissy, almost dreading his response.

'Last year.'

The answer surprised her and she checked herself. 'Last year? So you've had time to think about it? You haven't just done this on the rebound?'

'I almost did,' admitted Stef. He looked away. 'But I talked myself out of it. I told myself it would not be fair on you to jump out of her bed and into yours and I made myself stay in Italy. But I couldn't stop thinking about you. Then eventually, I swallowed my stupid pride and asked your brother for advice.' Suddenly, he grinned and looked back at her. His gaze was like a jolt of adrenalin as he continued to speak. 'Jon told me he was going to do this project with his friend Simon, and I invited myself to Whitby. Between us, we concocted this story of my helping him out. But really, he helped *me* out.'

'How?' Lissy was staring at him, hypnotised by his voice as he tried to explain what had happened. She'd barely noticed that he had slipped into his native tongue and she was answering, just as fluently, in Italian.

'Who do you think prepared all of this for me?' he whispered, indicating the lights. 'And the hamper had to be delivered somewhere, didn't it?' There was a smile hovering around his lips, and Lissy thought back to the day they'd just passed.

'When?' she asked. 'When did Jon do it?'

'When we were out today. That was why I received that call in Staithes. I wanted to know it had all happened, and he rang to tell me it was almost done, and could I just tell him where the champagne glasses should go. No wonder I looked guilty!'

'But Becky didn't say!'

'Becky didn't know,' said Stef. 'I knew she'd tell you and I wanted it to be a surprise. She thinks he's been doing a location shoot today. She'll know by now it was an untruth but I'm sure, under the circumstances, she will forgive him. Lissy, you have killed me these last few years. Not a day has gone by when I haven't thought about you or wondered how I could contact you. I had to do it somehow, I had to try and win you back. I had to let your heart speak to you in the moment and tell you what it wanted.'

'I can't believe Jon did all this and said nothing. I can't believe you planned all this! Sometimes, I could hate you, Stef, I really could. I hated you that day in Cornwall.'

'I know. Looking back, I hate myself. But if you'd only let me explain that day, it wouldn't have been too late. Nothing had really happened then. Still, no point thinking about it now. But what about tonight?' Stef lowered his voice and moved closer to her. 'Do you hate me tonight, Elisabetta?' He bent his head down to her upturned face and brushed her lips with his.

'No,' replied Lissy quietly. 'I don't hate you tonight. I think I love you – I absolutely do. I don't think I've ever stopped loving you. I wasn't admitting what we had to myself at all. I told people you were a summer fling, I kept saying it meant nothing and I danced off with other men, just to prove a point. But nobody could hold me – not one person.

'I know people think I'm vain and shallow and brittle, but none of those men meant anything. I'm an awful person, I really am. I kept saying I didn't care and Becky despaired of me, and even Simon, when he got to know me. He told me I had to accept that you and I were meant for one another.

God knows what Cori would have made of it all if I'd taken the time to keep in touch with her after Uni. Only I didn't and that's another awful thing about me. But I'm sure Simon has told her about you anyway.' She laughed, unamused at her failings. 'It was always you. But you see, before I met you, I thought I was in love with someone. Then it turned out he was married and seeing you with her just brought it all back.' She shivered.

That had been another terrible summer – the summer before she met Stef. In her mind, she had cheapened herself by sleeping with a married man. She had accepted his lies and his stories and been taken in by his tales – about how he had left his wife and how they hadn't slept with each other for years and about how she kept the children away from him …

Then she mentioned it to Becky, who asked, quite innocently, why he kept coming to her house and why she'd never been to his home. Why he could only see her at certain times of the week and why she could never contact him by phone.

Looking back, she felt stupid; she felt absolutely ridiculous. How had she not seen it? How had she, Lissy de Luca, been taken in by that? She'd been well and truly fooled by him.

And of course he was married. She'd followed him one evening, and seen him go home to a big, detached house with two cars on the drive and a play-house in the garden. She'd seen a pregnant woman come to the door flanked by a toddler and a school-age child. She'd seen him kiss the woman, and kiss the children, and walk inside laughing.

A bit more research confirmed that it was indeed his wife, and Lissy knew that she, Lissy, was a fool and an idiot and clearly not worthy of a decent relationship.

'You had good cause to be stubborn and hate me,' replied Stef. 'I wasted your time, my time and Kerensa's. I am so sorry.' He laid his forehead against hers and she closed her eyes, feeling his long eyelashes brush her skin as he nuzzled in. She breathed deeply and inhaled the warm, spicy scent of his aftershave.

'I'm very pleased you don't hate me tonight,' he murmured, 'but don't make a decision just yet. Don't forgive me until you see one more thing to prove I love you and I never stopped thinking of you. Shall I show you a picture of a girl in a red dress?'

'A girl in a red dress?' Lissy pulled away and stared at him, images of their perfect summer scrolling through her mind. 'I had a red dress.'

'You did,' replied Stef. 'So would you like to see the picture? Unfortunately, it isn't downstairs. I had to hide it away on Saturday, thank the Lord for my portfolio.'

Lissy felt her lips curl into a smile. 'Is it upstairs?' she asked. 'Upstairs in the bedroom, maybe?'

'I believe it is,' replied Stef, quite seriously. 'I do think that is where I last saw it.'

'Then I think I would like to see it.'

'I think I would too.' He moved away, just far enough so he could stand up, put his glass down and gently remove hers from her grasp. Then he took her by the hand and led the way up the steep little staircase, lit with stars.

In the bedroom, Lissy saw the photograph laid exactly in the middle of the double bed. The red of the model's dress was startling against the crisp, white drifts of sheets and pillows, and she picked the photograph up, holding the frame almost reverently.

It was exactly as he had said; a girl standing on a rocky plateau, staring out to sea. Her hair blew around her face, and the set of her chin was stubborn as she raised her head to the horizon. Far beyond her, the sea stretched out in a sparkling azure carpet, a suggestion of ships bobbing about on the water, and a flock of gulls soaring up into the heavens.

'Do you like it?' Stef asked.

'It's me,' she replied, quietly. 'It's like Harold Knight's *Bathing Pool*. Just like it.' She lifted her hand and traced the figure with her fingertip. 'I look happy,' she said eventually. 'It looks as if nothing can spoil the future.'

'The photograph is indeed full of hope.' Stef took the frame from her and looked at it. He frowned a little as if he was inwardly criticising his work. 'Still, it is one of my best, I think. That and your new Miranda picture.'

'That's because of the model.' Lissy looked up at Stef and felt that yearning grow that she had fought against for seven years. Nobody had ever come close to him. Nobody ever would. She'd spent her time meddling in her friends' relationships and matchmaking like there was no tomorrow – just to stop thinking about what she had failed to achieve for herself. She had built walls, moats and barriers – you name it. Nobody, now, knew the real Lissy; the happy, generous, less-than-perfect girl she was inside. They just knew the apparently spoiled, selfish girl who seemingly craved perfection and order. But she wasn't like that – not really. She was just trying to protect herself. And Stef was the only one who'd ever come close to finding the real Lissy she'd buried so deeply, so many years ago.

She was damned if she went ahead with this, and cursed if she didn't. Stef had once told her he had Gypsy blood somewhere along the line. She didn't know if she had – her father had never told her that was the case – and she couldn't predict the future. She didn't know which way the dice would fall and God knew she didn't have a crystal ball; but was it worth the risk? Was Stef worth the risk?

She made a decision. 'Put the picture down, Stef,' she commanded quietly.

Startled, he obeyed, placing the photograph on the bedside table as Lissy looked up at the skylights and saw the stars framed perfectly in the glass rectangles. 'Starlight,' she said. 'Rossetti's old *Sea Spell* planisphere is all above us. His star chart. It makes me feel very insignificant.'

'Insignificant?' Stef moved towards her, and lifted a length of hair from her forehead. He brushed it to one side, letting his hand linger for a moment. 'You could never be insignificant.'

'We are all insignificant compared to that place up there,' said Lissy, her attention not at all on the stars anymore. 'We can see constellations and galaxies and other worlds from here. It makes whatever we do down here seem like it matters very little.'

'It matters to me,' Stef traced the curve of her shoulder and ran his finger down her arm. The sensations shot fireworks around her body. 'It matters so much. It matters that I lost you for seven years.'

His hand had found her waist and was drawing her closer to him, her hands reaching out for him, her body answering his. Lissy found that it mattered very much to her too, although there was no longer any time or space for words.

Chapter Twenty-Four

Sea Scarr Hall, 1905

Dearest Lorelei,

I hate London. The parties are hideous and the company is worse. If I wanted someone who brayed, I would have fallen for a donkey.

I'm so envious of you, dear Lorelei. You were never forced into too-tight corsets and you never had to suffer boned collars in your day dresses so your head was held up nice and straight. The young ladies down here barely eat, because their gowns are as confined as the circles they move in. They are forever found sobbing in the corners because the young man they have set their sights on is now 'attached' to their best friend through no fault of their own. And it all happens so jolly quickly as well! I really feel I am at a meat market.

I want to come back to Yorkshire. I want to come back to you, dear Lorelei. And to Archie. Nobody down here can hold a candle to him.

Fondest regards,
Florrie

Lorelei smiled when she read the letter, then folded it up and put it to one side, ready to respond to later. Florrie wasn't a happy girl, but, as a young lady of her class, she had to put up with it. Lorelei would be sympathetic and agree with her, but she had to stay there, despite all her protestations. She was homesick, that's all.

Lorelei instead prepared to spend the day with Julian.

He called for her, very properly, at the Hall and suggested he take her into town to hunt for members of the Staithes Group. There was no need for anyone to know that she had sneaked back into the Hall, just as dawn broke. Her body ached deliciously in a way it hadn't for a long, long time, and she flitted through the deserted corridors, keeping to the shadows like a ghost, praying that she wouldn't encounter any servants on her way. And this morning, this beautiful morning, her prayers had been answered and she had managed to creep into her room, unnoticed by anyone at all.

'You make the Group sound like rabbits!' Lorelei laughed delightedly as Julian stood in the foyer, his hands in his pockets and his feet planted squarely apart. He had his suit on today – the one he had worn for the ball – and she thought he looked positively edible in it. Even more so, because she now had a very clear image in her mind of what lay beneath that suit and the thought made her go hot and cold and pine for more of the same.

'Not quite rabbits. More elusive than rabbits,' he replied. Lorelei pulled her veiled hat on and tied it with a scarf, excited beyond belief. Walter was still missing, so that was wonderful, and she prayed that he would spend another night with Harriet. In fact, she prayed that he would decide to spend *all* of his time with Harriet and leave her the hell alone.

It would be even better if he were to divorce her.

And so, here they were, in Staithes, pleasantly full after enjoying tea and cakes in a small tea shop in the town. Lorelei had pointed out Roraima House, a delightful three storey house built about ten years ago by the Sea Captain John Trattles and named after his steamship, the SS *Roraima*, and in return Julian had pointed out the cobbles and the fishermen's cottages and the way the houses huddled together in the streets as if they were sheltering from a storm.

These were all things Lorelei knew of and had noticed of course, but it was different having Julian with her. He made her look at them – really *look* at them – and then told her stories about the artists and how he had met with some of them and how that had spurred on his interest to come here.

'Of course,' he whispered to her as he refilled her tea cup, 'it all pales into insignificance now I've met you, Lady Scarsdale.' Lorelei giggled and accepted the cup.

Then she became serious. 'Julian, is what we are doing so very wrong?' she asked. 'I mean, to all intents and purposes I *am* a married woman. But part of me says "what's sauce for the goose is sauce for the gander".' She compressed her lips and stared into the tea cup.

Then she sighed. The Yorkshire girl was back.

'I don't really know when I sold myself down the river, Julian. I didn't love him when we married, but he could be quite charming at times. I thought by living at the Hall I could take up my painting again and drift around quite happily. But it's not enough. I think I was trying to escape my past. You know all about my history – and so does he, now.' She blushed and frowned. 'So I was never going to be an angel, was I? Maybe it's just me. Perhaps I expected too much of myself.'

'Your past doesn't matter to me, and neither does your present. I would like to be part of your future though. But I fear that may not be entirely possible either. That saddens me somewhat.'

'I wish you could live in the Dower House permanently.'

'Me too. But I have a home and a business in Scotland, in Edinburgh, and I have to go back there eventually.' He looked genuinely upset. 'I wish you could come with me.'

Lorelei said nothing. If she allowed the possibilities to take flight and carry her away, she might as well leap upon the man in the tea shop and let him have his wicked way with her right there and then. Both of those options seemed delightful – but not very well timed.

'Anyway,' Julian's voice brought her back to the present. 'I have something for you. I have to go and collect it, and I can't allow you to come with me. So I will, if I may, leave you here with another pot of tea and another slice of sponge cake, and I shall hurry back. Oh. And I have this for you as well. You can ponder it whilst I am away.'

He rummaged around in the breast pocket of his jacket and handed her a small, flat package wrapped in brown paper and tied up with string.

'What's this?' Lorelei looked down at the package and then back at him. But he was standing up, ready to leave. He winked at her and smiled. She was pleased she was sitting down as her legs suddenly felt very unsteady.

'Open it and see. I shan't be long. Just count up to fifty to make sure I've disappeared first.' And with that, he slipped out of the building.

Lorelei watched him striding down the street until he was out of sight and was ridiculously happy that she had chosen a window seat. Then she turned her attention to the package.

The paper was stiff and Lorelei had to pick at the string a little to loosen the knot, but when she unfolded that paper – well. She was utterly, utterly speechless.

Inside the package was a photograph – it was the first one Julian had taken of her on the rock; the very first one. She was sitting on the thing dressed in that medieval gown, tendrils of hair escaping from her plait. She had her arms wrapped around her knees and she was smiling at the camera. Or, more to the point, there was a little secret smile playing around her lips which was directed more at the cameraman than the camera.

'Oh, God!' She clapped one of her hands over her mouth. 'It's me. That's really me.' She looked up and glanced around the tea shop, horribly aware that people might be staring at her and wondering why her cheeks were on fire and why her hands were shaking so much.

Lorelei flipped the photograph over and saw the words *LS by JMC*. Julian had written that message neatly on the back of it, deliberately she thought, so that she could at least pretend Mrs Cameron – whose initials were the same – had been the photographer. Another little secret they could share between them.

'Oh, Julian,' she whispered. She looked up again and was surprised to see that nobody had, in actual fact, taken any notice of her. She felt her cheeks flush once more and she wrapped the photograph back up and thrust it into the little bag which hung from her wrist. It fit perfectly.

She moved the chair back with a very loud scraping noise and a waitress appeared out of nowhere.

'Can I help, miss?' the girl asked.

'I ... um ... I think I want to pay,' replied Lorelei, surprising both herself and the girl. The girl's eyes widened – so much was charged to accounts that ladies did not generally pay for much at all.

'Aren't you waiting for the gentleman to come back, miss?'

'Ah – no. No, I shan't, thank you. I will just pay,' said Lorelei. It felt strange being independent again. She quite liked it. 'In fact,' she continued expansively, 'let me make it clear that I am paying for us both.' She smiled confidently at the waitress and stood straighter. Yes, that had shocked her, hadn't it?

'Very well, miss.' The girl looked at her curiously. 'Let me just get the bill for you.'

'Thank you.' Lorelei followed the girl to the cash register. She had a feeling that was not allowed either, but she felt ridiculously free. It was that photograph, wasn't it? Julian had shown her the real Lorelei again, not the one who lived by society's rules in that gilded cage by the coast.

She took a few coins from the bag and gave them to the girl then hurried out of the tea shop. She dashed to the end of the street where she had seen him disappear, then realised that was where her plan of independence had failed her. Where on earth was he? Now she understood why he had told her to stay put. The road turned both left and right and—

'Lorelei!'

She swung bodily to the right and saw him hurrying down the street towards her, with that now-familiar loping stride and the ever-present camera-case slung across his body.

'Julian!' She couldn't help it – she called back and didn't care who heard her. She raised her gloved hand and waved at him, then waited until he approached her.

He flew at her and somehow his arms were around her and she was giggling and he pulled her into a side street.

'The photograph—' she began, but then suddenly there were no words, just his lips on hers and the sound of the seagulls crying far, far above them.

Julian pulled away first, his gaze travelling over every inch of her incredible face. When he had seen her there looking so alone, the urge to take her away from Sea Scarr Hall and Staithes and that vile husband of hers was so strong, he knew he was lost.

'What are we going to do?' he whispered, lifting his hand and running his thumb down the side of her face. 'I just know I can't leave here in a few weeks' time and go back to Scotland without you.'

'Oh, God, don't talk about it!' moaned Lorelei. She closed her eyes and leaned into him. His arms came around her and she fit so perfectly into the sphere of his being that he refused to think of a future where they were parted. 'I want to come with you, I do, but he'll find me. He'll come after me and he'll know.'

'Then the answer is simple. We can't go together, can we?' said Julian. 'I leave first, we have a torturous few weeks where we plan your escape, then you follow me. You could go first, but you don't know where I live and the servants might wonder why a mermaid had turned up on my doorstep.'

'Servants?' Lorelei pulled away and looked at him. 'You have servants?'

Julian laughed. 'Don't look so shocked. I might not be as wealthy as Walter, but I do all right. Did you think I lived hand to mouth in a garret somewhere?'

'I don't know what I thought. You don't seem ...' Her voice trailed off and she looked flustered.

'I'm not an arrogant, stuck-up prig like Walter?' he asked, smiling down at her. He pushed a tendril of hair away from her cheek so he could see her better. 'As I said, I do all right. I live in a reasonably large house in Edinburgh New Town overlooking Queen Street Gardens and I have a cook who is also my housekeeper. I have two maids and a butler. Can you live with so few staff, darling Lorelei?'

'I think I probably could.' She smiled back. 'It's more staff than I had when I was modelling.'

'It's perfect, then,' replied Julian. He dropped a kiss on the top of her nose. 'Now, if we are both serious, this will take a lot of planning.'

'Oh, I'm deadly serious.' Lorelei frowned into the distance. 'The thought of living with *him* for the rest of my life. No. I simply can't.'

'I'm serious as well. My worry is that your life would be considerably shortened if I left you there. And to show you how serious I am ...' His heart started beating much faster and much louder and he was aware that there was a little crack in his voice. 'I got you this to remember me by until we can be together properly.' His hand dipped into his breast pocket and he pulled out a tiny box. 'It's yours,' he said, knowing he must be scarlet by now, 'as a friendship ring to start with. It's yours for as long as you want it.'

Lorelei's stare moved from Julian's face to the box and back again, confusion and shock rendering her speechless for a moment. 'May I open it?' she asked eventually.

'Of course.' He handed it over and noticed that both their hands were shaking. Lorelei must have noticed it too. She stared at her hand as she held the box and laughed. 'God, what have you done to me today? I shook like a leaf in that tea shop when I opened the package. And I'm doing it again.'

'I don't know.' He caught her hand and brought it to his lips. 'Is that better? Because I don't know what I've done to you but God knows what I *want* to do to you. I should maybe have done this at the cove. It was probably more appropriate for the way I'm feeling.'

'And me,' she whispered. Then she gently extricated her hand and opened the box. 'Oh, my!' Her eyes became round in her face. 'It's beautiful. How did you ...' She let the words drift away and took the ring out of the box.

'Do you see the pattern?' Julian asked. 'I took a photograph, remember? Then I developed it and took it into a jeweller's and asked if that sort of pattern could be made into a ring and then I put the order straight in. I think he's done a beautiful job, don't you?'

Lorelei nodded and then peered at the stone. 'It's a diamond!' she exclaimed. She pulled her glove off and made to slip the ring onto the third finger of her right hand.

'Allow me,' said Julian.

She laughed and dropped the ring into his palm. 'As you wish!'

'Thank you. This, my love, is to recognise a special kind of friendship.' Julian slid it onto her finger and for a moment, his heart jumped as she caught his hand and their fingers entwined briefly before she reluctantly disconnected them.

She held her hand up and tilted it this way and that so the stone caught the light. 'I don't want to wear it on this hand,' she said quietly. 'I want it on my other hand.'

'One day,' replied Julian. 'One day, I promise you will be able to wear it there.'

'It's just not the right time, is it?' she said sadly.

Julian realised her eyes were shining too, glistening with unshed tears. 'It's not,' he replied, equally sadly, 'but we will know when it is.'

'Yes. Indeed, we will,' she answered. 'And until then, it will stay on this hand.'

The Road to Staithes, 1905

It was the hair that made him look twice. The woman had a hat on with a little veil and a scarf tying it to her head, but he had caught a glimpse of the midnight blue-black shimmer of her chignon at the back. Everything about her – the height, the bearing, the build – suggested it was his wife. And that man she had been with – louche, disreputable, too long hair ... it looked awfully like that Cooper man.

Walter, travelling back from his mistress's in an anonymous black carriage, slammed back in his seat and clenched his fists. That hair – that hair was what had attracted him to begin with. She used to wear it loose and he used to like it when she rode him, and trailed it across his naked flesh, laughing as he begged her to continue.

Now he hated it. He hated it when it escaped from its style. He hated it when a pin came undone or a curl escaped. He hated it when she tried to push it back into order. He hated it because it reminded him of his weakness and his desire. She was a whore. But more than that, she had ensnared him. She had woven a spell around him like a bitch on heat and he had sniffed around her until she had reeled him in.

God, he hated *her*.

And he loathed the fact that even now, as he laid his head back against the seat and groaned away his desire, he still saw her face laughing into his and her hair trailing across his torso. He couldn't stand the fact that his most base instincts still craved her body.

He had to make it stop. He had to let her know – let her and her disgusting lover know – he knew about them. And then he would beat an apology out of her to make sure it never happened again.

Chapter Twenty-Five

The Dower House, Present Day

There was a knock on the door of the Dower House and Lissy, hearing it from upstairs, leaned out of the window and saw Stef standing there, his camera slung around his neck as usual.

He raised his hand to rap once more and she shouted down to him. 'It's open! You should have just tried it!'

Stef looked up and his beloved, handsome face broke into a grin. 'Aha! I didn't want to just walk in on you. It might have been an embarrassing moment.'

Lissy laughed. 'There's nothing embarrassing going on in here. Did you bring your luggage?'

'I did. I've checked out of the B & B, and everything is in my car.'

'One of the rooms up here is going to be ideal for your studio,' Lissy replied. 'It's got the best view and one of those funny little sconces we saw up at the Hall. I'm desperately hoping it's the one that would light the way for the smugglers. Hold on. I'm coming down.'

She withdrew and hurried down the staircase, meeting Stef as he walked in through the front door. He caught her when she ran towards him and picked her up, swinging her around as she clung on, laughing.

'Are you sure that this will be all right?' he asked, finally setting her down with a kiss.

'More than all right,' she agreed. 'The lease is mine for the summer. Nothing says I can't invite a friend around.'

'A friend?' Stef raised his eyebrows. 'Is that all we are?'

Lissy blushed and looked away. 'We're maybe a little more than friends.'

'Maybe,' he said. 'Anyway – would you do me one favour, please?'

Lissy looked at him in surprise. 'Of course. What is it? Do you need some help bringing the equipment in?'

'I will later. But before that, would you mind walking up to the Hall with me again? I have been in touch with my friend and he asked would I be kind enough to take some photographs of the derelict building. We don't need to go inside, don't look such a scaredy-cat!'

'But how is he going to see what it's like if we don't go inside?' asked Lissy.

'Well *you* don't need to go inside, but maybe I do,' amended Stef. 'Anyway, I would like the company, *si*?'

'All right.' Lissy reluctantly pulled on a pair of trainers and tugged her camisole down to meet the top of her shorts. 'I'm ready, I suppose.'

'Good.' Stef took her hand and squeezed it. 'I really don't think it's such a horrible place, you know. I will look after you, I'm here now.'

'I just keep thinking of the things we saw up there,' said Lissy as they left the Dower House.

'Shadows, nothing more,' replied Stef and raised her hand to kiss it.

Lissy moved closer to him, and soon they were strolling up to the ruin, their arms around each other.

'I'd like to see around the back of the house,' mused Stef. 'I would like to try and get a few shots from that direction. The angle of the afternoon sun helps, I think.'

'Whatever you want, but I'm running away if I see anything odd again.'

'I can catch you though. You only have little legs.'

Lissy laughed. 'It's not my fault I'm short!'

'Good things come in small packages,' said Stef, quite seriously.

'So does poison. I've been told that one before. You know, like Circe and her jealous love.'

She cast a glance up to him, but he merely shrugged and kept his eyes fixed on the Hall as they approached it. 'Circe? Who is Circe? I've never heard that name before. Here we are! Around the back, I think. Yes, let's get it done immediately.'

He guided her around the edge of the building and as they took the corner, Lissy came to a sudden halt. 'What's that?' she demanded.

In the centre of the lawn, beneath an ancient, gnarled tree, was a rusted old wrought iron table and two chairs, equally in a state of disrepair. On the table was a flask and a white box.

'It seems to be a picnic of sorts – or maybe an afternoon tea,' said Stef, feigning surprise. 'Shall we investigate?'

Lissy held back. 'Did you do this? Where did you get the furniture?'

'Oh, I could never hide much from you, could I? Yes, I did do this, and I found the furniture in one of the old outbuildings. It has all seen better days, but it seemed a shame to leave it in there. Don't worry, I gave it all a good clean before I brought you here. I know how you dislike grubby things – like your poor niece.'

'I don't dislike her! I love Grace! But one must admit that she does attract the dirt. So—' Lissy took her hand out of Stef's and moved forward. 'A flask and a box. I presume it's a box of cake?'

'From a good old-fashioned bakery in Whitby. I had to queue for a long time to get served. It is a very, very popular place.'

Lissy just shook her head. 'And dare I ask what's in the flask?'

'Hmm. Well it's not champagne, as I think tea goes better

with cake. It's a very English thing. I tried to put hot chocolate in, but it just resulted in a gloopy mess. I'm sorry.'

Lissy burst out laughing. 'Tea is fine. Shall I get pouring and you can start your photos?'

Stef raised his camera and framed the table. 'I can start right now. And to be honest, I took plenty of photographs earlier when I came to set this up. We can just enjoy the tea and cake. I thought you could pretend you were Lady Scarsdale.'

'Simply delighted to be her.' Lissy dropped a beautiful curtsey.

Stef laughed and followed her to the table. He placed his camera on the surface, then pulled one of the chairs out for her.

As she sat down, he took the opposite seat. 'I'll unscrew the flask,' he said. 'You open the cakes. You can choose which one you prefer.'

'Anything that involves chocolate and cream will always be my first choice.' She lifted the lid of the box eagerly.

A wedge of chocolate cake greeted her, along with a slice of strawberry gateau, and she was about to comment on them, when she spotted something else. 'Oh! What's this?' She pointed at a small package, wrapped up in a paper napkin.

'Oh – that,' responded Stef. 'It's for you.'

'Really? Can I open it?'

'You can. I just hope it's not sticky.'

'It's not, it's well wrapped, whatever it is.' She unfolded the napkin and the world seemed to stand still. A battered red leather box, embossed with a jeweller's name in gold lettering revealed itself. 'Stef!' Lissy looked up and saw that Stef had slid from the wrought iron chair to the grass and was, even now, on one knee, looking up at her.

'Please? Open the box, *cara mia*.'

Lissy began to shake. 'Is it what I think it is?' she whispered, the years rolling back to Cornwall and an antiques dealer and a ring.

'I don't know what you are thinking,' replied Stef, 'but if you open the box it might help.'

Lissy nodded, speechless, and lifted the lid.

On a faded, red velvet cushion was a platinum ring. The centre was a solitaire diamond: a round, brilliant circle which, when you tilted it, would look like a glorious diamond spinning-top from the side. It was Edwardian and Old European cut and the shoulders were set with filigree leaves and flowers and what looked like tiny waves cresting over the decorations.

'Stef ...'

'If you don't want it to be an engagement ring, that is perfectly fine,' Stef said hurriedly. Lissy looked at him. Even when she had caught him with that girl, even after everything that she had thrown at him this summer, she had never seen him look so unsure of himself. This was a man who didn't know what was coming next. This man was terrified.

'It can be a friendship ring,' he continued. 'I went back to the shop the day we saw it and bought it for you then.' He made to stand up, his face flushed. 'I don't know what I'm doing down here at all. I think I may have dropped a lens or something—'

'Stef! Stop it.' Lissy didn't know whether to laugh or cry. 'Tell me what you are really doing down there, or I promise I shall leave you kneeling there in misery.'

'Honestly?' Stef fixed dark eyes on hers.

'Honestly,' she replied.

Stef took a deep breath. 'Lissy, I want to marry you. That is as honest as I can get. Will you do me the honour of being my wife? Not right now or not next month, and not even next year, not if you don't want to. Just tell me that sometime in our future, I can be your husband, your lover, the father, perhaps of your children. It is all I have ever wanted, ever since I met you. And now, now I think I might be in a position to ask you.' He looked down at the grass. 'I am certainly in the correct position by kneeling, I think. But if you feel it should be different, then—'

'Stop it. Just stop it.' Before she could think, she was on her knees before him, his face in her hands. 'Kiss me. Just kiss me. That will help me decide.'

'It can be a friendship ring, truly. If that is all you want, take it as that. Take it as—'

'Shut up, Stef.' She pulled his face towards her and kissed him.

It felt right to have the ring now. It was its time and its place. It felt right to be with Stef, on the lawn, in front of Sea Scarr Hall, the tiny box between them.

'It's not going to be a friendship ring,' she murmured as she pulled away. 'Not at all. I don't want to waste any more time without you.' She pointed at the box. 'It's your turn now, Stefano Ricci. You have to do this next bit.'

Stef stared at her as if he had never seen her before. 'Oh, my love,' he whispered as she held her left hand out and splayed her fingers. He picked up the box and took the ring out. A ray of sunlight suddenly caught the diamond, sparking iridescent rainbows across the lawn and over the rusted white table. Lissy squinted as the gleam caught her unawares and looked away briefly, blinking. For a moment, out of the corner of her eye, the Hall was no longer a ruin, the table not rusted. The unkempt grass wasn't cold beneath her bare knees, and her skin was protected by an ivory skirt. Her eyes were shaded by a cartwheel brimmed hat. The Hall was sturdy and thriving with people, laughter floated across the gardens.

But then, the images disappeared and she was back on her knees, in front of the man she loved; the man she had always loved.

And the ring fitted perfectly.

The Dower House, 1905

'Stop the carriage!' Walter rapped on the window and the carriage drew to a halt. He climbed out and threw some money at the driver, before sending him on his way.

The horses whinnied and their hoofbeats echoed as they disappeared into the distance, whilst Walter stood and surveyed the Dower House from the carriage drive.

'I shall find out, and I shall destroy you both,' he promised, and strode down to the little building overlooking the cove.

The fool had left the door unlocked, which made it much easier. He flung it open and stopped in the hallway, listening out for any sounds. It was silent. Walter looked at the staircase and felt his craving for her grow. He caught his breath, imagining her up there, coupling with that man. His eyelids fluttered briefly, then he focussed on the steps and began to climb them.

He prowled around the entire upstairs, sniffing the air, checking for her scent, hoping he would see her naked and— NO!

He turned and headed back downstairs, checking out room after room, scanning the place for a ribbon or a shoe or a petticoat or— NO!

His desire mounting, he pushed open the final door and stood stock still.

'You bastard!' he yelled. He raced over to a collection of photographic plates and grabbed them, staring at them, his eyes raking them, his breath coming faster and faster. It was her, in black and white, burned forever into a glass plate. She mocked him with her filth and her promiscuousness, her mouth full and sensuous, her body sleek and taut ... 'You disgust me!' He shouted at one of the plates. 'You both disgust me!'

He turned and stormed out of the room, the plates in his hands. He arranged them on a table in the stairwell and, his breathing ragged, stared at them, imagining what she— NO!

Tearing his gaze away from the pictures, he caught sight of a gun propped up by the coat stand.

Without pausing, without thinking about how his own body was reacting to the static images, he grabbed the weapon, took aim, and fired.

It was early evening by the time Lorelei and Julian returned to the cove. They had taken a carriage to the top of the cliff path and walked the rest of the way down.

Lorelei slipped at one point and Julian grabbed her to stop her tumbling down – and then, he told her, it just didn't seem necessary to let her go. She looked up at him, laughing, and agreed. So they wandered down the path in the cooling air, hand in hand, secluded from anybody who may have chanced to see them; like Walter.

Lorelei hoped again that Walter had stayed with Harriet. She would know soon enough. If there was a message from him about an imagined storm or a lame horse or whatever nonsense he trotted out this time, then she was determined to come back down to the Dower House and spend as much of the evening with Julian as she could.

She was just about to voice this plan to Julian, when she saw the front door of the Dower House swinging open and she stopped dead in her tracks.

'Julian! Did you leave the door open this morning?' she asked, pointing to it.

'The door?' Julian followed the direction of her finger and shook his head. 'No. I made sure it was shut properly. It's a wee bit stiff, so I gave it a good tug and made sure it was secure. There was a seagull inside three nights ago, so I determined to make sure of it ever since. Those damn birds get everywhere. I did leave it unlocked, because I didn't suspect anyone would come down here, but clearly I was wrong.' He frowned. 'It's definitely open.'

'It's because we are so near Staithes. The seagulls love the fishing boats, but someone *must* have been in – it's wide open!' Lorelei's stomach lurched a little. 'Oh, Julian! I hope they haven't stolen anything.'

'I'll bloody kill them if they have! I *never* bother locking it!' He took off at a jog and Lorelei hitched up her skirts and hurried after him. She was confident there were no thieves around here, but she had such a bad feeling about this ...

The sound of Julian cursing moments after he barged into the Dower House made her run even faster. She clip-clopped up the wooden steps in her sturdy, buttoned up boots and came up behind him.

'Look! Just look what they did!' he shouted. He jabbed his finger in the direction of the staircase. Lined up on the small table in the stairwell were the three negative glass plates that showed Lorelei sitting on the rock. Or, more to the point, there were the shattered remains of the three negative glass plates that showed Lorelei sitting on the rock.

Each plate had been decimated by a shotgun. And there were three holes in the wall behind the table to prove it, along with a gun that had been tossed on the floor.

'They even used my own shot gun! Bloody hell. I brought it with me in case there was shooting or hunting around here and I had a fear that I might be expected to attend a shooting party. *God*! What else have they done?'

He began to storm off towards the drawing room where Lorelei knew the bulk of his equipment was – but she reached out and touched his shoulder. He swung around and stared at her, a challenge in his eyes.

'They won't have done anything else.' Lorelei's voice was flat. 'It was Walter. I know it was him. And I guarantee that those are the only things he has destroyed. He hated me being a model. Said it corrupted me. Maybe he's right. He wouldn't want to think I was doing it again.'

'What? Well, I'll kill the bastard!' raged Julian. 'Right here. Right now. Just let me go to the Hall and—' He bent over and picked up his gun. There was an ominous click as Julian cocked the thing and began to stalk out of the house. Lorelei shrank back a little, suddenly scared. Julian was furious – she did not rate Walter's chances should he catch him.

'No. Julian, please,' she shouted. 'You can't go up there. You can't go to the Hall, you simply can't. If you did kill him, what on earth would we do then? You'd be hung or something and I couldn't cope with that.'

Julian paused and looked at her. 'I don't care what he does to me or what the consequences are. I care about *you*. I'm worried that when you go back there, he'll hurt *you*. I can't let that happen.'

'Julian, *please*,' she said on a sob. 'Don't go. Let me go back to the Hall. Let me get some things together and we'll go away somewhere. We'll go away tonight. We'll go somewhere he can't find me.'

'Where? Where will we go? We've already established he'd come to Edinburgh.'

'Then we'll go somewhere different. We'll go to London or Paris. I have friends there. They'll help us. Or I'll just go. You go to Edinburgh and send for me later.'

Julian put the safety catch on again and threw the gun down in disgust. He shook his head and went out onto the terrace. He sort of folded up so he was sitting there, facing the sea, and put his head in his hands and swore.

'He won't do anything to me,' said Lorelei desperately, wanting to believe it, wanting Julian to believe it. 'He won't.

He has too much to lose. He has a reputation to protect and this is easiest all round. We'll just get the first train that comes in at the station. We'll go anywhere it takes us. I can gather some things and I have a little money set aside.'

'We don't *need* your money!' thundered Julian. He looked up at her with those dark brown eyes, so full of pain, and her heart twisted in her chest.

Lorelei dropped down beside him and took his face in hers. 'Maybe not. But it can only help, can't it? Let me go. Give me an hour and I'll be back. I promise.'

'What if—' Julian began; but Lorelei pressed her fingers to his lips and shook her head.

'Shhh. No "what if"s. I won't allow them. I simply won't.'

'But—'

'Same for "but"s, I'm going. I'll be back in an hour. You pack what you need and we'll go. I'll get the carriage and we'll load it up, then simply disappear.'

She stood up and looked out at the sea. Her heart twisted again. She wouldn't miss anything about her life here at all – apart from the sea and the cove. But they were just hers by default anyway, weren't they?

Resolutely, she turned her back to the sea, dropped a kiss on Julian's head and began to run to the Hall before he could protest any more.

Chapter Twenty-Six

The Beach Hut, Present Day

Lissy's phone bleeped: a text coming through, demanding her attention.

'Do you ever switch that thing off?' asked Stef, mumbling into the pillow.

'Nope.' Lissy rolled away from him. 'And anyway, it's a message from Becky.'

'Ah, Becky.' Stef rolled over. 'I like Becky.'

'Me too,' said Lissy. 'She says she's got something interesting for me and she's on her way here with it. That's nice.'

'I don't like Becky so much now,' grumbled Stef. 'She interrupts our afternoon.'

Outside the sun was shining and it was warm through the skylights of the beach hut. They'd started off with good intentions of spending time on the beach after a late lunch, but the drowsy heat and the enormous pub meal had made them sleepy. So they had slipped into the beach hut to rest – but one thing had led to another and well, they were both basically naked now.

'She'll be at least half an hour.' Lissy turned towards Stef and trailed her finger down his cheek.

He smiled, his eyes still closed. 'A nice idea – but half an hour does not give us much time to truly make love.' He turned his head and opened his eyes, deep pools of dark, honeyed chocolate staring into hers. Her stomach did that fizzy thing again, but she knew he was right.

'Okay.' Lissy sighed and sat up. 'I'm not showering though. The sea is too warm to waste.' She slipped the ring off her finger and laid it carefully on the bedside table. She still marvelled at how similar the pattern was to the sconces in the Dower House. One could almost imagine ... But no. That was just silly.

She grabbed the pillow and threw it at Stef. 'Catch me if you can!' she cried, and with that, she raced down the stairs, grabbing a towel and a purple chiffon cover-up. She ran out of the hut, tossing the towel and the chiffon onto the sand and hurtled straight into the sea. She gasped as the water hit her legs, revelling in her nakedness.

Had Lorelei done this with her lover? That mystery man in the painting? Who knew – but Lissy was enjoying herself. It was a very, very long time since she had let go like this. She ran out as far as she dared before lifting her legs and swimming a few strokes, then she turned around, treading water until she saw Stef race out of the hut, clutching a towel. He had stopped to put shorts on – but even so, his torso looked ever-so tempting and she immediately started swimming inland again, just to be near him.

She didn't care that her hair was plastered to her head, or that she didn't have a scrap of make-up on, or that the salt water was playing havoc with her hairstyle. Instead of the sleek, dark bob that she straightened carefully every morning, her natural waves were kinking in, and the ends would curl up once it all dried in the sunshine. It felt good to find herself again.

Twenty minutes later, she spotted a lone figure trekking down the path towards the beach. She could tell by the dark hair and the slim shape it was Becky. Her friend was also lugging something that looked like a portfolio with her, which Lissy assumed she had pilfered from Jon's studio.

'You were right – we wouldn't have had much time,' she said to Stef.

'We'll have plenty of time after she has left,' he said, flashing that to-die-for smile.

'Well, just let me out of this water before Becky sees anything she shouldn't!' Lissy laughed, ducking under Stef's arm, and swimming quickly to the shore.

She splashed onto the sand and pulled her cover-up on without even bothering to dry herself. The filmy material clung to her, but that was better than Becky seeing her stark naked.

Becky waved as she saw Lissy on the beach. She shifted the portfolio onto her other shoulder and picked her way down the path. Lissy walked forward to meet her, curious to see what she had brought.

'Hey Lissy!' Becky grinned. 'Having fun?'

'Yes, thank you. Where's Grace?' She looked around as if the child would pop out of nowhere.

'At the studio with Jon. She's really grumpy today and I didn't think you could give this,' she said, patting the portfolio, 'your full attention with her around. Don't worry, we'll bring her tomorrow. Oh!' She put her hand on Lissy's forearm. 'Did Cori send you the scan photo of her baby? Isn't it wonderful?' Her eyes sparkled. 'I think it's a girl.'

'Wonderful – but I hope it's not giving you ideas,' said Lissy; a little bit of her perhaps hoping that it *was* giving her ideas. 'Please say you're not going to get pregnant as well. I couldn't cope with another Grace.'

'What? Me? Why ever not? Grace would *love* a little sister or brother, and you know they're so cute when they're babies – what? Stop staring at me like that!' Becky looked from Lissy to Stef and back again and grinned. 'Grace wants to know when you two will have a baby as well! Isn't that funny? I told her you were going to get married and she said people who lived together had babies and would you have one soon please. It'll be so lovely. Your children will need plenty of cousins, you know. I'll have to have words with Jon and we'll have to get onto it…'

'You're an awful person!' Lissy shuddered theatrically, but she was smiling nonetheless. 'Stop it. Right now!'

'*Grazia* will be the first to know if it ever happens for us,' promised Stef with a grin. 'So what have you here for my fiancée?' He smiled at Lissy, who could feel herself turning bright red. *Fiancée*. She'd been many things, but it was the first time she'd been a fiancée.

'Oh, all right. This is just something I thought you'd like to see. Don't ask me how I got it. Just know that I have sources.' She laid the folder down on the sand, sitting cross-legged next to it. 'It has to go back, but,' she looked up at Stef again and nodded towards him, 'I thought you could take a photograph of it. We'll pretend we don't know the meaning of copyright, yeah?'

'Oooh, I'm intrigued.' Lissy sat down in front of Becky. 'What is it?'

'Well – Simon spotted it in the Tate archives.' She waved her hand in one of those dismissive gestures she was so good at. 'And it just so happened that it was earmarked to be sent up here to Whitby. There's an exhibition running at the Pannett Gallery—'

'Pannett Gallery!' interrupted Lissy. 'Ugh. The Hand of Glory.'

'The very same,' agreed Becky, 'said to be the severed hand of a felon, taken from his body when he was on the gallows; used also to aid and abet burglaries by allegedly inducing comas into the residents of a home.' Becky's eyes lit up again.

'I hate the way you seem to enjoy that image.' Lissy looked at Becky in horror. 'It's disgusting.'

'But it's history. And you love history.'

'I don't like severed hands.' Lissy folded her arms and compressed her mouth into a small, tight line.

'Okay. So don't go into the severed hand gallery then. Anyway. As I was saying, there is going to be an exhibition there.' Becky bent forward, tucking a strand of hair behind her ear then going to work on the zipper. 'And it's going to be about the Staithes Group of artists. It will have a smattering of Pre-Raphaelite portraiture, and some Julia Margaret Cameron photographs. Aha – that got your attention, didn't it? So, this little beauty slipped through the net, as it were. And it took, shall we say, a little diversion to our studio. And no.' She held up her hand and shook her head. 'Don't ask how. If I tell you, I'll be forced to kill you.'

Lissy loved a mystery. 'You have to tell me.'

'I can't.' Becky held her stare. 'I really can't. So as I say, this little beauty was misinterpreted—'

'You *never* said that,' interrupted Lissy, jumping on the words. 'I don't even know what it is, never mind how it was misinterpreted.'

Becky ignored her. Lissy didn't know whether it was by accident or design, but she was inclined to go with the second. This, then, was potentially Becky getting her own back. There weren't often things like this that Becky knew something about and Lissy didn't, and the suspense was knotting her stomach up.

'The dates on what I have here are all wrong for what they originally thought it was,' continued Becky. 'Cameron died in Ceylon in 1879. She moved there in 1875 and she didn't take many pictures in her later years because she couldn't get the supplies. All of her photographs were copywritten and she kept records on each and every one of them. What I have here, had no records.'

With a gigantic flourish, Becky ripped the zipper open and folded the portfolio out.

'What is it?' Lissy bounced up and was on her hands and knees before she was really aware of it. 'Who is *she*?'

It was a black and white photograph of a woman sitting on a rock, her long, dark hair blowing out of its intricate plait in the breeze behind her. She was dressed in a mediaeval style and had her arms wrapped around her knees. The photographer had caught her just as she turned her head and faced the camera.

'Ohhh,' said Stef. 'Very nice. I wonder what the exposure time was?'

Stef was ever the technical guru. But he had a point. Even Lissy knew that the lady must have smiled at the photographer for quite a while, given the fact that most old photographs depicted grumpy-looking people who had to hold that expression for a good few minutes. Hence, they rarely smiled. And what a gem it was to *find* an old photograph of Victorians and Edwardians smiling – they did exist. But she had never seen them in reality, like she saw this one.

'See the rocks?' asked Becky, her voice breaking into Lissy's thoughts. 'Look.' She pointed out over the cove at the collection of rocks Stef had taken Lissy's *Miranda* photograph on. 'Can you see the similarity?'

'They're identical,' said Lissy. 'But what's that got to do with dates?'

Becky gently pushed Lissy's hand away as she tried to pick up the photograph. 'In the late 1890s there was a terrific storm out here. It broke down the defences of the cove – prior to that, there was a private jetty leading out from your Dower House.'

'So,' said Lissy, suddenly understanding, 'this picture has to be from later than the 1890s.'

'Exactly,' said Becky. 'And it gets better. The back of the photograph has something interesting on it. It says *LS by JMC*. An easy mistake to make, yes, if you're looking for Cameron shots?'

Lissy nodded; she knew her eyes must be round as saucers by now. '*LS*. It has to be Lorelei Scarsdale. It simply *has* to be. Dammit! Who the hell is JMC then?'

She looked at Becky as if her sister-in-law could tell her.

And apparently, she could.

'Julian MacDonald Cooper. There are a few pictures of his left in private collections around the world. He never made it particularly big, but he did well enough. There are some invoices and things with certain pieces of his work, giving a North Yorkshire dealer's address around about this time. He did a lot of work on the Staithes Group, especially when the Group began to fracture near the end. That's who the current experts think this guy is anyway. It's a long shot but ...' She shrugged her shoulders and looked at Lissy. 'I hope it helps. And the rumour is that he fell in love with your Lorelei Scarsdale, but much of it is lost to history, unfortunately. It was probably just a summer fling, but it's a link, anyway. I think his great-grandson lives down south somewhere, and he's the one who verified this work could be Cooper's, when they started to look at it more closely.'

'Becky!' Lissy threw her arms around Becky. 'Thank you, thank you, thank you!' She sat back, knowing she had a ridiculous smile on her face. She could feel her cheeks almost splitting with it. 'Julian. He's called Julian,' she told Stef.

'I'm sorry he is not a romantic smuggler type for you to lust after.' He squeezed her shoulder. 'You thought he was.'

'I'm not writing him off as un-smugglerish.' Lissy grinned. 'It was just a theory I had. Why else would she have lights in her windows to guide him in?'

'So they could have privacy, perhaps? So he could come and visit under the guise of *being* a smuggler?' suggested Stef. 'It was maybe less dangerous to use that cover story? We will never know the truth of it. Perhaps they just used to light the lamps so they knew the other was thinking of them.'

'I like that idea.' Lissy turned back to the picture and stared at it. 'I love this story. I haven't found *any* pictures of her at all before this one. But him,' she said, pointing to the picture, 'I think we do perhaps know what he looked like.'

'The watercolour?' asked Stef. 'Very possibly.'

'Yes. The watercolour. And other – stuff. You know what I'm talking about Stef. But I'm almost positive.'

'He doesn't scare you now?' Stef smiled at her.

Lissy shook her head. 'No. I've given it a lot of thought. Nobody in love could have ever been scary. But I think their stars must have burned very, very brightly to leave their memories here for so long.'

'Maybe she blazed into his life like a comet, the way you blazed into mine?' suggested Stef. His voice made Lissy's toes curl with pleasure.

'Um – I have no idea what you're talking about, but do you want to take a picture of this now?' asked Becky. 'Then I can kind of get it away from here? Before it's kind of missed? You know?'

Lissy brought her thoughts back to the task in hand. 'Stef?'

'Certainly, Lissy.' He laughed. 'I will be one minute.' He turned and ran across to the beach hut. Lissy watched him go and she shivered a little, but not in an unpleasant fashion.

She wondered if their stars, their comets, would burn as brightly; if the way their worlds had collided again would leave an imprint on this little cove, or even in Sea Scarr Hall, along with the shades of Julian and Lorelei – for that was who she had decided haunted that place, for better or for worse.

It must have been one hell of a summer fling.

Becky's fingers pressed lightly on her arm and she dragged her attention away from Stef.

'So can we stop worrying about you now?' asked Becky.

'Worrying?' replied Lissy, confused. 'Why on earth should you be worried about me?'

'Because you're far too stubborn, that's why,' replied Becky. 'And you two. Hell, you guys are caught in a perpetual riptide. You need to just ride it out and let it sweep you away. Seriously. Make this work, okay?'

Lissy's eyes drifted to the photograph, and she remembered the photo Stef had hung up in the beach hut – the one of the girl in the red dress. She was slowly getting back to being that girl, slowly letting people back in. It would take time, but she would get there.

A few grains of sand had drifted onto Lorelei's photograph and Lissy blew them away gently. The woman in the photograph looked back at Lissy, her eyes warm and gentle. Lissy smiled at her and didn't feel stupid in the least.

'Riptide?' She looked back up at Becky. 'Well, next summer, we're going to get an old VW van and we're going to Cornwall again, to finish what we started down there. Then we'll visit Portofino and I'll stay there for a little while. We can easily commute back and forth between Portofino and London. And because I don't really work at the Tate I can just reduce my volunteering. They'll have me back anytime I want to go there, I know that. I won't be far away, really, and Stef just does his own thing for his job. Plus, it's only two hours or so, direct from London to Genoa.' Her gaze drifted over to the beach hut again, then she looked straight at Becky, making her mismatched eyes as frank and as honest as they could ever be. 'We'll be okay this time.'

'To be okay is all we want for you, Lissy.'

'I promise you, everything will be fine.' Lissy looked back at the beach hut and waved at Stef as he came out, his camera in his hand. Stef raised the camera in an answering wave and Lissy's heart bounced around in her chest.

Yes. They'd be okay.

In fact, they'd be just fine. They'd be utterly fine – this time.

Chapter Twenty-Seven

Sea Scarr Hall, 1905

Lorelei was in her sitting room, throwing some of her most precious belongings together in a carpet bag when Walter found her. The photograph Julian had given her today had been one of the first things she packed, along with her ring. The photograph was her touchstone. It was for her to remind herself who she really was – she was still, beneath all the veneer, that girl on the rock, smiling with such hope into her future.

'So the whore has returned,' came the voice from the doorway. Lorelei didn't need to look at him to know that he was drunk. His words were slurred and part of her thought that was very useful; he wouldn't be able to put up much resistance when she barged her way through the doorway and hopefully knocked him flying like a six-pin. Oh, she could dream …

'No, the whore has *not* returned,' she said, quietly, although the fear was rising within her. 'There was never a whore in this room, therefore she cannot return.'

Walter swore and stumbled into the room. He raised a fist, flailed a little, aimed, then lost his target. A wardrobe got the full force of it this time. He tried again, and she was too slow; he managed to land a stinging slap across her cheek.

Lorelei cried out and scurried away from him, her cheek burning, her eyes filling with tears. He came after her, reaching out to grab her, but thank God he was so very drunk he couldn't seem to manage it.

With a stream of vitriol on his lips, he continued to stagger towards her, tripping over a hatbox on the floor. The white

Lady of Shallot dress was partially stuffed back into it and Walter leaned over, making an erratic grab for the gown.

He caught hold of it on the third pass and stood upright, swaying slightly. 'This,' he said, brandishing it, 'is a whore's clothing. And you've been wearing it to rut with that wastrel visitor in the Dower House.'

'I have no idea what you're talking about.' Lorelei's voice was shaking, her heart thumping. She just wanted to be away from him, but she knew she had to edge around him to gather her hairbrush and comb from the dressing table.

'Oh, yes you do,' he said. She made a move, and this time, he did manage to catch hold of her arm and hang on tightly.

She gave a little startled yelp and tried to shake his clawing fingers from her flesh. 'Get *off* me!' she shouted. 'Do *not* touch me. Don't ever touch me again!'

'Oh no, I bet he's doing enough of that for both of us!' yelled Walter, pushing his face right up to hers.

Lorelei felt sickened as she saw the bloodshot eyes and smelt the stench of alcohol on his fetid breath. 'Leave me alone!' she yelled, shaking her arm so violently he managed to lose his grip and reeled drunkenly, staggering to get his balance back, tripping up over the white dress he still held onto.

Lorelei, her arm numb where he had grabbed it, took advantage and ran past him, tossing a few more things into the carpet bag. What she hadn't managed to pack and what she couldn't send for, she could easily buy. Of course, she would have to be careful about the address she had the belongings sent to – oh, it was too difficult to think about right now.

Still, a trunk of clothing was already in the carriage; she had seen to that before Walter had roused himself enough to realise she was back. She wished she hadn't left the art exhibition programmes, her most precious things, at the

Dower House. She hoped that Julian would remember to bring them. Everything else, she thought, looking quickly around the room, was expendable.

She had a momentary fluster when she remembered her wooden paint box and the picture of Julian – but really – she was going to live with him, wasn't she? Her stomach fluttered and, she reasoned, she could always buy new paints. The thought of trying to squeeze past that obnoxious, slavering creature again to retrieve her paints and the picture from the cupboard turned the fluttering into nausea. No, best to leave them behind.

'I'm going,' she said. 'I shan't be back and I shall send for the rest of my things in due course. If you want a divorce, I will be more than happy to oblige.'

She turned and half ran out of the sitting room. She was aware that Walter let out a roar and stumbled along behind her shouting. Judging by the rustling, dragging sound following them along the corridor, he still had hold of that bloody gown. Well, he was welcome to it. It reminded her too much of the fancy-dress ball, despite the fact she had worn it for her photograph on the rocks.

She had rescued the photograph and the ring from her life at Sea Scarr, and that was all that mattered.

Walter hurried along the corridor after Lorelei, furious at her. He shouted obscenities until he could shout no more, and became more and more agitated when she resolutely ignored him.

The whore swept down the staircase, carrying that bulging carpet bag, and walked out into the foyer and he had the awful image of himself scurrying like a lapdog behind her. *God!* If the servants saw him … He'd done enough begging and crawling at her feet and it shamed him to remember any of it. The bitch! The whore! That disgusting creature he despised yet yearned for … NO! No, he didn't. He mustn't. He hated her.

He had a brief glimpse of a carriage – *his* carriage – waiting on the gravelled drive as she pulled the door open, and he saw a footman bow to her as she climbed on. As the door started closing on itself, Walter picked up the nearest thing, a priceless vase bursting full of flowers, and hurled it at the opening. The vase smashed and shattered onto the floor and as the puddle of water began to spread over the black and white tiles, he, Walter Scarsdale, Lord Scarsdale of Sea Scarr Hall, turned and marched into the library.

He should *never* have allowed himself to fall for that witch. That little bitch had tricked him into marriage with her fluttering eyelashes and her innocent demeanour. And yet, she was no better than a prostitute. He didn't care to know how many men she had been with; it sickened him to even try to work it out. And that photographer was the latest on the list.

And to think, he had welcomed him into his home the night of that ball.

Memories flashed into Walter's mind of Mary Percy – Florence's mother and the woman he had tried and failed to impress for years, and the anger and frustration grew, a tight ball that strained at his chest muscles. Mary Percy was the one he had really wanted. If only she had yielded herself to him. Imagine, if they … He felt himself break out into a cold sweat and staggered over to the little table near the fireplace.

On it was a decanter or two of good brandy and a set of glasses. Walter made a grab for one of the decanters, but it slipped out of his clutches, splintering on the floor. A pain shot along his arm and he gasped. He stared down at his hand, which no longer seemed to belong to him. Then he realised he was still carrying that bloody dress. Well – it could go in the fire. He tried to toss it into the grate, but his co-ordination seemed to have vanished and he didn't quite manage to get the whole thing in.

He got enough of it in though. Enough for the flames to lick at the fabric and start burning along the seams and the skirt; enough for those flames to reach the rug where the skirt lay, half in and half out of the fireplace.

The flames were big enough to sniff around the library and find the shattered decanter and follow the trail where the brandy had soaked into the rug and splattered up the bookcases and onto the books.

The flames were also large enough to curl around Walter, who lay on the floor senseless, one hand clutched to his chest, his eyes staring sightlessly up to the ceiling.

His last thought before the heart attack claimed him was not of Mary; neither was it of his mistress and nor was it of Sea Scarr Hall.

Bizarrely, it was the negative, black and white image of his beautiful whore sitting on a rock in the cove, wearing that God-forsaken dress and laughing at him as he held the shotgun up and blew apart the glass plates she was etched upon.

Her hair had looked blonde and the dress had looked black and she was perched on a giant white thing as black-tipped waves washed up onto the grey beach.

She truly did look like the Angel of Death; a Siren upon a rock, luring the next man who thought he loved her to his demise ...

Till he, the fated mariner, hears her cry,
And up her rock, bare breasted, comes to die ...

Julian had packed all his belongings and was ready to leave. It hadn't taken him long. He was, after all, simply a summer visitor and he had only enough items to last him for his holiday. What had taken up most of his time was the securing of his camera equipment, and the careful storage of all the photographic plates he had taken of Staithes and the artists and the coastline. Those, and Lorelei's catalogues.

At least, he thought wryly, his time here hadn't been a complete waste. It made him go hot and cold to think of what might have happened to all those negatives in light of the fate of Lorelei's pictures.

Remembering that brought his gaze to the shotgun which was propped up by the door. He hadn't put that back into its case. No; that would stay out until he and Lorelei had left Staithes and were safely in the carriage on their way to wherever. If Walter was capable of shooting those glass negatives, then there was no knowing what he might do to Lorelei.

Julian thought back to when he had first seen her swimming, to that collection of bruises around the top of her arm, just like a set of fingerprints: *Don't worry. A wave took me too close to the rocks.*

Some bloody wave.

Julian was desperate to head up to the Hall and collect Lorelei; to protect her in some way and bring her safely to the Dower House. But he knew he couldn't do that. Instead, he picked up the gun and walked down the steps onto the beach. He would wait for her there on the shoreline – then at least he would be visible to her when she came down the winding path and she would see that he was ready for her.

Julian had seen the family carriage go up and down that road during his stay – it was the only route to the Dower House, then it curved up again and climbed the hill towards Staithes. He looked in that direction and remembered Lorelei coming down there and slipping. Had it really only been a couple of hours ago? Not even that, perhaps. He stared at it and simply couldn't comprehend what had happened since.

As his mind turned over the bizarre shift in fortune, he heard a crash from the bathing machine behind him.

Julian swung around and pointed the gun in that direction. 'Who's that?' he demanded. 'I'm armed and I'm not afraid to use it.'

More crashing and thudding. Then a bang. Then the door flew open and he cocked the gun, pointing it at the wooden creation.

'Please. D-don't shoot me,' came a quavering voice; a very young, very terrified voice.

The dirty, tear-stained face of a young girl appeared at the door. 'I'm a friend of Lady Scarsdale,' she said on a sob, 'but I'm not causing any bother, I promise.'

'What the hell?' Julian didn't immediately rush forward, but he lowered the gun and stared at the girl.

She was in a considerable state of disarray. She was flushed and her fair hair tangled, while her eyes were too bright. Beneath it all, Julian recognised the visage of the girl who had been the star attraction at the ball he had attended at Sea Scarr Hall and the young lady who had enjoyed so much cake at her farewell tea party.

'Florence?' he asked.

'Yes. Or Florrie. Lorelei sometimes calls me Florrie.'

'What in God's name are you doing in there?' snapped Julian.

'I escaped from London. I wanted to come back. I love Archie and I don't want to be a debutante anymore. Oh, it's horrible down there and I hate it. I wanted Archie. So I came back. I wrote to Lorelei and I told her I was going to leave. I was going to see her, because I know she'll help me and she'll talk to my mother, and—'

'Sir?' The door opened a little wider, and a tall, gangly young man with too-long reddish hair stepped out of the bathing hut, looking equally guilty.

'Archie?' Julian stared at the young man. 'What the *hell*?'

'It's just as much my fault,' admitted Archie. 'She wrote

to me and we arranged it. We arranged to meet here. I'm so sorry, Sir.'

'We didn't mean to be in here so long, but we heard gunshots and we were terrified to come out.'

'And Florrie has hurt her ankle,' added Archie, 'because she slipped on the dunes.'

'It does hurt quite tremendously,' said Florrie. 'It's very puffy but I daren't take my boot off.'

Julian was exasperated; he wanted these youngsters out of the way so he could watch for Lorelei coming, but he couldn't just leave them. They were innocent children, in love, completely unaware that he was about to elope with Lady Scarsdale. And what a Society scandal that would make. Plus, one of them was injured.

Julian thought quickly. 'Look – Lorelei will be here soon and we'll sort this out before we go to watch the fishing boats come in – so I can take some photographs. Let's get inside the Dower House, and we can at least get you some food, and try to see what's wrong with your ankle.'

'Oh, thank you!' Florrie edged out of the bathing hut and stood awkwardly on the top step. 'But I don't think I can walk all the way to the Dower House.'

'Lean on me, Florrie,' said Archie, gallantly. 'Let me take you in my arms.'

'Good God,' muttered Julian again, turning away and raking his hand through his hair. He did not need two love-struck children in his keeping, today of all days. 'All right,' he said in a louder voice. 'Take it cautiously. You don't want to damage your foot any more. I'll get some soup heating for you, while you make your way across.' He prayed that it wouldn't take long to set the stove and prepare the bowls for these two uninvited guests. And he guessed it would be a good idea to get a doctor at some point as well.

His mind was spinning as he ran across the beach and

climbed the steps into the Dower House. Perhaps the youngsters could come with them as far as the nearest town. Then they could try to find a hotel and a doctor and hopefully leave them there. Or maybe they could deposit them at Archie's house and the boy's mother could deal with them. He sighed again.

What a bloody day.

He also prayed that he wouldn't miss Lorelei coming down towards the cove in the carriage while he was looking after the youngsters in the Dower House.

Lorelei did not miss the sight of the Dower House appearing as the carriage trundled down the winding road towards the cove. In fact, at the very point where she knew she would catch her first glimpse of the place and remain invisible for a few seconds to the occupant of the house, she pulled the window down and leaned out so she could look for Julian and remember the wonderful sight of her future waiting for her.

And it was precisely at that moment where she wished she hadn't seen him at all.

Two dark figures were standing in the shadowy entrance to the beach hut, their arms around each other locked in an embrace.

'Stop!' commanded Lorelei, banging on the carriage and startling the driver. 'Don't go any further!'

The driver did as he was bid and the carriage drew to a halt. Lorelei gazed in dismay as the couple closed in on one another and began to kiss. Lorelei felt sick to her stomach as she watched them, and saw the man – a tall, rangy man whose hair was too long – lean down and lift the girl's skirt, his hands running up beneath her petticoats in a very tawdry fashion.

Julian was with another woman. Someone he didn't want

her to know about. Why else would she have been in the bathing hut? Was this, then, a farewell to the woman – another little flirtation he had enjoyed as the summer lazed away?

Lorelei's head was spinning with questions and suppositions. Who the hell was she? And what was Julian doing with her? It was a private beach – nobody had access to it, and certainly nobody had access to her bathing hut. It was like a slap in the face, like he was flaunting some woman he had bedded in Staithes, and saying farewell to her in the only way she understood.

Lorelei raised a shaking hand to her face, aware that her cheeks were wet. She hadn't realised she had been crying. But she knew she had two choices. She could go down there and confront the bastard, the way she had always dreamed of confronting Walter about the Harlot. Or she could just get the hell away from Yorkshire and forget about the whole damn lot of them. She should just accept that she was unloved and unlovable and nobody would ever be faithful to her. It had happened too many times; it *always* happened. She'd hoped Julian was different, but he wasn't. They never were.

I have youth and a little beauty, she thought, her insides twisting as she recalled the last time she had used that phrase. She had made the mistake of trusting Julian and he, like others before him, had simply used her.

Lorelei took a deep breath and straightened her shoulders. 'Please continue,' she commanded the driver in a voice that sounded stronger than she felt.

'Where to, Madam?' asked the driver.

'To Whitby. To the railway station.'

'Very well, Madam,' replied the driver. And the horse began to move again.

Lorelei sat very still as she drove away from her dreams, and the wind from the sea dried the salt-water tears on her cheeks.

Chapter Twenty-Eight

The Dower House/Sea Scarr Hall, 1905

Julian installed Florrie and Archie in the kitchen, Florrie showing him her pudding-like ankle in despair.

'Archie had a look before we came in here, but he says he thinks it's just sprained,' she told Julian. 'He couldn't feel anything sinister, could you, Archie? After this, shall we go to the Hall and see Lorelei?'

'She might come here,' Julian said. 'She's supposed to be on her way. Just eat your soup and rest your ankle up for now. She won't be long and I'd rather keep you here than take you up there in case Lord Scarsdale gets a little cross with you running away and contacting young Archie.'

He took himself back outside after what seemed an age and looked up at the driveway. It was empty and he felt, for the first time, a creeping sense of panic.

'Where are you, Lorelei?' he muttered, unwilling to admit that he thought Walter had possibly discovered her plans, flown into a brutal rage and finally killed her. *Damn it, I should have gone with her after all.*

It was when he saw the column of smoke rise over the trees and heard the faint crackle of flames that he took to his heels and ran up to the Hall, oblivious to the gradient or the fact that anyone might see him.

He ran as fast as he could, all the while aware that the smoke column was growing thicker and the noise of the fire was becoming louder. His heart was pounding, and not just from the exertion. What if Lorelei was in there? What if she was trapped? What if she was already dead, strangled or stabbed by her husband's own hand?

Julian arrived at the gravelled pathway where he had been greeted by Lorelei on the afternoon of that tea party. He could still see her in his mind's eye, even through the thick smoke, as she flitted here and there in that white dress, holding onto her big hat, looking up at him and laughing.

All around him, people were shouting and screaming. There seemed to be a surfeit of servants rushing around and he reached out his hand, grabbing one of them as they ran past him. It was a young girl of about fourteen years old. He recognised her as little red-headed Phyllis.

'What's happened?' he asked.

'Fire broke out, Sir. In the library. It's taking over the house. The master and mistress are missing!' The girl stared up at him with round, terrified eyes, her face streaked with smoke and her red hair escaping from her hat. 'What shall we do, Sir?'

Julian shook his head, releasing her. 'I don't know. I don't know what can be done.' He looked around helplessly, searching for someone a little older and less excitable. His eyes alighted on a man – the one who had greeted him the evening of Florrie's ball: Heimdall. His stomach churned as he remembered that Florrie and Archie were still in the Dower House, oblivious to any of this and he ran over to the man.

'Has anyone found Lady Scarsdale?' he asked. 'Please. Just tell me if anyone has found her. And you should know there's a lady in the Dower House who needs medical attention as well, once help arrives.'

The footman or butler or whatever the hell he was looked at Julian, his expression as terrified as the young girl's had been. 'The authorities will have to come, Sir. They'll see to the lady you mention. But there's a body in the library. Yates said he saw someone in there on the floor but he couldn't get in to rescue them. We don't know who it is. The flames chased us out.'

Julian stared at the man dumbly as the world went in and out of focus. 'Lorelei,' he managed eventually. 'Is it her?'

'I don't know, Sir. I just don't know.' The man looked torn between politeness to Julian and supporting the staff – an innate need to be courteous trying to win over a desire to help.

'Please. Go to the staff, do what you can,' choked out Julian. 'I'll help. I'll do whatever I have to. I'll tell the authorities when they come—' He couldn't go on.

'Thank you, Sir.' The man bowed slightly and hurried off.

But Julian, despite his offer of immediate assistance, froze for a moment and could do nothing but stand and stare at the burning, crumbling Hall before him and pray that the body in the library wasn't Lorelei's.

But if it wasn't Lorelei, where was she?

And then he truly felt the world shift as he sank to his knees and realised that he might never see her again. Because if she wasn't in the Hall, and God knew nobody who was still in there could have survived, then she hadn't come to the Dower House in the carriage for him after all.

Was she alive or dead? Was she even now lying in the burning Hall before him, or had she simply driven away and lied to him about everything? He didn't know how or if he would ever find out.

And he had no idea which alternative was the worst.

Julian didn't want to consider that Lorelei Scarsdale and the bright future he had imagined for them were lost to him forever, so there was not even a second's hesitation.

He got to his feet and stared at the building. There was a hope, a very faint hope that she was somewhere in there – somewhere hidden away and terrified. Somewhere away from the flames.

He scanned the building – the wing where he knew her sitting room was had escaped the worst of the fire just now.

So before he was even aware of what he was doing, Julian ran towards Sea Scarr Hall, pushing past the crowds of people, intent on finding Lorelei.

He didn't even stop at the side door and think about where he was heading. He ran through the opening and vanished inside.

What, after all, did he have to lose?

Cornwall, 1905

Lorelei had, in fact, ended up in Cornwall. She had just boarded the first train she could and headed in whichever direction it took her.

The direction happened to be south. And Cornwall seemed as good a place as anywhere. After all, hadn't her parents lived at Newlyn for a while? Then they had gone to Lamorna, she remembered, after she sang the praises of the Bohemian community that had lived and worked there.

But Lorelei discovered that her parents had moved on and she had no real idea of where they were now. She guessed they would send a letter to Sea Scarr Hall and tell her, when they remembered they had a daughter who might like to know where her family was. But she didn't want to think about how she would actually *get* that letter now.

One of the artists she met in Lamorna told her he thought Lorelei's 'friends' – she had been very careful not to tell him her relationship to them, just in case – had gone to Wales.

'I could introduce you to some of the other artists,' the young man told her. 'They might know more than me.'

'It's all right,' Lorelei said hurriedly. It had been a long time since she worked with anyone in Cornwall, but she certainly didn't want anyone asking too many questions. She didn't, after all, have a very common name. 'I might try St Ives or

Polperro. I'm sure my friends have links to those places. Thank you for your time.'

'Well, if the subject comes up, who shall I say was asking?' The artist smiled, his face open and honest, although he had a quiet, serious demeanour about him for such a young man.

'Well, my name is Laura,' she told him, lying far too easily, but the less he knew about her the better. Walter or Julian might come looking for her. She felt a little sick thinking about Julian and that woman again, and she certainly didn't want to give her real name to anyone down here.

Lorelei had already sold the ring and the photograph – she'd pretended the picture was an actual Cameron print and the dealer she had spoken to in Penzance had been ridiculously excited and she'd made an awful lot of money from it. The ring she had sold to a jeweller – and again, had made a tidy profit. She wanted nothing to remind her of Julian. Both items had to go.

'And your surname?' prompted the young artist, breaking into her thoughts. He shifted his canvas from under one arm to the other and Lorelei made a mental note to buy some more paints. She was glad she had left them and the seascape behind at the Hall. Two more items that held too many memories.

'My surname?' she asked.

'Yes, your surname.' The artist smiled. 'I take it you've got one?'

'Yes. Yes, of course I have.' Lorelei looked out at the blue sea twinkling in the cove and the quarry-like rocks that protected the place. She thought for a moment she saw a young woman in a red dress scrambling over them, and a man who looked an awful lot like Julian waiting for her. But then she blinked and they were gone; just one more trick of the light.

Her heart twisted and she guessed that pain was something she was going to have to get used to.

And then she spoke, almost without thinking. 'My surname,' she said, looking back at the awfully patient young man, 'is Cooper. Yes. My name is Laura Cooper.'

The Dower House, Present Day

'It's definitely been a summer to remember.' Lissy drained her third glass of champagne, perched on the table somewhere between the remains of Grace's birthday cake – a rather impressive hedgehog with chocolate button prickles – and the remains of a bottle of champagne she had taken custody of, a little while ago.

She and Stef had decided to make good use of the twinkling lights from the beach hut and had draped them across the railings of the terrace, and all around the windows and doors of the Dower House. They had looked so pretty, Lissy had then decided it was a shame to waste the twinkles – and waste the last few days of summer – and hosted a party on their final night in Staithes. Their cases were more or less packed, their luggage ready to be piled into their cars, ready for them to travel tomorrow; and then they would be heading back to Lissy's apartment in London. Stef would stay with her until the Mayfair exhibition and, they both knew, he would be staying even beyond that. They had to plan their campervan expedition for next summer, after all.

'It's definitely been a wonderful summer,' said Becky, a little tipsy by now. 'Your engagement, Cori and Simon's engagement and Grace's fourth birthday. Cheers to you all!' She raised her own glass in the direction of her friends.

'And of course, we can't forget Cori's baby news,' added Lissy. She smiled at Cori who was certainly a lot more curvaceous than she had been two months ago, and in much better spirits. She was currently sitting on one of Lissy's reclining chairs, her hands resting on her rounded stomach and a Virgin Mojito within easy reach. She and Simon were staying in the studio flat that night, so there was no real hurry to go anywhere. Becky had been right with the scan – Cori was having a girl, and Cori and Becky had joked that the pressure was now on Lissy to have one too.

Grace, the birthday girl, who of course thought the whole party was for her and her alone, had delighted in pressing her ear to Cori's tummy, and placed a tiny fairy cake on the hard, neat bump, whispering to the baby that it was for her. Grace had shrieked with laughter when a tiny fist or a strong little foot had thrust itself out and made the cake topple off, and she had subsequently tried to make it happen several more times, until Becky finally made her stop.

The birthday girl, however, had hit the wall about half an hour ago, and currently lay sleeping, sprawled out on her back on one of the sofas in the Dower House. Her arms were flung above her head like a starfish and her legs were bent up, frog-like, in that attitude all small children display when they are fast asleep and completely and utterly relaxed.

From where Lissy sat, she could see Stef, bare-footed and bare-chested, poking around at the barbecue, the few, wispy clouds behind him rose-pink in the low sun. A little thrill ran through her body as she saw the glow of the coals reflected on his skin and a scowl of concentration on his face. His hair was flopping forwards, but not enough to hide the sharp edges of his chin and his cheekbones, and not enough to cover his eyes. One dark, wayward curl was hanging over his forehead, tantalisingly close to his eyes, and she longed to move it away, just to touch him, just to be close to him – but she had all night to do that. She had the rest of their lives. The thought excited her and she smiled over in his direction.

Jon and Simon were near Stef, huddled together, looking at the barbecue in the way that only men can do. Jon had a bottle of cola and Simon was clutching a bottle of beer, waving it around as he extrapolated on something probably quite academic. Simon laughed loudly at, quite possibly, his own joke, and Jon nodded sagely.

'I can guess who's driving you guys back to Whitby, Cori.' Lissy pointed at Simon. 'He is *well* on his way to getting drunk. I don't think I've ever *seen* him drunk.'

'Well it's only fair,' replied Cori with a laugh. She shifted in the recliner and pulled herself more upright, the twinkling lights sparking off the emerald on the third finger of her left hand. 'It's Simon's engagement as much as mine, and I've got the best excuse in the world to stay sober. Only three and a half months to go. Fourteen weeks, give or take.'

'Not that you're counting,' teased Becky. 'Oh, but it's making me broody. Jon! Jon!' She cupped her hands around her mouth and pretended to be calling him. 'We need another one!'

'Seriously?' Lissy stared at her. 'And you're far too loud!'

'Am I? Battery's dead.' Becky waved her hand around her right ear and pulled a face. 'Anyway. I *will* act on it. Unless you want to be the next one? Best enjoy the champagne while you can.'

Lissy laughed and pushed Becky's shoulder gently. 'What with you and Stef – leave me alone. Please!'

'Hey, do we need to change the music?' Cori looked around. 'It's stopped.'

'I'll do it. I'll check on Gracie as well while I'm in there. My goodness, though, I hope Jon and Simon don't try any Dad-dancing.' Becky stood up. 'Well, Jon's allowed to do it, I suppose, and Simon should get in some practice, I guess.' She giggled and wobbled a little. 'What do you want on?'

'Just choose something. Anything,' replied Lissy.

'It makes no difference to me,' grumbled Becky. 'Battery's dead. I told you. Can't hear a damn thing. Dance music maybe? It's got a beat to it. I might feel it through the floorboards, poor old me. Still – big secret – we're looking into cochlear implants. Can't wait! Jon reckons with the expected income from Mayfair, especially with Stef putting *his* photos in the exhibition, we can go for it quite quickly. I wonder if I can still switch it all off though, if Grace whinges too much?'

Her pretty face creased into a thoughtful frown and Lissy stifled a giggle. 'Stef's got plenty of dance music on the laptop.' She chivvied Becky up gently. 'His music, his choice – not mine. But it is a party after all.'

'Then dance music it is.' Becky stumbled off, not quite walking in a straight line, but heading in the general direction of the laptop.

'God love her,' said Lissy, shaking her head as she watched her sister-in-law leave. 'You can tell she's out of practice with this champagne thing.'

Cori laughed. 'This is lovely though. Thanks for inviting us. It's a shame to be going home tomorrow – I'd much rather laze around by the sea for a few more days, but we've got work and that's the thing.' She rubbed her tummy gently. 'This little one, though, I'm going to make sure she visits the seaside as much as she can. You can't beat it, can you?'

'No,' replied Lissy. 'The seaside is simply heavenly. It's been a perfect summer.' She smiled at the group of people she loved the most – her best friends in all the world, her family and her future, all together on this perfect evening. 'I don't think I could be any happier,' she said thoughtfully. 'Not at all.'

Stef looked up at that point and waved at her. His smile lit up his face and she waved back. For a moment, they were the only two people in existence and everything else melted into insignificance, as it always had done when she was with Stef.

'No,' she reiterated. 'Not at all.'

Chapter Twenty-Nine

Newlyn Art Gallery, Cornwall, 1906

The exhibition displayed some outstanding work – everyone agreed. There were pictures from Harold Knight and Laura Knight and many of the others in the Newlyn group.

But one picture, in particular, caught his attention.

'Excuse me!' Julian approached the gallery owner and smiled. He held out his hand, and saw the man recoil a little from the scarring. It was fading now, but the flames had licked at his skin unforgivingly – if it hadn't been for Heimdall appearing out of nowhere, grabbing him around the middle and pulling him bodily out of the place, he would have been dead for sure – not just burned.

Julian had travelled to Cornwall this summer; it was a good excuse to build on his work with the fisher folk and artists of Staithes, and his buyers agreed – but in reality, the draw of the place was too strong to ignore. Whilst he'd been recovering from the burns, he had thought of nothing but Lorelei, mourning the fact that, had he only been at that exhibition a few days earlier, he would have met her sooner and he would have loved her longer. And all the heartache would have been avoided, for both of them. He would have protected her with everything he possessed.

But now – now, he wondered if some other reason had brought him there. He hardly dared to hope; but he did.

'Yes, Sir? Can I help?' The owner hesitated a moment, then took his hand and shook it.

'Aye. That painting there – the one of the beach and the rock in the cove. Can you tell me more about the artist?'

'This one?' The gallery owner walked over to a watercolour and pointed at it. A rock stood proud of the churning sea, waves crashing alongside it and spilling onto a beach. Storm clouds gathered in the sky, but in the corner was a depiction of a house, one of the windows lit up, warmly glowing against the gloom. Some careful strokes of the brush had depicted a couple of shadows on the rock, which may or may not have been two people standing closely together.

'That's it,' said Julian. 'That's the very one.'

'The artist is called Laura Cooper,' replied the owner. 'She's one to watch.' He nodded and studied the picture. 'Comes from the north, but she's been here a twelve-month or so now. Very highly regarded. This is an incredible piece.'

Julian gazed at the picture, his heart thumping, his mind transported back to last summer in Yorkshire. The summer where he had met, loved and lost Lorelei Scarsdale.

'Laura Cooper. I don't suppose you have an address for her? Anywhere I can find her?'

'I do know where she lives, but I don't think it's at all correct for me to be telling you where she is.'

Julian nodded. 'I understand.' He looked away from the painting and at the man. He smiled and fixed him with a very direct look. 'How much would it cost me to find out where she lives?'

'Excuse me?' exclaimed the man. 'Are you attempting to bribe me?'

Julian laughed. 'Aye. I am. Look – I don't know if you'll believe me, but this – this mess on my hands, on my arms – it's because I tried to rescue her. I thought she was dying in a burning building. And I went in after her. But I didn't reach her, and for this twelve-month you mentioned, I've thought she was dead.'

'Sir!' The gallery owner was astonished, but Julian could tell that the man, romantic Cornishman that he was, was drawn in by the story.

'When I knew her, she was Lorelei Scarsdale. Lady Scarsdale. My name, if you're interested, is Julian MacDonald Cooper.'

'Cooper?' The man stared at him. 'MacDonald Cooper the photographer? But she's calling herself Laura Cooper.'

'It seems that she is,' agreed Julian. 'Intriguing, isn't it? And, if it's all the same to you, I'd really appreciate a chance to talk to her. Please.'

The gallery owner stared at Julian for a moment, and Julian could almost see the cogs whirring in his mind.

'I'll tell you what, Cooper,' said the man slowly, his Cornish twang softening every word. 'I don't think I can be telling you where the lady lives, but if you take one of our catalogues, it has details of all our artists in the back. You will see, Sir, that it also advises where the studios are located, should anyone wish to contact the artist.'

Julian nodded. He took the catalogue the owner proffered and dug into his pocket to pay for it.

The owner shook his head. 'On this occasion, I am happy to waive the fee, Sir. I wish you every success in your venture.'

'Thank you.' Julian smiled at the man, his heart pounding. All he wanted to do was rush out of that place and run to Laura Cooper's studio. He flicked to the back page and scanned it for the details. He pointed at it and tapped it with his forefinger. 'Can you—'

'Out of the door and turn left, then keep going until you reach the bend in the road, then you'll be amongst the cottages. You should be quite close to the studio then.'

'Thank you, again. And you're right …' He looked at the picture. 'It's an incredible piece. I'm going to come back and buy it, I swear. But now – now, I have to go.' He nodded and turned, hurrying out of the gallery and onto the street. As he had been instructed, he turned left and ran as fast as he could towards the old cottages.

Lorelei was drying her paintbrush and studying a seascape she had just completed. Fishing boats dotted the ocean, and the cliffs rose up on either side, directing the viewer's eye to the far distant horizon. She didn't know what was on that horizon – as always, it felt out of reach.

It wasn't the most imaginative of compositions, but she was happy with seascapes and they seemed to be awfully popular. She had been working on the way the light dappled the waves and the motion of the water rolling onto the beach and the way the clouds scudded the sky. She was reasonably happy with it, anyway.

She turned and was laying the brush beside the palette of watercolours, when there was a knock at the studio door; an insistent knock. A knock that was more like someone hammering the door down; one that she could not ignore.

'I'm coming!' she shouted. She tossed her hair over her shoulder, revelling in the fact that she could wear it loose here and nobody would criticise her for it. Nobody ever asked any questions, either, which was an almighty blessing in itself. Her dress today was simple and white, belted with a sea-green sash and she tugged it straight to neaten herself up; some old habits died hard.

Lorelei flung the door open and stood staring at the man who stared back at her. She hung onto the doorframe, terrified the floor would slide from beneath her and she would crumple at his feet. He was there on her doorstep, his fist curled up, ready to knock one more time. His face was as dear and as handsome as she remembered, his dark hair longer, his brown eyes wide and unsure.

'Lorelei.'

He didn't need to say any more. Lorelei swept her gaze from the top of his head down his body and to his feet.

She looked again at his raised fist, and saw his other hand clutching a rolled-up brochure from the art gallery.

She saw the shiny, puckered red skin and, despite what she had witnessed at the Dower House, her heart twisted: 'What happened?' Her voice cracked and she was surprised she had even managed to formulate a phrase. He was here. He was here, in front of her.

'There was a fire.' His eyes burned into hers. 'I tried to rescue the woman I had given my heart to. For a whole year, I thought she was dead – burned to ashes, just like her husband.'

Lorelei's stomach churned. 'He's dead?'

'Yes. There's nothing left of her house but a shell. Nobody lives there anymore. Nobody knew where she had gone. Everyone thought she had been trapped. But I hoped. I never stopped hoping.'

Lorelei couldn't move; she could barely even think. Images of that day flitted through her head. Images of the people on the beach kissing, the man holding the young woman closely. 'But you were with someone else. I saw you.'

'Me? I wasn't with anyone else!' cried Julian, looking horrified. 'I was waiting for *you*! It must have been Florrie. She was there with Archie, hanging around that bloody bathing hut, and I told them—'

'*Florrie?*' Lorelei burst out. 'Florrie was there? She should have been in London! She should have …' Her voice died away as she remembered the letter from Florrie she had put to one side; the hysterical outpourings of a young girl despairing of her place in Society. It might have been herself, once upon a time – only she, Lorelei, wanted to *be* someone in Society. Florrie, on the other hand, didn't. She wanted to settle into matrimonial anonymity; marry a solicitor's son and raise a brood of children as round and blonde and sturdy as butterballs, living happily in the countryside.

'Yes. I left them together. Florrie had hurt herself and I was going to go for help, and then I saw the smoke. By the time I got to the Hall, it was like a furnace and I thought you were—' His voice caught and he looked at his hand, flexing his fingers. 'There was the fire, you see.'

'Oh, Julian. I'm so sorry.' She reached out and touched his hand, feeling once again the warmth and the energy of the man she had loved so deeply that summer; her summer visitor.

Her art and all the upset of the last few months slid into nothingness, wispy as the threads of clouds in her watercolour sky. 'I should have waited. But Walter – Walter *made* me like that. He made me distrustful and jealous, and I couldn't bear that anyone else should have you if I couldn't. I should have stayed. I should have marched down to that beach and found out what was going on—'

Tears sprang into her eyes and she stopped speaking as his hand curled around hers and desire darkened his eyes. 'I would never treat you like that. Never. I'm not Walter. And I'm yours for as long as I live. Please, Lorelei. Please don't make me wait any longer. Sea Scarr is a shell – there's nothing left except our cove and our beach and the Dower House. You still own it all – it's still yours, for what any of it's worth. We can go back there. Or we can stay here. Or we can go to Edinburgh. Or I can just walk away and you can go back to being Laura Cooper. But ... you chose my name. That gives me hope. May I hope, my love?'

His voice was low, his eyes fixed on hers. He held her hand as if he would never let her go again.

Lorelei entwined her fingers more deeply within his. She felt the ripples of scars against her own skin and knew he had done it for her. He had risked his life for her. And she had abandoned him without questioning why. She had been wrong – so very, very wrong.

Lorelei leaned up to him tentatively, her lips parted.

Gently, she kissed him, and then she pulled away. 'Come inside, Julian MacDonald Cooper,' she whispered. 'Come inside. And help me decide.'

And as he stepped into her little studio and the door shut behind them, the distant horizon was at last within her grasp.

Epilogue

Lissy had waved off her friends, packed up the rest of her belongings and was leaning on the balcony, staring out to sea, enjoying the resulting peace and quiet of her final evening in the Dower House.

'Elisabetta.' Stef walked up to her and stood beside her, mirroring her stance and looking across the water. 'It is a beautiful evening. I shall be sorry to go, but it has been an incredible summer, has it not?'

'It has, my love.' Lissy removed her hand from the railing and rested it on Stef's. He twisted his around, so their fingers were entwined and Lissy determined to remember that feeling of safety and security and *rightness* forever.

'Look, *bella*, look!' Stef suddenly leaned forward and pointed to something near the beach hut. 'People. Strangers. In your cove! On your beach!' He sounded amused, but Lissy didn't take offence.

'I see them,' she said with a smile. 'And do you know what, I'm feeling magnanimous, so I'm not even going to chase them away. They're welcome to the place. It's served us well, hasn't it?'

'It has,' agreed Stef. 'Yet I wonder who they are? Well – it is not my problem, as they say. My problem is this.' He turned to face Lissy and lifted her hand to his lips. He brushed her skin with a kiss and Lissy shivered, despite the warmth of the late evening. 'My problem is how to convince my Elisabetta that *bambinos* are not too bad after all – having spent a few weeks in the company of Grace, I am wondering whether my Elisabetta would ever be tempted to have a Grace of her own.'

Lissy laughed and shook her head. 'One day. One day, when we decide we've had enough of our campervan and I start to miss the cuddles and the stickiness too much, *then* we'll have one. I wouldn't want to have a *bambino* with anyone but you, Stefano Ricci. And I never thought I'd hear myself say that.'

'That is a very good answer,' replied Stef with a grin. 'Imagine how beautiful our children would be if they took after you!'

Lissy laughed and stood on her tiptoes to kiss him properly. 'Very beautiful,' she agreed. 'But only if they take after *you*.' She took one last look out at the cove and the couple who were, even now, standing hand in hand on the beach, gilded by the silver light of the moon.

A light breeze that Lissy couldn't feel lifted the woman's long, dark, wavy hair as she pointed out to sea. The man beside her, his hair equally dark, leaned towards her to speak; then he stood up, let go of her hand and raised something up towards the horizon. A camera, Lissy saw.

She narrowed her eyes and studied them a little more closely – the woman's pale dress was long, floating around her ankles, a ribbon blowing around in the wind. Her sleeves were trimmed with more fluttering ribbons and her feet were bare on the sand. The man's feet were bare too – his shirt was white, gleaming against the backdrop of the ocean, and his hair was too long, whipped up gently by the same breeze that lifted the woman's curls. There were no footprints in the wet sand, where they stood, looking out to the horizon.

Lissy had a good idea who they were, and she felt nothing but peace and joy for them.

'Goodbye Lorelei and Julian,' she whispered, 'and thank you.'

And good luck to them, wherever they chose to go.

It had been a beautiful evening and Lissy didn't have long

left in Staithes. So she was going to enjoy every moment she had there.

'Isn't it funny?' she mused as she turned from the sea and began to lead Stef inside. 'From here, the horizon doesn't seem far, does it? Except I know, in reality, that it's miles away.'

'But we can still reach it,' he answered, 'It's still ours.'

Lissy smiled. He was right. It had always been theirs; she had only needed to believe that they could reach it together.

And a little distance away, in the window of Sea Scarr Hall, a glint of moonlight caught the corner of the glass and glimmered for a brief second. The gleam was mirrored, just for a moment, in the upstairs window of the Dower House.

Thank You

Thank you for reading *The Girl in the Photograph*. I hope you enjoyed Lissy and Stefano's story as much as I enjoyed writing it. Lissy has been a wonderfully head-strong character in my previous novels, *Some Veil Did Fall* and *The Girl in the Painting*, and I thought it was high time she had a book of her own – and so did she, apparently, because one day she danced straight out of her life and right onto my page, demanding I tell her story! So what could I do but oblige her?

All authors, as well as loving their characters, really value their readers. The road to publication is a magical one and seeing your book out there, being enjoyed by people like yourself, is a fantastic feeling. It's even more special if people like you take the trouble to leave a review. It's lovely to hear what readers think and we all value their feedback.

If you have time therefore, something as simple as a one-line review on Amazon, a note on a book review site such as Goodreads or indeed a comment on any online store would be hugely appreciated.

Please do feel free to contact me anytime. You can find my details under my author profile and I very much hope that you'll enjoy my other books as well.

Happy reading, and again, a huge thank you!

Lots of love

Kirsty

xxx

About the Author

Kirsty Ferry is from the North East of England and lives there with her husband and son. She won the English Heritage/Belsay Hall National Creative Writing competition in 2009 and has had articles and short stories published in *The People's Friend*, *The Weekly News*, *It's Fate*, *Vintage Script*, *Ghost Voices* and *First Edition*. Her work also appears in several anthologies, incorporating such diverse themes as vampires, crime, angels and more.

Kirsty loves writing ghostly mysteries and interweaving fact and fiction. The research is almost as much fun as writing the book itself, and if she can add a wonderful setting and a dollop of history, that's even better.

Her day job involves sharing a building with an eclectic collection of ghosts, which can often prove rather interesting.

Follow Kirsty on:
www.twitter.com/kirsty_ferry
www.facebook.com/pages/Kirsty-Ferry-Author

More Choc Lit

From Kirsty Ferry

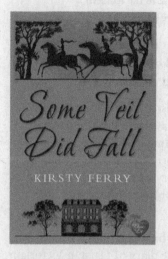

Some Veil Did Fall

**Book 1 in the Rossetti
Mysteries series**

**What if you recalled memories
from a life that wasn't yours,
from a life before …?**

When Becky steps into
Jonathon Nelson's atmospheric
photography studio in Whitby,
she is simply a freelance
journalist in search of a story.
But as soon as she puts on the
beautiful Victorian dress and poses for a photograph, she
becomes somebody quite different …

From that moment on, Becky is overcome with visions and
flashbacks from a life that isn't her own – some disturbing
and filled with fear.

As she and Jon begin to unravel the tragic mystery behind her
strange experiences, the natural affinity they have for each
other continues to grow and leads them to question … have
they met somewhere before? Perhaps not in this life but in
another?

Available in paperback from all good
bookshops and online stores. Visit
www.choc-lit.com for details.

The Girl in the Painting

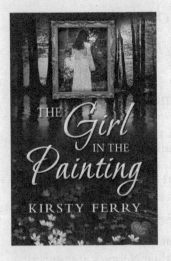

Book 2 in the Rossetti Mysteries series

What if you thought you knew a secret that could change history?

Whilst standing engrossed in her favourite Pre-Raphaelite painting – Millais's Ophelia – Cori catches the eye of Tate gallery worker, Simon, who is immediately struck by her resemblance to the red-haired beauty in the famous artwork.

The attraction is mutual, but Cori has other things on her mind. She has recently acquired the diary of Daisy, a Victorian woman with a shocking secret. As Cori reads, it soon becomes apparent that Daisy will stop at nothing to be heard, even outside of the pages of her diary …

Will Simon stick around when life becomes increasingly spooky for Cori, as she moves ever closer to uncovering the truth about Daisy's connection to the girl in her favourite painting?

A Little Bit of Christmas Magic

Book 4 in the Rossetti Mysteries series

Any wish can be granted with a little bit of Christmas magic …

As a wedding planner at Carrick Park Hotel Ailsa McCormack has devoted herself to making sure couples get their perfect day, but just occasionally that comes at a price – in this case, organising a Christmas Day wedding at the expense of her own Christmas.

Not that Ailsa minds. There's something very special about Carrick Park during the festive season and she's always been fascinated by the past occupants of the place; particularly the beautiful and tragic Ella Carrick, whose striking portrait still hangs at the top of the stairs.

And then an encounter with a tall, handsome and strangely familiar man in the drawing room on Christmas Eve sets off a chain of events that transforms Ailsa's lonely Christmas into a far more magical occasion than she could have ever imagined …

Visit www.choc-lit.com for details.

Every Witch Way

Time for a Halloween road trip …

Nessa hates her full name – Agnes – which she inherited from her great-great grandmother – but is that all she inherited? Because rumour had it that Great-Great Granny Agnes was a witch, and a few unusual things have been happening to Nessa recently …

First, there's the strange book she finds in her local coffee shop, and then the invite from her next-door neighbour Ewan Grainger to accompany him on a rather supernatural research trip. What ensues is a Halloween journey through Scotland in a yellow camper van (accompanied by a big black cat called Schubert), a mystical encounter in an ancient forest and maybe just a touch of magic!

Visit www.choc-lit.com for details.

KIRSTY FERRY

Watch for Me by Moonlight

Book 1 in the Hartsford Mysteries series

"It was the first full moon since that night. She waited and watched by moonlight, as she had promised …"

When her life in London falls apart, Elodie Bright returns to Sussex and to Hartsford Hall; the home of her childhood friend, Alexander Aldrich. Once upon a time, Alex and Elodie were on the brink of something more than just friendship, but a misunderstanding left their hopes of a future together in tatters.

After a freak storm damages the church roof at Hartsford and the tomb of Georgiana Kerridge, one of Alex's eighteenth-century relatives, Elodie and Alex find a strange reconnection in a shocking discovery – and in the series of uncanny events that follow.

Slowly they begin to piece together Georgiana's secret past involving a highwayman with a heart of gold, a sister's betrayal and a forbidden love so strong that it echoes through the ages …

Visit www.choc-lit.com for details.

Introducing Choc Lit

We're an independent publisher creating
a delicious selection of fiction.
Where heroes are like chocolate – irresistible!
Quality stories with a romance at the heart.

See our selection here:
www.choc-lit.com

We'd love to hear how you enjoyed *The Girl in the Photograph*. Please leave a review where you purchased the novel or visit: **www.choc-lit.com** and give your feedback.

Choc Lit novels are selected by genuine readers like yourself. We only publish stories our Choc Lit Tasting Panel want to see in print. Our reviews and awards speak for themselves.

**Could you be a Star Selector
and join our Tasting Panel?**
Would you like to play a role in choosing which novels we decide to publish? Do you enjoy reading women's fiction? Then you could be perfect for our Choc Lit Tasting Panel.

Visit here for more details…
www.choc-lit.com/join-the-choc-lit-tasting-panel

Keep in touch:
Sign up for our monthly newsletter Choc Lit Spread for
all the latest news and offers: www.spread.choc-lit.com.
Follow us on Twitter: @ChocLituk and Facebook: Choc Lit.

Where heroes are like chocolate – irresistible!